The Finder of Lost Things

THE FINDER OF LOST THINGS

by Kathy Lynn Emerson

Chapter One

The Keeper of Colchester Castle's gaol, Luke Fludd by name, was a small, wiry man with beady little eyes and a bird's nest of a beard. His manner was as rough as his speech. He had no respect for the gentle birth of his prisoner. To him she was merely a source of income. He knew full well she would pay for exemption from ironing and for all the little amenities he could offer her too.

Unaccustomed to taking orders from such a ruffian, Blanche Wainfleet found it difficult to hold her tongue when he presented her with his list of fees. Her natural inclination was to argue. Common sense kept her silent. She had been warned about this.

It cost her most of the coins in her purse to bribe Fludd not to place manacles on her wrists, fetters or shackles on her ankles, or an iron collar around her neck. Additional charges covered the rental of a blanket and a charcoal brazier and granted her permission to keep the small bundle she'd brought with her. It contained clean linen, a spare bodice and kirtle, and her comb and tooth cloth. For these privileges, she paid without demur. It was the twenty-first day of January, the coldest time of the year. She had no intention of freezing to death while she was imprisoned in this ruin of a castle.

The keeper demanded further payments for food and for charcoal to burn in the brazier. Once he had pocketed Blanche's money, he informed her that the amount she had just handed over would cover her expenses for no more than two weeks.

She longed to wipe the smug smile off his face, but it was far too late now to change her mind. She had been committed to Colchester gaol for an indefinite period of time, charged with repeatedly refusing to attend church and with failure to pay the fines leveled for that refusal. No one, least of all Luke Fludd, would believe that until a week ago she had been a member in good standing of the Church of England.

She supposed she could catch Fludd by surprise and attempt an escape. Given the tumbledown condition of the castle's walls, it would take no great effort to scramble to freedom, but the presence of a scattering of armed guards might present a problem.

Blanche suppressed a sigh. More than stone walls and iron locks held her captive. She had to discover the truth, and this was the only way open to her. Failure was a possibility, especially when she'd had only six days to prepare, but she was determined to do all she could to avoid a premature end to her self-imposed mission.

She had studied hard and taken it upon herself to speak with an aged family retainer in her brother-in-law's household, a man who had been imprisoned for his beliefs back when Queen Mary sat on the throne. Thirty-four years ago, that had been, but his memory of the ordeal was still vivid.

"Do not make the mistake of thinking I exaggerate in order to frighten you," he'd warned her. Then he'd launched into an account that spared no detail of the time he'd spent locked up in the Marshalsea, one of London's most notorious prisons.

Given that she and other prisoners of gentle birth had the wherewithal to bribe their jailers, Blanche hoped to receive better treatment, but she was well aware that she could not count on anything. *Pretend to be meek and submissive*, she reminded herself. *Cowed and downtrodden. Fearful. A martyr to your faith but one with monetary resources yet to be tapped.*

Blanche liked to think of herself as brave and bold but in these circumstances even the most valiant person would quail. She *was* afraid. She would be a fool if she were not.

The keeper thrust a moth-eaten woolen blanket into her arms before escorting her into a cold, dank passageway lit only by smoking torches set into brackets at irregular intervals. With every step, Blanche felt safety and security fall farther behind. The tap of her leather boot heels on the stone-flagged floor had an ominous ring. The keeper's heavier footfalls sounded abnormally loud. Every step they took echoed off thick stone walls that, at least in this part of the castle, were solid and surpassing formidable.

Without warning, Fludd's vise-like grip on her upper arm tightened, jerking her to a halt. For a small man, the keeper had strong hands. He nodded to a guard, who in turn unlocked a heavy oak door studded with nails. Enormous wooden beams encased it.

"See there." He pointed to two places where the beam above the door had been worn smooth. "That's where prisoners are wont to grab hold. They cling and plead and try to prevent my men from dragging them inside." He smirked, his beady eyes gleaming in the light of a nearby torch.

The illumination was not bright enough to show her what lay beyond the door, not until Fludd lifted the torch from its bracket and gestured with it. Reluctantly, she stepped inside the small, windowless, unoccupied room, wondering if this was to be her prison cell. If so, she had already failed in her quest.

What had been but a distant murmur in the passageway sounded much louder in the confined space. She heard people talking and moving about, although she could see no one. Foul odors had begun to assault her sense of smell the moment she left the keeper's rooms. Now they reached a pungent level. Blanche had been told that sanitation in prison was primitive, but she had not expected the stench of human waste to be so overwhelming.

"You'll grow accustomed to the stink," Fludd said. "After a day or two, you will not even notice it."

She hoped he was right.

When the keeper shoved her forward, Blanche realized that they had not been standing inside a cell after all. Rather they were in a sort of anteroom. He unlocked one of two doors that appeared to lead deeper into the prison.

"These accommodations will be available to you when you run out of money." He opened the portal far enough to give her a clear view of what lay beyond.

The stone cell was bare of comfort, unlit, and frigid. At least a dozen women, faces ravaged and clothing ragged, huddled together in the dark and cold. They blinked at the sudden influx of light. One of them held a tiny, emaciated baby to her breast. It shifted and began to cry, but so weakly that Blanche feared it would not live to see another day.

As abruptly as he had opened it, the keeper slammed the door shut. Relieved though she was to cut short this glimpse of Hell, Blanche barely suppressed a cry of protest. It was cruel and inhuman to leave those poor souls in torment.

"That one is for the men." Fludd indicated the second door.

Cowardly as her sentiment made her feel, Blanche was pathetically grateful that he did not insist upon opening it. She could imagine well enough the plight of those within.

His point made, Fludd led her still deeper into Colchester gaol. Once again he stopped before a thick wooden door, this one reinforced with iron bars. The guard stationed before it detached one of several heavy keys from his belt and inserted it into a rusty lock. After a brief struggle, the key turned and the door creaked open to reveal a flight of stone stairs descending into blackness.

Was she to be confined in the castle dungeon? Blanche froze, unable to force herself to step over the threshold until the keeper gave her a shove to get her started. She caught her balance, narrowly avoiding a nasty fall. She still felt unsteady on her feet when the guard slammed the door shut behind her.

Chapter Two

B lanche stood stock-still, afraid to move in the darkness lest she tumble down those treacherous stone steps. Her heart hammered so loudly that the sound filled her ears, drowning out everything else except the way her breath began to sough in and out. On the edge of panic, it seemed to her as if the only source of air had been cut off along with the light.

How much time passed before she had control of herself again, she could not say. Bit by bit, the worst of her fear lessened and she could think rationally once more.

This is all part of the plan, she told herself. *You are in no danger.*

Although she was no longer certain she believed she would ever be free again, she knew what she had to do. What choice was there but to descend the stairs and discover what lurked below? If all had gone according to plan, she would find other women prisoners there. As long as they believed she was who she said she was, they would pose no threat to her safety.

Tucking the blanket and her bundle of clothing under one arm, Blanche felt with her free hand for something to steady herself during her descent. At first, she had the disorienting sense that there was nothing there to find. Then her flailing fingers struck a rough stone surface.

The wall was so cold that she could feel the chill right through her fur-lined leather gloves. She jerked her hand away, but immediately reached out again, craving even the small reassurance she could take from its solidity. Her brief glimpse of the stairs by torchlight had shown her that there was no railing, not even a rope to hang onto.

Cautiously, she felt with her right foot for the edge of the step. Finding it, she drew in a deep breath. She told herself again that she had nothing to fear. The recusant women held in Colchester gaol were not starved or beaten. No torture was employed to make them renounce their beliefs or betray others of their faith.

Blanche shuffled her way downward. The steps were heavily worn in the center, giving them an uneven surface made even more hazardous by the absence of light. Her anxiety increased when the stairway twisted back on itself. The thick walls seemed to press in on her until she felt as if she was descending into a well.

Blanche stopped and squeezed her eyes shut, then slowly opened them again. In the most logical part of her mind, she knew that the stairwell would soon open out into the chamber below. It would no longer be pitch black. The women housed there had the wherewithal to afford candles.

Inhaling slowly, she took heart. Yes, that was tallow she smelled burning. Although other, less welcome odors also drifted up to her, this place was not suffused with the sickening miasma she'd encountered in that horrible little cell Luke Fludd had shown her.

As she continued on, she experienced a slow diminution of the blackness. She increased her speed, anxious to be out in the open again, and was almost running by the time she rounded the last turn and once again found herself on level ground. Her gaze went at once to the source of the light, a half dozen flickering candles augmented by the glow from two charcoal braziers. They illuminated a small circle of kneeling women, their heads bent in prayer.

None of them looked up, giving Blanche time to make a quick survey of her surroundings. She was not locked in a dungeon, but rather in a vaulted underground storage room. No shackles were set into the walls. No iron maiden or rack stood ready for use. Although this place was uncomfortably cold, it was neither damp nor unduly noisome.

A stray draft plucked at the feather in her high-crowned hat, briefly drawing her attention upward. She pictured a window high above their heads, although there was not sufficient light to confirm her guess. It was possible what she felt was only the wind creeping in through hairline cracks

CHAPTER TWO

in the walls. A pervasive coldness did seep out of the stone of which they'd been built, the accumulation of centuries of winters. Even wrapped in her fur-lined cloak, Blanche felt the chill of her underground prison begin to creep deep into her bones.

That brought her attention back to the braziers, their only source of heat, and she frowned. She had paid for a brazier for herself, and the charcoal to fuel it. Would it be forthcoming, or was it Fludd's practice to cheat those he locked up, knowing they had no recourse?

The women were still praying, still oblivious to her presence. Too chilled to remain where she was, Blanche cleared her throat and began to walk slowly in their direction. The rustle of fabric sounded loud in the semi-darkness as her fellow prisoners at last turned her way. She felt their eyes boring into her, but no one spoke. Faced with suspicious, even hostile stares, her steps faltered. She stopped halfway to the circle of light.

After a moment, a solitary figure rose to her feet and detached herself from the others. She moved with slow dignity, marking her as a person of importance, at least in her own mind. The dim light behind her cast her in silhouette as she approached Blanche, making it difficult to discern much about her appearance. Blanche could tell only that she was stout without being fat. She was, in truth, shaped like the trunk of a tree and appeared to be just as solid.

The woman halted an arm's length away, her wariness a palpable force. She squinted in the dim light in an effort to make out Blanche's features. After a moment, she gave up the attempt and fumbled in the pouch depended from her waist to bring forth the stub of a candle. She thrust it into Blanche's hand.

"Hold this."

Blanche obeyed. A moment later, she heard flint strike against steel and saw it spark. The tallow smoked and stank, but it provided sufficient illumination for the two women to examine each other in detail. By its flickering light, Blanche beheld a face that was exceeding pale under an old-fashioned French hood. The skin beneath the woman's eyes had the bruised look of someone who had not slept well for some time, but her eyes,

7

dark as midnight, were fierce.

What she saw when she looked at Blanche was less certain. Blanche's mirror told her she was no great beauty, although some considered her a handsome woman. She was in her twenty-eighth year, of medium build and slightly above average height, and had blue eyes and pale yellow hair. Most important, she bore little resemblance to any of her sisters.

Blanche waited for the older woman to speak first. Clearly she was the leader of the recusant women imprisoned in Colchester Castle. Unfortunately, she did not look pleased to have a stranger thrust upon her.

This was one of the most crucial moments in Blanche's mission, the point at which everything could go terribly wrong. If the other prisoners saw through her disguise and decided she was a spy, she would never find the answers she sought. She might not even survive her first night of internment in Colchester gaol.

Meek and mild, she cautioned herself. *Show yourself to be timid, but not too timid. And very, very afraid.*

At last, the gentlewoman spoke. "I am Lady Otley. The others imprisoned here are my neighbors and my servants. I do not know you."

Blanche sketched a hasty curtsey that set the feather in her hat bobbing. She had chosen her clothing with care. A minor adjustment in the way her cloak fell gave Lady Otley a glimpse of her peach-color underskirt, embroidered after the French fashion. That her partlet was open at the throat was a signal that she was unmarried. That lie was necessary. They must believe she had no one to whom she could appeal for help.

"My name is Blanche Wainfleet, Lady Otley."

"You are not native to this part of Essex." The gentry in rural areas knew each other, by name if not by sight, especially the Catholic gentry.

"No, ma'am. After my father died, I came here from London to live with a distant cousin and her husband."

"What man is he?"

"Arthur Chapell." He was a member of the lesser gentry who lived on the far side of the county from Otley Manor. In truth, he was not married to a cousin, but rather to Blanche's sister Joanna.

8

"I have heard that name." Lady Otley drew herself up a little straighter in recognition of the fact that Arthur was not one of her co-religionists. He was a good and faithful servant of Queen Elizabeth and attended church services in his home parish without fail. "Why were you arrested? Did you abuse his trust?"

"I am not a thief or a murderer!" Blanche protested. "I was caught reading a forbidden book." She managed to coax out a tear. "Then everyone was wroth with me, ready to condemn me as a heretic simply for being curious. My sin was reported to the magistrate and he insisted upon bringing charges against me, after which my cousin's husband declared that he washed his hands of me and forbade me ever to set foot in his house again."

Sad to say in these perilous times, such a small offense *could* send someone to prison.

Initially, it might have been more effective to claim that she was a secret Catholic who had been imprisoned, as Fludd had been told, because she would not conform to the requirements of the state church, but she lacked the knowledge to play the part of a long-time recusant. Her ignorance of "the old religion" would soon have tripped her up, had she tried that ploy. Instead, Blanche had invented a story that spared her the necessity of pretending she already shared Lady Otley's beliefs and at the same time, or so she devoutly hoped, would earn that gentlewoman's trust.

"Are you...recusants?" she asked in a timid voice.

"That is why we were arrested." Lady Otley was short with her. Suspicion seemed to radiate from her person.

"Then mayhap, while I am confined here with you, you might tutor me in your faith. I am most anxious to learn more."

"You wish to embrace Catholicism?" The possibility failed to soften Lady Otley in the least.

"I think I do. What I have read inclines me to that belief."

Blanche bowed her head, hiding her expression. Had the reports that Lady Otley was zealous in her proselytizing been wrong? She had hoped the mere suggestion that she would be open to conversion would be enough to win the other woman's trust. She needed Lady Otley to take her under her wing.

9

How else was she to succeed in her mission?

"What forbidden book?" Lady Otley asked.

"*The Exercise of a Christian Life.* The copy I had was translated into English but the original was written in Italian by a Spanish Jesuit named Gaspar Loarte." Blanche blurted out the explanation in an eager voice and then held her breath.

"I know of it." Lady Otley sounded slightly less hostile and her stare, although it could not be said to have softened, did not seem as intensely suspicious. "This book was printed in England a few years ago on one of the printing presses loyal Catholics keep hidden from the queen's men."

When the gentlewoman fell silent, as if in thought, Blanche took the opportunity to examine her person in more detail. The black velvet gown Lady Otley wore had rolled shoulder pieces and full sleeves turned back with cony fur. The front was closed against the cold, hiding her underdress. What did show was a bodice fastened all the way up to a high collar that supported a small ruff. The latter was much the worse for wear. The starched linen had wilted and where once it had been white, it was now discolored by sweat and grime.

"How did you obtain a copy of this book?"

Lady Otley snapped out the question, making Blanche start, and her answer came out in a breathless rush.

"It was given to me by a friend in London. I brought it with me to Essex, never dreaming that my cousin's husband would prove so radical in matters of religion."

"Is this Londoner a secret Catholic?"

Blanche feigned hesitation, as she thought anyone would do if the story were true. "She has never said so, but when I confided in her that I longed for a life of quiet contemplation and did much regret that girls could no longer take their leave of worldly matters and enter nunneries, she suggested that I might benefit from reading certain prayers and meditations."

Lady Otley nodded, this time in grudging approval. "What words in *The Exercise of a Christian Life* did you find most meaningful?"

A quotation came easily to mind and Blanche repeated it without hesitation. "After troubles quietness."

In truth, she had found several passages that spoke to her. The book was written with a simplicity that made it easy to comprehend, even by someone ignorant of the rites and rituals of the Catholic church. It offered exercises the author believed should occupy every good Christian. Fortunately for Blanche, it also explained the essence of the Catholic faith. An entire chapter was dedicated to the mysteries of the rosary. In the short time she'd had to prepare before entering Colchester gaol, the text had been a godsend.

"We will speak of this more anon," Lady Otley said. "If you are sincere, I will instruct you in the true faith and discover if you have a vocation, but be warned that if you try to cozen me, I will know it."

And do what to me in retaliation? Blanche wondered. *What punishment did you inflict on Alison Palmer when she changed her mind about converting to Catholicism?*

Once Lady Otley indicated that Blanche should follow her back to the circle of women and the warmth of the braziers, she went willingly but remained wary. In a way, she was glad of Lady Otley's caution. It was a good reminder that even if these recusants seemed kindly disposed toward her, they were not to be trusted. If Alison had stayed away from them, she would still be alive.

Blanche's sister's death weighed heavily upon her. It was the reason she had come here, to the place where Alison had died.

Chapter Three

None of the women to whom Blanche was presented looked capable of murder. Three were gentlewomen. Mistress Kenner, Mistress Farleigh, and Master Farleigh's elderly unmarried aunt, Matilda, were Lady Otley's neighbors. The other two were her servants, Edith and Sarah Trott. The remaining prisoner was a child of nine, Mistress Kenner's daughter Jane.

"Come and sit." The younger Mistress Farleigh patted the floor beside her. "Place your blanket beneath you to ward off the chill from the stone." The glow of the nearest brazier made her face look sallow and revealed bladelike features—a pointed chin, a long, narrow nose, and sharp cheekbones.

It was only after Blanche accepted the invitation that she realized how good it felt to be off her feet. She dared not let down her guard, but she felt some of the tension leave her neck and shoulders. Curled beneath her, her lower limbs relaxed for the first time since she'd entered Colchester Castle.

Mistress Kenner was little and round and although her face wore a worried look, she managed a faint smile of welcome. The reason for her concern clung to her side. Beset by a hacking cough, Jane Kenner appeared to be a sickly child. Her brown hair hung in lank clumps. Her brown eyes had a haunted look.

Without prompting, Lady Otley provided Blanche with a brief account of their arrest in a raid on Otley Manor. Caught celebrating mass, they had been sent straight to Colchester gaol, where they were to remain at the pleasure of the queen. Even now, their husbands were petitioning for their release.

No one mentioned Alison, but Blanche knew she had been brought to Colchester Castle with the others and that she had not survived her first night in prison. The cause of her sudden death had not been investigated by the authorities. Indeed, Alison's body had been released to the family only because their sister Joanna's husband had arrived at the castle before it could be buried in a pauper's grave and forgotten.

Alison might have died of natural causes. Sudden fevers could carry off even the healthiest of individuals, but it was also possible that one of these women had killed her. If they knew she'd changed her mind about converting to Catholicism, they'd have had good reason to silence her, especially if they feared she'd tell the queen's men where to find the Jesuit priest who had escaped from Otley Manor during the raid.

There had been no visible wounds on Alison's body, but she had been afraid for her life in the weeks before her imprisonment. She had said so in a letter she had written to their oldest sister, Philippa.

When the four of them had been children together—Philippa, Joanna, Blanche, and Alison—Blanche had always been the one who could most easily find mislaid toys and lost pets. She had been so consistently successful at such endeavors that the other girls had dubbed her "the finder of lost things." Only later had they realized she also had a talent for discerning when someone was lying. She had learned at an early age how to recognize dozens of little telltale signs of deceitfulness. These two abilities, combined with the temporary absence of her husband, made Blanche the best suited of Alison's sisters to uncover the truth about her death.

"And so we molder here," Lady Otley said, concluding the tale of their arrest and imprisonment.

"Were your husbands arrested, too?" Blanche already knew the answer but she was curious to hear how they would reply to her question.

"Praise God, no men were present that day to be taken into custody." Mistress Kenner's eyes glistened with unshed tears as they met Blanche's across the glowing coals.

Lady Otley made a small, ambiguous sound, but the way she pursed her lips suggested disapproval. Blanche could not tell if it had been the question she disliked or Mistress Kenner's answer.

Mistress Farleigh leapt to the defense of the absent gentlemen. "Despite their true beliefs, they dutifully attend services in the local parish church."

"If our husbands were to recuse themselves as we do, our families would soon be impoverished." Lady Otley's flat voice conveyed no emotion. She was simply stating a hard truth. " Sir Stephen must pay a fine every time I absent myself. To double or triple that each week would be ruinous."

Despite Blanche's suspicion that one or more of these women might have had a hand in Alison's death, she felt a pang of sympathy for their plight. Every loyal Englishman and woman was required to go to church on Sunday or be fined, but the Pope had forbidden Catholics to attend the services of the Church of England. Those sincere in their faith faced a difficult moral dilemma. If they chose to continue to worship in their own way and were caught, fines, arrest, and imprisonment were the least of what they might face. The threat of execution hung over the heads of all those who clung to the Old Religion.

"Why are you in Colchester gaol?" Mistress Kenner asked.

Blanche repeated the lie she'd told Lady Otley, although she suspected she had been overheard when she related her story the first time. By the conclusion of the tale, when she once again expressed an interest in pursuing the contemplative, religious life, Mistress Kenner and Mistress Farleigh were nodding their heads in approval and Matilda Farleigh reached out one skeletal hand to touch Blanche's sleeve.

"I was called to serve the Lord," she said in a voice that quavered with age. She was almost cadaverously thin, with a deeply lined face and faded blue eyes.

"She means she was once a nun," Lady Otley explained, "back before King Henry dissolved all the religious houses in England."

Blanche stared at Matilda Farleigh in awe. That had been more than fifty years ago and made her a very old woman indeed.

"Will you tell me what that life was like?" Genuinely eager to hear more, she leaned forward so that, for the first time since she'd taken her place in the circle of recusant women, her upper body was fully illuminated by the

14

light from the candles.

A startled gasp warned Blanche what was to come even before Mistress Kenner said, "Your hair is white!"

Lady Otley's penetrating gaze fixed on what could be seen of Blanche's tresses beneath her hat and coif. The single tallow candle she'd used earlier to inspect the newcomer had not given off sufficient illumination to reveal their unusual lack of pigment. Blanche's hair was such a pale shade of yellow that most people perceived it to be colorless.

Belatedly, Blanche realized she should have expected this reaction. On first encountering a young woman with hair better suited to an aged crone, people often looked at her askance. Some superstitious folk even made the sign against evil, thinking she must be so afflicted for a reason.

Affecting a rueful expression, she gave the true explanation and hoped it would suffice. "I was born this way and named Blanche because of it. My mother made light of how different I look and was wont to say that in the old days this shade would have been called silver-gilt and much admired. I fear I have always found it a great trial."

"God gives us all our burdens to bear," Matilda Farleigh said. "Some are greater than others."

Blanche wanted to ask if it was true that nuns shaved their heads when they entered a convent but feared such a question might be seen as frivolous. Instead, in the hope of turning the conversation away from her unfortunate appearance, she nodded solemnly and uttered platitudes.

"Those of your faith have been most cruelly persecuted. I admire your fortitude."

No one else spoke and while their silence continued Blanche was left to fret about what they were thinking. Had this mere accident of coloring increased Lady Otley's suspicions, or would it elicit her sympathy? The others would follow that gentlewoman's lead, and if they decided to reject her entirely, she would be hard put to learn anything of Alison's fate.

Meek and mild, she reminded herself. *A follower, not a leader. You are humbly attracted to the "true faith" these women believe in. Given time, you will be able to earn their trust.*

She had a week.

"It grows late," Lady Otley said.

When she bowed her head and the others did likewise, Blanche hastily followed suit. The practice of lengthy communal evening prayers was one both the Old Religion and the New had in common. What was strange to Blanche was the way Lady Otley addressed the Lord through intermediaries—the Virgin Mary and several unfamiliar saints—until the very end of her devotions. Then she lifted her eyes to Heaven and spoke directly to God.

"And we pray You grant us our freedom," she said in a loud, clear voice, her entreaty sounding more like a demand than a humble request, "and do so in all haste, for we have been confined in this place far too long already."

After Lady Otley made the sign of the holy cross she stood up and the others did likewise. Blanche had practiced this papist custom most diligently before leaving her sister's house and copied their movements, but the gesture still felt unnatural.

"And so to bed." Lady Otley gathered up the blanket she had been using as a cushion and spread it out on the cold, hard floor.

Blanche regarded the sleeping arrangements with a jaundiced eye. "I had imagined there would be pallets to lie upon, or at least a pile of straw."

"Be grateful there is solid stone beneath us," Mistress Farleigh said. "It could be naught but hard-packed earth."

"We suffer gladly for our faith." Lady Otley's pious statement, although it seemed to contradict the last words of her prayer, made the statement into a rebuke. "You would do well to recall the advice given in that book of yours. Does it not warn you not to love too dainty and soft a bed?"

With a sigh, Blanche produced the relevant quote from *The Exercise of a Christian Life*: "Call to mind that narrow and hard couch of the cross, which for thy sake our Savior lay upon."

Lady Otley nodded in grudging approval before settling herself for sleep.

Blanche admired self-sacrifice, but she preferred to keep her own suffering to a minimum. She had dressed warmly in preparation for her imprisonment. Wrapping herself in her cloak, she used it as both mattress and blanket. She folded the inadequate piece of wool she had been given for the latter purpose into a rudimentary pillow, resting her head upon it as she curled herself into a tight ball.

She was still cold. The nearest brazier warmed only one side of her, and that not well. Her cloak and the thickly-lined, quilted gown and undergarments she wore beneath offered little protection from the pervasive chill at her back. It required a leap of faith to close her eyes and will herself into unconsciousness. At length, as she began to drift off, she launched a plea of her own toward Heaven, the heartfelt prayer that she would not freeze to death while she slept.

Chapter Four

Blanche awoke stiff, sore, hungry, and cold. She could not remember when she had felt more like a block of ice. For the first time, she admitted to herself that Alison might have sickened and died as a result of her imprisonment alone. Frostbite and chilblains must afflict many prisoners. There was such a thing as gaol fever, too. But so quickly? No one else seemed to have been ill, save for the child, and it was likely she'd been sickly to begin with. Alison had been blessed with a robust constitution. She should not have succumbed so easily.

Blanche struggled to her feet and made use of the latrine pit in a far corner. *No*, she thought, *if I survived my first night in this place, Alison would have done the same*. There had to be more to her death than natural causes.

By the time she rejoined the other women, another physical need had made itself known. "Do they mean to starve us here?" she asked. "Is there no food in this place?"

"All in good time," said Lady Otley. "This is the hour for silent prayer and meditation."

Still bleary-eyed from an uncomfortable night, Blanche looked around her. The others were already on their knees. When Lady Otley joined them, Blanche assumed the same position.

She envied them their ability to subdue the need for material sustenance and surrender their hearts to God. All eyes but her own were closed in spiritual contemplation. A serene smile lit Matilda Farleigh's wrinkled countenance. No one fidgeted, not even the child.

Belatedly, it occurred to Blanche that she could see the features of her kneeling companions much better that she had been able to the previous night. They were illuminated by feeble rays of sunlight. She sought the source and located a small, barred window high up on one wall. Pale beams full of dust motes also revealed bare stone walls, uneven flagged flooring, and a scattering of bundles containing the few possessions the prisoners had been allowed to bring with them when they were arrested.

By day, the chamber was no more appealing that it had been in darkness. The high, vaulted ceiling gave the storeroom a cavernous aspect, but in truth it was not so very large. Blanche wondered what it had been used for before it was turned into a prison cell. Wine, mayhap, or munitions? Provisions for a siege? Her brother-in-law had told her that Colchester Castle was ancient, older even than the Tower of London.

A shoe scraped on stone as the wearer shifted her weight. When Blanche's gaze drifted in that direction she locked eyes with Edith Trott, one of Lady Otley's two servants. Blanche offered up a tentative smile but the young woman did not return it.

She would question the maidservants first, Blanche decided. Household retainers always knew more about their betters than their employers realized. If she could persuade Edith or the other maid, Sarah, to confide in her, she was certain they could tell her something about her sister's last hours. They'd likely known her as well or better than Lady Otley had, for Alison's role in the household had been as Lady Otley's companion. As such, she'd have had daily dealings with the staff and, knowing Alison as well as she had, Blanche felt certain she'd have tried to befriend them.

The creak and thud that announced the opening of the door at the top of the stairs put an end to morning prayers and to Blanche's ruminations. The two servants sprang to their feet and scurried toward the sound.

Lady Otley rose more slowly, accepting Blanche's proffered arm to lean on. "We are fed twice a day," she explained. "The guards deliver the food. Edith and Sarah serve it."

On a nonexistent table, Blanche presumed.

Two burly, brutish, uncouth fellows in leather jerkins and grimy Venetians appeared at the foot of the stairs. They carried a wooden box between them.

With an air of contempt, they dropped it on the floor, showing no care for the contents, and would have left without speaking if Blanche had not called out to them.

"Wait. Please. I would have a word with you."

They ignored her approach and continued on toward the stairs.

Such callous and disrespectful behavior infuriated Blanche. Between her lack of rest and her general discomfort, she could not maintain her accustomed command of her temper. Always a trifle volatile, it snapped with the ease of a branch in an ice storm. Hiking up her skirts, she hurried after the guards, almost trotting in order to intercept them before they began their ascent. She thrust herself in front of them, shoulders squared, and folded her arms over her chest as she glared up at them.

Her resolution wavered as she got a closer look at their unkempt beards and cold, hard eyes. She expected to be brushed aside like a troublesome insect, if they did not simply walk right over her, but when the larger guard's pig-like eyes went from cold to hot, she experienced a more primal sort of fear. Her heart in her throat, she froze, momentarily incapable of either movement or speech.

The guard leered at her. "Lonely are you, sweeting?"

His companion laughed. His gaze dropped to her bosom and he licked his lips.

Each of the men was a head taller than Blanche and far stronger, but once again her temper rose to the fore, a force strong enough to overcome incipient terror. Since she had nowhere to run, she was left with only one choice—defiance. She thrust out her chin and glared at her tormentor.

"I was promised a brazier. Where is it?"

The first man hawked and spat. "'Twill cost you."

"I have already paid. I want that brazier and adequate charcoal to fuel it and I want it now." Her voice grew steadier with every word. She was determined not to show weakness. That way lay certain disaster.

From behind the bulk of the two ruffians, Blanche heard one of the women gasp. Too late, she remembered that she had intended to give the impression that she was a quiet, inoffensive woman, not only to those who were keeping them here, but also to the imprisoned recusants. She'd been warned that prisoners, if they were wise, did nothing to call attention to themselves.

That ship had sailed.

When the guard reached for her, Blanche ducked, evading his grasp. At the same time, she reached for the small sharp eating knife no one had thought to take away from her when she was admitted to gaol. Hidden beneath her cloak, the sheath had gone unnoticed.

Common sense reasserted itself an instant before she revealed that she was armed. She had no illusions about what would happen if she used a weapon to defend herself. The guards would have no difficulty taking the knife away from her. Afterward, at the least, she would be clapped in irons. If the keeper was truly annoyed by her actions, he'd likely throw her into that noisome cell he'd shown her on the way to this one.

Knowing it would be madness to risk such a fate, or a worse one, Blanche moderated her tone while at the same time making sure she stayed just out of reach of the two men. She lowered her eyes and attempted to present a cowed and penitent demeanor. She did not need to affect the tremor in her voice. That came of its own accord.

"Please, sirs, I beg of you, bring me the brazier. A body could freeze to death in this terrible place."

Sensing it was futile to appeal to the prison guards' better nature, since it was doubtful they had one, she began to back away. She started at the sound of Lady Otley's voice.

"Mistress Wainfleet is correct, and may I remind you that we are none of us here under sentence of death. We have not yet been tried for any crime, let alone convicted."

The first guard's lips curled in contempt. "'Twould be no great loss if another of you died."

He turned his back on them and started up the steps.

"Just one less papist to worry about," said the other, and followed after his partner.

Blanche stood stock-still staring after them. What did they know about Alison's death? And had she just ruined any chance of persuading them to share that information with her?

Then a more alarming idea reared its head. What if Alison, so like Blanche in spirit, if not in appearance, had also challenged the guards? Had she paid the ultimate price for her defiance?

The door above slammed shut.

Careful to school her features, Blanche turned to Lady Otley. There was a catch in her voice when she asked, "Would they have struck me?"

"I do not doubt it, had you continued to defy them. Worse, you put your virtue at risk."

Blanche did not have to feign her reaction. Her knees went suddenly weak and what little warmth there had been in her body drained away, leaving her hands clammy and her entire body shaking. Despite the innuendos and the lecherous looks, a part of her had refused to believe she was in danger of being violated ...until now.

"Have those men forced themselves on others? Have they gone so far as to kill helpless prisoners?"

"Our safety so far rests in the fact that they have other duties and would be reprimanded if they took too long to complete any one task, but they are dangerous all the same. What if they had taken you away with them? You'd not have been so brazen as to challenge them then, would you?"

"I should not have confronted them," Blanche admitted.

In truth, her real mistake had been in trying to play the role of a biddable female in the first place. It had been folly to attempt such a ruse when it was not in her nature to let anyone run roughshod over her.

Lady Otley regarded her with disfavor. "You appear to be accustomed to standing up for yourself."

"I can see that you disapprove, but I did tell you, madam, that I lived in London for most of my life. In that great city, as elsewhere, it is good to be silent and obedient at home, but in London's marketplaces one needs must be assertive. My mother taught me young to demand only the best cuts of meat and the freshest bread and to brook no argument from shopkeepers."

Lady Otley acknowledged the sense of this with a curt nod and turned her attention to the provisions the guards had left behind. Edith and Sarah had already begun to unpack the wooden box.

Relieved of her most immediate fears, Blanche remembered that she was hungry. Her stomach growled in anticipation as she hastened to join the others and receive her share of the food and drink.

Chapter Five

The heel of dark brown bread was so hard it rivaled the paving stones in the floor. The wooden bowl Blanche had been handed proved to be half full of lumpy porridge. Repulsed and slightly nauseous, she set both aside.

Catching sight of her expression, Mistress Farleigh sent her a sympathetic look. "I fear our diet varies little, but it is sufficient to keep body and soul together. Despite that brute's words, no one wants us to die in captivity."

"They would rather keep us alive until we can be sentenced to be executed in public." Lady Otley made short work of her portion of the porridge. "Little do they realize how glorious a fate it would be to be martyred."

Appalled, Blanche stared at her. "Surely the queen does not execute women!"

"What is to stop her? Her father had no qualms when it came to ridding himself of enemies, male or female. We need not mention the two queens he ordered beheaded, but have you never heard of the Nun of Kent? She was executed at Tyburn in old King Henry's time."

"Burnt at the stake," said Matilda Farleigh, gnawing doggedly on her share of the bread.

Female felons were hanged, Blanche remembered. Heretics were burnt at the stake. She shuddered and reached for the pint of beer that went with the meal. It was watery and sour, but better than nothing.

"Only time will tell what our fate will be." Lady Otley seemed to relish the prospect of dying on a bonfire for her faith, a viewpoint Blanche could not begin to understand.

Although the meal was unappetizing, Blanche knew that Mistress Farleigh was right. She had to eat. If she did not, she would grow weak in both mind and body. That would not do. She needed to keep her wits about her.

She nibbled cautiously at the bread, surprised that no one had yet lost a tooth trying to bite into it. Dunking it in the porridge did no good. What was in her bowl was so cold and congealed that it had no effect. Dipping the bread into her beer softened it a trifle but did nothing to improve the taste of either.

On the far side of the brazier, Jane Kenner sat huddled in her woolen cloak, the hood pulled up to cover her light brown hair. She had not touched her food.

"Taste just a little," Mistress Kenner urged her, but when she tried to bring a spoonful of the porridge to her daughter's mouth, the girl turned her head away.

"Is there ever any meat?" Blanche asked.

"This is Friday," Lady Otley reminded her. "A fish day."

That remark, and the tone of voice in which it had been uttered, discouraged further conversation.

While Blanche consumed her unsatisfactory meal, she thought with great longing of the far more satisfying offerings that would be set before her if she were at home. In Holborn, where she and Kit had purchased a fine, large house right after their marriage, she'd be breaking her fast with good ale made from pure water. She'd be served the finest manchet bread money could buy and there would be cheese and fruit and a bit of beef or ham, even on a fish day.

Under the law, loyal Englishmen were not supposed to eat meat on Wednesdays, Fridays, or Saturdays, or during Lent. Although they could be fined for it, noncompliance was widespread, and because Blanche had no great fondness for fish of any kind, she frequently ignored the prohibition. Given Kit's wealth, she could indulge in a great variety of flesh and fowl on any day of the week.

She wondered where he was now, her wandering merchant husband. He had set sail months ago aboard one of his own ships, hoping to negotiate new contracts to import foreign goods into England. He might return at any time, but she did not truly expect to see him before the warmer winds of spring made travel by sea less hazardous.

Blanche used the last of her bread to scrape the porridge bowl clean. The food left a nasty taste in her mouth. Too late, she wondered if it was tainted. A case of the belly gripes would be disastrous, confined as they were in this dismal place.

Once again it occurred to her that she might be wrong about the cause of Alison's death. Her sister could have been carried off by something as simple as food gone bad. Or she might have injured herself stumbling down those treacherous stairs, or come into contact with a broken stone or a rusty nail. Even a small wound could spell death if it became inflamed. Blanche had once seen a man who had died that way. Great red streaks had run up his arm from a shallow slash on his palm. She'd been told that when they reached his heart, it stopped beating.

"There is better coming." Mistress Farleigh sent Blanche an encouraging smile. "For our second feeding on fish days, they give us a wedge of cheese, or sometimes one good herring, and on flesh days we each receive four ounces of meat, although it is impossible to say what manner of creature it comes from."

Blanche forced herself to return the smile. "That is good to hear. Even the frigid air does not seem so cold when one's belly is full."

"Likely it will be herring for supper." Matilda Farleigh accompanied this pronouncement with a loud smacking of her lips.

"Aunt Matilda was a nun in her youth," Mistress Farleigh reminded Blanche. "At Barking. She is accustomed to fasting and to mortifying the flesh."

"What need of food when the spirit is strong?" the old woman quipped.

Blanche bit back a tart reply. She had shown quite enough spirit for one day and was loath to do anything else to arouse Lady Otley's suspicions.

Once the food was gone, they had none of the usual female occupations with which to pass the time. Blanche did not regret for an instant the lack of needlework. She had always questioned the common belief that a woman's hands must be kept busy. She had decided years ago that this was an idea devised by fathers and husbands to keep their female relations from meddling in matters they considered to be the exclusive province of men.

And yet she could not help but think with great longing of her normal routine. Once she broke her fast at Wainfleet House, she was accustomed to speak with the cook about the day's meals. After that, she usually worked on the accounts, both household and business, as she was responsible for Kit's enterprises in his absence. When that duty was done, she often walked in the garden for exercise, even on cold January days. Then, if she had time, she liked to curl up on one of the gallery's deep window seats and read. At home, she had a small collection of favorite books, not one of them religious in nature.

After sleeping in her clothing, Blanche felt grubby and disheveled, but there was no water to wash with in Colchester gaol.

You can endure this for a week, she told herself. At the end of that time, Joanna's husband Arthur and his friend Master Peyton, a justice of the peace, would come in person to the prison with an order for her release.

Only seven days.

Six now.

She must not waste her time wishing she was safe in the house in Holborn with Kit at her side. She must focus on the task at hand, to learn all she could about the circumstances of Alison's death

"My hair came undone during the night," she said aloud. "I fear I have never been any good at dressing it." The long, pale strands hung down her back in unruly clumps to corroborate this statement. "I would be most grateful, Lady Otley, for the loan of one of your maids to help me set it to rights."

"Edith will see to you," Lady Otley said. "She is less fumble-fingered than her sister. But I must warn you, Mistress Wainfleet, that neither of the Trott sisters has been properly trained to dress hair." Lady Otley's ample bosom heaved with a deep sigh. "I have been seeking a tiring maid for some time with no success. Until we were imprisoned here, my companion assisted me with my attire and my hair, but she proved too frail to survive the ordeal of imprisonment. She died the day after we were thrown into this vile pit."

Blanche had to bite her tongue to keep from blurting out a spate of questions. She must not appear too eager for information, lest they suspect her of taking an undue interest in Alison's fate. She was not supposed to know anything about the woman who had died.

"How unfortunate," she murmured instead.

"Edith," Lady Otley called. Both maidservants had been relegated to the outer circle, farthest from the candlelight and the heat of the braziers. "Come here, girl. I have a task for you."

Blanche studied the young woman as she approached. She was sturdily built, a useful attribute in a maid-of-all-work. She appeared to be twenty at the most and was probably younger. Her countenance was sullen, which did not improve upon its features—close-set chestnut-colored eyes, a snub nose, and full lips slightly parted to reveal a slight gap between her two front teeth.

Given her orders by Lady Otley, Edith trailed after Blanche to the place, a bit removed from the braziers where the other women were gathered, where she had left the small bundle she had brought with her into prison. Blanche produced her comb from the pack and settled herself tailor-fashion on the blanket.

When Edith knelt behind her to begin her task, Blanche drew in a slow breath. She could not hope for any better opportunity to interrogate the maid. If they kept their voices low, no one else would overhear more than a stray word or two.

Chapter Six

B y the time Edith braided Blanche's hair and fashioned it into a coil at the nape of her neck, Blanche despaired of learning anything from her. Edith Trott was the most close-mouthed servant she had ever encountered. Despite several attempts to ease the girl into casual conversation, asking her how long she had been in service and if she wished to be trained as a tiring maid, she'd received only monosyllabic answers and no encouragement to move on to broader topics. Lady Otley's maid had volunteered not a single word the whole time she'd been combing Blanche's hair and lacing it with flat-woven inkle braids. Did she fear her mistress would disapprove of idle chatter? Or was she simply shy with strangers? Without much hope of success, Blanche made one last attempt to initiate a conversation.

"There was a queen once who had hair as pale as mine. She was the wife of King Edward the Fourth, if memory serves. That was more than a hundred years ago, but my mother could remember her grandmother telling her—"

She broke off when Edith abruptly let go of her hair. She turned her head just in time to see the girl cross herself.

"Whatever did I say? The kings and queens in those days were all good Catholics."

"Not that one." Edith spoke with a trace of country accent, but her speech was near enough to that of London and its environs for Blanche to have no difficulty understanding her. "Some do say she was a witch. Why else should a king marry a low-born widow woman?"

She reached for the elaborate hat that lay discarded on the bundle of

Blanche's possessions. It was a pretty thing, decorated with colorful ribbons and a feather, but useless when it came to supplying added warmth.

"It would be foolish of me to wear that in here," Blanche said. "Better to raise the hood of my cloak against the cold."

When Edith's gaze remained fixed on the hat, Blanche had no difficulty guessing her thoughts. She was imagining how it would look perched on her own mud-brown hair. A few errant strands had escaped from the plain linen kerchief she wore. Acting on impulse, Blanche detached one of the ribbons and presented it to the younger woman.

"With my thanks," she said.

Edith looked surprised by the gesture, and not altogether certain she should be pleased, although she did not hesitate to accept the gift. For safekeeping, she tucked it into the pocket hidden in the folds of her kirtle.

Blanche watched the maidservant walk away, mystified by her attitude. Most retainers went out of their way to fawn over their betters. Mayhap she'd thought Blanche had nothing to offer her but gratitude.

Edith tucked her bare hands into her armpits as she joined her sister just behind the circle of gentlewoman. At that distance from the braziers, so little of the heat reached them that Blanche thought they must be well-nigh frozen. It was a wonder, in truth, that Edith and Sarah remained in good health. Within her own thick layers of fabric, she shivered in sympathy.

The two servants were not warmly dressed. Their cloaks had hoods, but the cloaks themselves were made of plain wool cloth lined with fustian, a mixed fabric of cotton, flax, and wool. They gave nowhere near as much protection from the cold and damp as Blanche's heavy, fur-lined garment. Beneath the cloaks, the sisters wore garb typical of serving maids of the lesser sort—plain blue kirtles that stopped at the ankles and bodices made of the same cloth, most likely dorneck, the linen customarily used for the clothing of domestic servants. In the normal way of things, maids spent their days doing chores that soiled hems and cuffs, washing floors and the like, so their sleeves were short, too. The long aprons and the neckerchiefs they wore around their shoulders did little to add warmth.

The braziers were inadequate to the task of warming a subterranean storeroom. Even in a much smaller space, they would have been erratic as a source of heat. As a child, Blanche had spent many hours sewing beside a similar brazier on a winter's day, face and hands dewed with perspiration while her backside froze. When she settled herself next to Lady Otley in the inner circle, she saw to her dismay that even that small amount of warmth would soon vanish. Their supply of charcoal was nearly depleted.

"Time for prayer," Lady Otley announced.

Once again, everyone knelt with heads bowed, but this time Lady Otley prayed long and loud in Latin. It pained Blanche to listen to her. Like most women, Lady Otley had never studied the language. She had learned the words by rote and recited them in a monotone that suggested she had little understanding of their meaning. Blanche steeled herself to endure. What choice did she have? Under other circumstances, she might have been amused by her realization that Catholic women prayed more frequently and fervently than the most evangelical of Puritans, but as Lady Otley droned on, Blanche fell into a sort of trance, her mind blank and her body unmoving.

"Mistress Wainfleet?" A poke in the ribs came hard upon the heels of someone speaking her name, ripping her from a waking stupor.

Startled out of her doze, Blanche looked down into young Jane Kenner's wide brown eyes.

The girl managed a tentative smile. "Prayers are over. We are permitted to get up now."

After kneeling for such a long time on the hard stone floor, rising was slow and awkward. The icy cold seemed to have penetrated every muscle and bone. Blanche's knees ached and her back felt as stiff as the proverbial board.

"You show a true vocation with your piety."

At last, Blanche heard a faint hint of approval in Lady Otley's voice. Slanting a wary glance at the gentlewoman from beneath half-lowered eyelids, she searched for any hint of sarcasm, but Lady Otley seemed sincere. It appeared she had mistaken Blanche's closed eyes and somnolent state for piety.

"This is the hour at which we take our daily exercise," Lady Otley announced. "It is our accustomed practice to circle the perimeter of our prison at least two dozen times."

She proceeded to promenade with Mistress Kenner while Mistress Farleigh and her aunt walked side by side at a slower pace behind them. Edith was paired with Jane Kenner, leaving Blanche to take her place at the rear of the procession with Sarah.

Edith's sister was the younger of the two by several years. At most sixteen, mayhap no more than fourteen, she had the same square face and snub nose, but her lips were not as full, nor was her body as voluptuous as Edith's. She walked with her head down, as if she was too shy to do more than cast an occasional covert glance in her companion's direction. Blanche allowed the first few circuits to pass in silence, but she was not about to lose an opportunity to question the girl.

"Do you hope to train as a tiring maid?" she asked, as she had of Edith. The servants responsible for dressing their mistresses held a privileged position in most households, only a small step below companion, governess, and housekeeper.

"One day, mayhap. I have not been at Otley Manor long." Sarah sniffled the way one did when holding back tears. "I arrived but a few weeks before the soldiers came and brought us here. I wish …"

"What do you wish?" Blanche probed when Sarah's voice trailed off. She was careful to keep her voice low and her manner encouraging.

"That I could go home again."

"Did you live near Otley Manor?"

Sarah shook her head. "Edith and I come from Stisted. Mother and Father were pleased when Edith found employment with Lady Otley two years ago. It is good to be trained in a gentlewoman's household."

Blanche nodded but said nothing.

"When my sister sent word there was a place there for me, too, Father said I must go." Sarah worried her lower lip with her teeth, looking as if she wanted to say more but did not quite dare.

Blanche slowed her steps, creating a little more distance between the two of them and the others. Lowering her voice to a whisper, she asked, "What troubles you, Sarah? You can tell me. I will not repeat a single word you say. I swear it."

Sarah's eyes widened slightly. They were an ordinary brown in color but Blanche imagined she saw in them a flash of relief before the girl once more ducked her head. "It is all this praying in Latin, mistress." The words were mumbled and hard to make out. "And the rosary beads. And the reason we were taken into custody in the first place. I am not a papist, mistress," she added in a frightened whisper. "My parents worship in the manner of all good English Christians."

Blanche patted her hand. "It is wrong to force you to go against your conscience, Sarah, but I caution you to bide a while yet in silence. Stay in Lady Otley's good graces if you can."

Outwardly, Blanche was calm, but her heart had begun to beat faster at Sarah's words. That they were an echo of what Alison had written in her last letter to Philippa did not bode well for the maidservant's continued safety. Had Alison known how Sarah felt? Had she befriended her, as Blanche desired to?

At the corner, they turned. "It must have been unsettling," Blanche said, still speaking softly, "not only to be thrust into prison but then to have one of your party die so soon after."

It was difficult to be certain in the poor light, but Blanche thought Sarah's already pale face lost even more color at the mention of Alison's death. The girl sent a nervous glance over her shoulder and an equally wary one toward the women walking ahead of them. Only when she was certain no one was paying any attention to their exchange did she sidle closer to Blanche and speak in a halting whisper.

"There is more going on at Otley Manor than forbidden papist rites. There is true evil there."

Blanche's steps faltered. The conviction in Sarah's voice made her feel certain that the girl believed what she was saying, but evil was a strong word. "What do you mean?"

Before she answered, Sarah once again made certain no one was looking their way. "Mistress Palmer did not just die, Mistress Wainfleet," she confided. "She was bewitched to death."

Chapter Seven

The stricken expression on Sarah's face told Blanche that the girl regretted her accusation as soon as it was out. She was frightened, not because she thought Blanche doubted her but because she had admitted something that someone, most likely Lady Otley, had ordered her to keep to herself.

Alison had been bewitched to death? Nonsense!

Although Blanche longed to throw subtlety aside and ask the questions burning inside her, she knew it would be foolish to press Sarah for details at this juncture. The maidservant was too upset, and the others were too near at hand. Even as she cautioned herself to be patient, Lady Otley signaled the end of the day's exercise.

The next hours seemed endless, enlivened only by the delivery of Blanche's brazier and a fresh supply of charcoal. The extra warmth, little as it was, was exceeding welcome and went a long way toward endearing Blanche to her fellow prisoners.

Throughout that long, dismal day, her thoughts returned often to what Sarah had said. Although Blanche knew there were laws against witchcraft, and that most people believed curses and spells could kill, she found it difficult to accept that her sister could have succumbed to another person's ill-wishing.

That evening's meal included the promised herring, along with the usual allotment of porridge, bread, and weak beer. Blanche managed to choke down the unappetizing food but her stomach very nearly rebelled and that night she slept poorly.

Blanche was accustomed to finding her own thoughts good company, but the next day they grew bleaker and more unprofitable with each passing hour. In dire need of distraction, she almost envied her companions. As true believers, they took comfort in the long sessions on their knees. Each time she pretended to pray with the other women, she was wracked by self-doubt, wondering if she had made a huge mistake in thinking she could discover the truth about Alison's death on her own.

As she continued to feign piety, her thoughts turned to her husband. Would she have entered Colchester gaol if Kit had been at home to reason with her? He was good at solving problems. At a relatively young age, he had acquired three fine ships. He traded with ports as far away as the Canaries and Muscovy, exchanging good English broadcloth for rare and expensive luxury goods. In the ordinary way of things, he no longer sailed with his little fleet, but he had chosen to make this voyage to France in order to meet with his factor there. Certain French merchants had indicated they no longer wished to do business with him, and he had been convinced that if he met with them face-to-face he would be able to convince them to continue the current, profitable arrangement.

Kit might well have thought of a better way to get at the truth of Alison's death, but lacking his guidance, Blanche had devised the best plan she could. Aided by her sisters, she had taken sensible precautions. In less than a week, she would be set free, whether or not she had succeeded in her quest for information.

She shivered. As cold and miserable as she felt at this moment, she wondered if she would last that long. If she did not freeze to death, she might well go mad from boredom.

Time passed so slowly that for once in her life Blanche would willingly have embraced the usual pastimes of gentlewomen, even those that had never been to her taste. Given the choice of remaining in prison with nothing to occupy her but prayer, and supervising the brewing and baking, she'd choose the latter in a heartbeat. She'd even endure being read to from improving books over Lady Otley's brand of spirituality. When the alternative was to do nothing at all, Blanche caught herself longing for the most mundane of chores. She'd strew rushes on the storeroom floor if she had any, and if they had been provided with chamber pots instead of that noxious latrine pit, she'd gladly have emptied them. At least the keeper had been right about one thing. She had become inured to the smells around her.

Walking in circles provided the only exercise. At home, Blanche rode, and she had learned to shoot both longbows and crossbows as a child. She'd set up targets in her garden and could almost always hit what she aimed at. She engaged in another sort of healthful activity when Kit was at home, but she thought it best not to dwell on that pastime. The other deprivations were frustrating enough.

By the afternoon of her second full day of imprisonment, Blanche could bear inaction no longer. Neither did she wish to continue to wallow in self-pity. She had been warned what conditions would be like in prison. She had made her choice in the hope of answers. It was time to begin a concerted effort to obtain them.

You are here on a mission, she reminded herself. *You have less than a week remaining. The sooner you learn the truth about Alison's death, the better.*

So far, every time she had tried to steer Lady Otley into a discussion of life at Otley Manor, that gentlewoman had launched into another lecture on the tenets of the Catholic faith. The obvious solution was to separate the other gentlewomen from their leader and attempt to elicit information from them.

Anything approaching private conversation was exceeding difficult to manage. For warmth, everyone stayed in a tight group close to the cluster of braziers. Only when Lady Otley sought the far corner of their prison to use the latrine pit did Blanche have an opportunity to talk to the others.

She shifted the blanket she was using as a cushion closer to Mistress Farleigh and offered what she hoped would sound like a casual comment. No matter how much she wanted to, she could not raise the subject of Alison's death directly, not without arousing unwelcome suspicions about her interest.

"Is it not a great pity," she ventured, "that we have no cards or dice with which to pass the time?"

"Indeed, it is," Mistress Farleigh answered, "but I miss music even more. At home I play the lute, the virginals, and the harp." For a moment, she looked as if she would weep.

"How clever of you." Blanche felt a twinge of envy. She was as hopeless when it came to performing on a musical instrument as she was at needlework.

"I have some small talent, and Aunt Matilda has a most splendid voice. She received extensive training when she was young."

Matilda Farleigh's wrinkled face wore its usual beatific smile. Despite the occasional flash of intelligence in her deep-set eyes, Blanche had begun to suspect that the older woman had reached the age where her wits were wont to wander. Matilda mumbled her prayers and fingered the beads in her rosary and spent much of the rest of her time staring off into space.

"She was a nun at Barking back before King Henry closed down all the religious houses in England." Mistress Farleigh's voice swelled with pride.

"So you said." *More than once.*

"She took holy orders as a young woman in the hope of rising to become an abbess."

Blanche tried to remember what she had been told about the dissolution of the monasteries. It was ancient history as far as she was concerned, having happened so many years before she was born. Genuinely curious, she asked what Matilda had done afterward.

"What could she do? Former nuns are not permitted to marry. She came back to her family and helped with the children. My husband inherited her care when his father died. She collects an annuity from the Crown every year, but it is a mere pittance, scarce sufficient to keep body and soul together."

"It is most unfair the way the world treats single women," Blanche said, at last seeing a way to bring the conversation around to Alison. "Why, we are but slaves to our fathers until we marry, and then we become naught but chattel in a husband's keeping. If we do not marry, now that all the nunneries are gone, we have nowhere to go to escape from the rule of men. Even in service, we are beholden to the head of the household." Except in the case of widows, that was almost always a man.

Matilda's hands stilled on her rosary and she turned her head. Zeal flared to life in cloudy blue eyes. "God has a plan for every one of us. It was His will, too, that we were cast out of the abbey."

"I know what it is to be an outcast," Blanche murmured.

"You are young yet." Mistress Kenner was only a year or two Blanche's senior, but she was married and a mother, which gave her seniority.

"I have seen much that is distressing," Blanche argued. "The very reason I am here is unfair."

"The authorities have no good reason to keep any of us in prison."

Lady Otley had returned so silently that Blanche had been unaware of her presence until she spoke. Silently, she cursed her slowness in leading up to the subject she most wanted to discuss. Another minute and she might have been able to ask how the death of Lady Otley's companion could have been part of God's plan.

On the other hand, she'd heard no disapproval in the gentlewoman's comment. Lady Otley seemed to be in agreement with her sentiments. Emboldened, she embroidered upon her theme.

"It is not just fear of another's beliefs that makes men cruel. There was a poor, simple woman in London who was accused by the Royal College of Physicians of illegally supplying her friends and relatives with herbal remedies. She was not licensed as an apothecary, so the physicians brought a complaint against her, threatening to lock her up and take away her livelihood. Only intervention by the queen herself saved her from imprisonment."

"The queen is—"

With a slashing gesture, Lady Otley cut off whatever Mistress Farleigh had been about to say. "Do you speak of a cunning woman?"

Something in Lady Otley's voice warned Blanche to be careful, but she kept stubbornly to her course. She had wasted too much time already. She needed answers.

"Only an herbalist," she said, "as are many goodwives."

Lady Otley nodded, appeased.

"But there *was* a cunning woman who lived near us in London, a poor old body who never did anyone any harm. Her simples helped heal almost everyone who consulted her, all but one lad who fell out of a tree and cracked his skull. The boy's parents blamed her because she could not save him. They accused her of bewitching their son to death!"

Having every eye upon her, unblinking, gave Blanche a moment's pause. Had she gone too far? The silence continued until she thought she would scream just to break it. Then Lady Otley let out a gusty breath.

"Your compassion speaks well of you, Mistress Wainfleet, but it is never wise to express sympathy for a witch. They are far more clever than you know. Many of them disguise their evil behind good deeds."

Blanche widened her eyes and pasted what she hoped was an incredulous expression on her face. "Never tell me you have encountered such a woman yourself?"

"Rest assured that if I did, I would have had her taken up by the constable for her crimes."

"Crimes?" It was a simple matter to sound bewildered. Blanche had difficulty following Lady Otley's logic.

"What I have seen is the result of wicked witchcraft, and in my own household, too. A short time before we were arrested, the companion I told you of, the one who died here in Colchester gaol, was possessed by a demon as the result of a witch's curse."

"Possessed?" Blanche's astonishment was unfeigned. If she had her doubts about the effectiveness of spells, she had even more difficulty believing that a demon could inhabit a person's body.

"We were unable to discover the name of the witch. They are clever creatures. But by the grace of God and the good efforts of those who understand such things, poor Alison was freed of possession."

"They performed an exorcism," Mistress Kenner said.

"It was a miracle," Matilda Farleigh lifted her face toward heaven, her eyes piously closed.

"But she died all the same." This last remark, spoken in a surprisingly loud voice, came from Jane Kenner. As soon as the words were out, the girl buried her face in her mother's skirts.

Blanche hardened her heart. She felt sorry for the child, but if she did not pursue this matter now, she might never have another opportunity. *"How did she die?"*

Lady Otley grimaced. "The exorcism was not as successful as we first believed. It did naught but cure her of the most obvious symptoms of possession. The demon remained inside her."

"Symptoms? What symptoms?"

"Uncontrollable sneezing," Edith said. She and Sarah stood together on the far side of the braziers, shoulders hunched in identical fashion.

Blanche slanted an incredulous look their way.

"She flailed about with arms and legs, jerking her whole body in a most unnatural manner," Lady Otley said.

Jane looked up long enough to bleat out a few more words: "Great ugly blisters appeared on her hands!"

"Not at first," Lady Otley corrected her, adding a stern look that strongly suggested children should not join in the conversations of their elders. "The Devil's marks appeared only after the demon once again made itself known. That occurred just after we were locked up in this room. Alison went into convulsions and there was naught anyone could do to save her life."

"How terrible." Blanche's voice was choked and she was close to tears. Only with immense effort did she keep control of her emotions. She could not afford to let the others see how affected she was by what she'd heard.

Lady Otley's manner turned brusque. "We will speak no further of such distressing matters. Instead we will pray for assurance that the evil is gone for good."

Blanche bit back a groan. Lady Otley meant her words literally.

Obediently, they all knelt, but when Lady Otley began to chant in her execrable Latin, Blanche closed her eyes and gave her thoughts free rein. At first they swirled in a confused jumble and she could make no sense of anything she had been told, but after a bit her mind circled back to young Jane.

Despite her apparent frailty, the girl's voice had been strong when she supplied that detail about the blisters. Many children had a morbid fascination with all things gruesome. Was she one such? Jane might have squealed and covered her eyes during Alison's death throes, but she might also have peeked through her fingers.

For the remainder of the time she spent on her knees, Blanche formulated and discarded a half dozen ploys by which she might persuade the child to confide what else she had observed.

Chapter Eight

I t was much later before an opportunity to question Jane presented itself, and circumstances were such that Blanche nearly changed her mind. Sickly, frail-looking, and undersized for her age, the child suffered a fit of coughing that left her as weak as a kitten. Her mother carried her a little apart from the others, bundled her in both Jane's blanket and her own, and was trying with little success to coax her to eat.

Tears flowed freely down Mistress Kenner's cheeks as she offered her daughter a bit of beer-softened bread. "You must keep up your strength, my dearest."

Young Jane held her mouth tightly closed and kept her eyes squeezed shut. She was no longer coughing, but her thin chest rose and fell in an erratic fashion.

"Shall I try?" Blanche asked, joining them. "My mother used to make a game of it when I was ill and disinclined to take nourishment."

She settled herself on the other side of the ailing girl, reaching across her small form to take the bread from Mistress Kenner. She shifted so that she was holding the morsel a few inches in front of Jane's face.

"It is a horse," she said.

Jane's eyes fluttered open to stare at her in astonishment.

"It is on its way home to the stable. There is a storm on the way. Do you want the horse—your favorite horse—to be left out in the thunder and lighting and rain?"

Slowly, Jane shook her head.

"Then open your mouth and let him in."

Jane thought this over before she obeyed, but in the end she let Blanche feed her. She made a face at the sour taste, but she did not spit out the offering.

When Jane had chewed and swallowed, Mistress Kenner handed Blanche a spoon and a bowl with a bit of porridge congealing at the bottom. It was one of the most disgusting things Blanche had ever seen and smelled worse than it looked but eating anything was better than starving to death.

"She might do better without everyone staring at her," Blanche told Jane's mother. The other women had been watching their every move, partly out of concern for Jane's well-being and partly from simple curiosity.

Or boredom.

Mistress Kenner hesitated, but she saw the wisdom in the suggestion. Easing herself away from her daughter, she shifted Jane's frail person closer to Blanche. Jane squirmed restlessly until she was nestled against Blanche's side. Of its own volition, Blanche's free arm came around the girl's thin shoulders.

They sat that way for several minutes, giving Mistress Kenner time to join the rest of the recusant women. It was nearly time for evening prayers. Under the circumstances, Blanche hoped Lady Otley would excuse her from participating. While everyone else was distracted, she would coax Jane to eat a little more, but she would also take the opportunity to question the girl about what she had observed when Alison lay dying. Blanche repressed any qualms she might have had about taking advantage of a sick child. It was scarce *her* fault that Jane was ill.

Quiet conversation resumed around the braziers. At any moment, Lady Otley would order them to their knees. Calling on all the patience she possessed, Blanche scooped up a bit of the noxious porridge and informed Jane that it was food for the horse and must be delivered to the stable before the poor animal starved to death.

Jane looked at her askance. They both started as a loud voice pierced the quiet of the subterranean chamber.

"You stole my new ribbon," Edith Trott accused her sister. "Give it back."

"I never did!" Sarah's outraged voice was nearly as loud as Edith's.

"At home you were always taking my baubles."

"I was child then."

Lady Otley intervened, ordering them both to their knees. "Let the Lord show you the truth," she said, and launched into a lengthy prayer.

When Blanche turned her attention back to Jane, she was just in time to see a brief flash of guilt flit across the girl's face. Closer inspection revealed that Jane had one hand clutched around the small pouch suspended from the embroidered belt she wore at her waist.

"Eat all the porridge," Blanche whispered, "and I will see to it that the ribbon is found in a place were no blame will attach itself to you."

Jane tried to feign innocence but her resolve wavered beneath Blanche's unyielding stare. In sullen silence she took the bowl and spoon and ate every bite. She pretended not to notice when Blanche removed the ribbon from her pouch.

It was much the worse for wear, grubby and discolored and scarcely recognizable as the bright ornament it had been when it graced Blanche's hat. That was all to the good. Secreting the purloined scrap of fabric in her pocket, she bent close to Jane's ear.

"What do you remember about Alison Palmer?"

Jane's eyes widened in surprise. "She died."

"You said you saw blisters on her hands. No one else mentioned those. What else did you see? You are a clever girl, Jane. You notice more than most."

The look Jane leveled at Blanche was filled with resentment. She had not liked being forced to eat the porridge and she hated that Blanche had guessed she was a thief. If she had seen anything beyond what she'd already revealed, it was clear she meant to keep it to herself.

"I would take no joy in revealing—"

"I ate the porridge," Jane interrupted. "That was the bargain."

Jane's smirk irritated Blanche, the more so because she had the right of it. They had struck a deal. She would have to find some other means to persuade the girl to talk.

Accepting the temporary setback, Blanche got to her feet and held out her hand. "Come. We must join the others at prayer."

When Jane ignored her, Blanche reached down, seized her by the shoulders, and hauled her upright. She shifted her grip to Jane's arm, tugging her toward the circle of women. She half expected the girl to launch into another fit of coughing. She'd not be the first to use a sickly appearance to elicit sympathy.

Once they were on their knees, Blanche kept an eye on the girl while Lady Otley droned on. Jane cast a sideway glances at her from time to time, a calculating look in her eyes, confirming Blanche's guess that she knew more than she was willing to admit about Alison's death. Bribery might convince her to cooperate. What a good thing that there were three more ribbons on that hat.

When at last the evening prayers came to their conclusion, Blanche made her way to the latrine pit. When she returned, she clutched the ribbon she had retrieved from Jane's pouch.

"You must have dropped this," she said to Edith.

Edith stared at the soiled strip of silk in distaste, her nose wrinkling. "How did you find it? I looked everywhere, even there."

"In this dim light, it is no wonder you overlooked something so small. I stepped on it before I realized what it was." At Edith's disbelieving look, she found herself adding, "I have always had great good fortune when it comes to finding lost things." Although this statement was true, it was not something she had intended to share.

"You must offer up a prayer of thanks to Saint Anthony of Padua," Matilda Farleigh murmured.

Intrigued, Blanche turned toward the former nun. "Who was he?"

"He is the patron saint of lost items and lost people."

"Did he make a practice of finding them?"

With a faintly superior smile, Lady Otley answered. "He gained his reputation because of an incident in Bologna more than three centuries ago. When his book of psalms was stolen, he prayed for its return. The thief, who had been a novice at the monastery, was moved by divine intercession to return the psalter and rejoin the order."

"How ... remarkable," Blanche said.

46

Her own skill did not rely upon prayers, nor was it dependent upon luck. A few questions and a bit of common sense were usually sufficient to yield a list of logical places in which to search for what was lost. Once she had even been able to determine the identity of the guilty party in an instance of theft. It had been a simple matter of observing others. The way the guilty party had reacted to her questions had given him away.

"I told you I did not take it." Sarah glared at her sister.

Edith's fierce scowl made it unlikely she meant to apologize.

Blanche took the opportunity to walk over to her bundle, pick up her hat, and detach its remaining decorations. She gave one ribbon to each of the Trott sisters and the third to Jane. The feather she presented to Lady Otley.

Chapter Nine

Blanche slept poorly that night and by the time she opened her eyes on Sunday morning she was once again chilled to the bone. Lady Otley pounced as soon as she saw her sit up on her makeshift pallet. "You say that you have studied *The Exercise of a Christian Life*. In what order must you therefore dispose your life and exercises on this holy day?"

Blanche was never at her best when she first awoke, but she did possess an excellent memory for anything she had read. "After I arise from my bed, I must offer and commend myself unto my Lord and maker, as on other days, but I must make my prayers somewhat longer, preparing myself to go to mass and receive the blessed sacrament."

"Excellent," said Lady Otley.

"But there can be no mass celebrated here," Blanche objected, "nor even, I think, a service of the Church of England."

"All the more reason for us to pray together throughout the day. What does your book say about the time after church?"

"I must employ my spare time until night in doing some deed of mercy, as in visiting a hospital or prison, comforting and performing some charitable office to those weak and comfortless creatures. Failing that, I may associate myself with virtuous companions, to report or hear some spiritual discourses, or read from godly books, or occupy myself in honest exercise. If I walk abroad for recreation, it should be to some secret and solitary place where other secular persons will not come to disturb me, thereby withdrawing my mind from God with profane conversation."

Blanche was about to point out that finding a private space while imprisoned was likewise impossible, and that they were themselves "weak and comfortless" creatures in prison, but Lady Otley had not finished her catechism. "What does your book say about the lives of saints?"

Suppressing a sigh, Blanche answered. "That to read or meditate upon their lives is a very good exercise upon such saints' days as are kept holy."

"As is imitating them," said Lady Otley.

Not in the manner of their deaths, or so Blanche devoutly hoped, but aloud she agreed and continued with her account of approved Sabbath behavior: "At the end of the day, I must meditate before supper, and before I go to bed I must examine my conscience."

Having acquitted herself well enough to please Lady Otley, she was allowed to visit the latrine pit.

The next hour, before the prisoners broke their fast, was spent on their knees in prayer. At least the prayers, one long and tedious and the other shorter, were familiar to Blanche, having been included in *The Exercise of a Christian Life*. The Lord's Prayer followed, but just when she thought they might be finished with the ritual, Lady Otley began all over again.

As Blanche dutifully mouthed the words, she could not help thinking they were not so very different from those she was accustomed to. In part, she supposed, that was because they were reciting them in English rather than in Latin.

"Illuminate my soul," Blanche prayed, "and stir up my lumpish heart, oh son of true sapience and justice, with the brightness of thy countenance, that I may here with a grateful and devout memory call to mind that sacrifice of obedience, patience, and most esteemed charity which thou, being wrapped in extreme woes and ignominious reproaches, did offer to thy celestial Father for our sins. Amen."

Her enthusiastic performance capped off two days of earnest playacting. When Blanche rose from her knees, Lady Otley's invitation to sit beside her was accompanied by a warmth that had hitherto been lacking.

Blanche warned herself to be wary as she accepted an unappetizing bowl of porridge and a serving of watered down beer. It might be only her own desperate need for acceptance that made her think the gentlewoman had mellowed.

"If you continue to prove such an apt pupil," Lady Otley said, "and show a true vocation, I will arrange for you to travel to a nunnery in the Spanish Netherlands. There are excellent houses at both Louvain and Mechlin."

Blanche needed no artifice to show excitement at that prospect. The justice of the peace who had helped Arthur arrange her false imprisonment had hinted that he would be grateful if she could provide him with intelligence about the means recusants used to smuggle Jesuits into England. It seemed likely that the same routes were used in reverse by those wishing to escape to the Continent.

"Is that possible?" she asked, feigning surprise. "I did not think one could leave England without a passport."

"It is true that passports are required to travel abroad and that they are denied to Catholics, but we have our ways. Our young women are made welcome in convents throughout the Netherlands and Spain. Our young men go to Douai."

"To the Jesuits?"

"Where else? When they are fully trained, they return to minister to English Catholics."

And plot against the Crown, Blanche thought. For as long as she could remember, she had been told that Jesuits were devils sent to stir up trouble in England. They were conniving, duplicitous, and downright evil, bent upon overthrowing, perhaps even assassinating Queen Elizabeth and replacing her with a Catholic monarch.

Aloud she said, "What if I discover I am not suited to the religious life, after all?"

"Then you will find satisfaction as a lay person, as we do, we poor souls who are too full of sin to be otherwise."

Blanche poked at the lumps in her porridge. "Do you suppose this food is a penance for some sin I am unaware of having committed?"

"We all sin," Lady Otley replied. "That is why we go to confession and are absolved of them."

"What do you do when there is no priest to confess to?"

"We suffer," Mistress Kenner said, "and carry our failings with us until such time as we are able to confess them."

Blanche doubted Jane Kenner's mother bore much of a burden. As for herself, she added to her list of sins every day. Almost every word she spoke to her fellow prisoners was a lie.

"It is a pity we are held here in Colchester Castle and not in the Tower of London," Lady Otley said after she had eaten some of her own porridge.

Blanche repressed a shudder. "I should think that the Tower is the last place you would wish to be. Those imprisoned there are closely guarded and a good many of them will only leave their cells to mount the scaffold." She had no difficulty sounding shaken when she added, "I still remember when they arrested Francis Throckmorton. He lived hard by my father's house near Paul's Wharf in London. I always thought him a kindly man who did not deserve to die for his faith."

He had, however, deserved that fate for plotting against the Crown. He had been executed at Tyburn some eight months after being taken into custody.

As she had hoped, the mention of Throckmorton released a great outpouring of sympathy from her fellow prisoners. Nearly seven years had passed since he'd met his fate, but he was still remembered by his co-religionists.

"At that time, there was someone in the Tower who was a great friend to all Catholics," Lady Otley confided. "Before Sir Owen Hopton left his post as Lord Lieutenant."

"Never tell me Sir Owen was a secret Catholic!"

"Not he." Lady Otley chuckled. "But his family lived with him in the Lord Lieutenant's lodgings. It was his daughter, Cecily, who embraced the true faith."

Blanche's astonishment did not need to be counterfeited. "How did that come about? I should think anyone living in such a place would have a horror of breaking the law."

"It was a man," Mistress Farleigh put in.

Lady Otley quelled her with a look, making it clear this was her story to tell. "As the Lord Lieutenant's daughter, Cecily had the run of the place. Some years ago, a toothsome young fellow named John Stonor was held prisoner in the Tower for eight months and more. He and Cecily met and fell in love and he converted her."

An all too familiar tale, Blanche thought. Alison's attempt to win the affection of a man who followed the Old Religion had been her downfall, too.

"After Stonor's release," Lady Otley continued, "Cecily dedicated herself to helping the Catholic cause in every way she could."

"But what could she do?" Blanche asked. "If she tried to free one of the prisoners, she would have been arrested herself."

"Nothing so bold, but you say you knew Francis Throckmorton. When he was a prisoner in the Tower, Cecily guided his brother George to a secluded spot beneath the tower containing his cell. It was not possible for them to meet face to face, so he wrote messages on playing cards and threw them out his window."

"George Throckmorton," Blanche murmured, furrowing her brow and pretending it was a strain to remember what she had heard about him. Although the events they spoke of had taken place years before, she and her sisters had taken a special interest in every tidbit of news relating to their neighbor and his kin. "I thought that George himself was a prisoner in the Tower."

"Not then. Only later."

"And Cecily? She was not caught?"

"Not then," Lady Otley said again. "In the ordinary way of things, since she was the Lord Lieutenant's child and a woman of gentle birth, she would have been the last person anyone would think to accuse. When she *was* examined by the authorities, she at once confessed, but not, you understand, to everything she had done."

"If they questioned her, they must have had a reason." No doubt they had suspected her of treason.

"She was seen escorting a stranger—a man suspected of being a priest—away from George Throckmorton's cell. At first, she denied all knowledge of him, but eventually she admitted that she'd been tempted into circumventing the rules because Throckmorton gifted her with a string of pearls. She gave her inquisitors the impression that she was just a silly girl easily swayed by baubles."

Blanche could not help but approve of Cecily's ploy. "I suppose it went against all they believed in to think a woman capable of such cleverness, and yet, since she was seen with a priest—"

"She claimed to have encountered him already on the grounds and had no notion he was a Jesuit. When he asked her to escort him to George Throckmorton's cell door, she saw no harm in the request. After all, the two men could only speak to each other through the keyhole."

Blanche's admiration grew greater with every word Lady Otley spoke. England's Catholics were reputed to have a system for moving priests from place to place in secret, but it had not occurred to her before that they would be able to share news with their co-religionists in the same way.

"When they asked Cecily what the two men spoke of, she told them she'd heard nothing, and indeed she had not. She went into Mistress Somerville's cell while they talked. Clever girl. She had long since obtained her father's permission to visit with the more gently born of the female prisoners."

"This Cecily of yours appears to be a most convincing liar."

"Indeed. She proved her innocence of any serious crime by confessing to small sins, including her failure to tell her father at once when George Throckmorton asked her to help his brother escape. She insisted that she had been so appalled by the suggestion that she ran away. The authorities decided she was not complicit in any treasonous plot and she received naught but a reprimand and a warning not to be so overfamiliar with prisoners in the future. She remained in residence in the Tower as long as her father held his post and continued to serve the true faith."

"Were those who questioned her simple?" Blanche asked. "A child should have been able to see through such a ruse."

"I understand that Cecily is a handsome lass," Mistress Kenner said with a smile, "and those who interrogated her were men."

"Even so," Lady Otley said. "Cecily took a great risk and did so again every time she helped a fellow Catholic. Just as she was the first link in a chain that conveyed Francis Throckmorton's last letter to his wife, so was she instrumental in delivering many messages from prisoners in the Tower to those held in the Marshalsea. Even now, living in London with a kinswoman, she manages to assist those who share our faith to communicate with one another."

"How is it that you know so much about her?" Blanche asked. "Never tell me you were also imprisoned in the Tower of London at the time!"

Lady Otley looked regretful when she shook her head. "After Mistress Somerville was released, she shared the story. As you have surely gathered, small enclaves of true believers remain in touch with one another and our priests carry uplifting stories from place to place." Abruptly, she sobered. "Poor woman."

"Mistress Somerville?" Blanche had no idea who she might be.

"Aye. Her husband attempted to kill the queen and as a result both she and her parents were arrested and charged with conspiracy. In time, the women were pardoned, but Mistress Somerville lost both her husband and her father in that terrible place."

"And yet you would rather be imprisoned in the Tower than in Colchester Castle?" Blanche could not understand how the older woman's mind worked. If she truly sought martyrdom, then she would not look so favorably on the clever tricks Cecily Hopton had employed to avoid that fate.

"At least there we would hear news from the outside," Lady Otley explained. "Cecily may be gone, but others have taken her place. For the right bribe, several of the yeomen warders can even be persuaded to smuggle in a priest."

"Then it is a great pity that we have no Cecily Hopton here in Colchester," Blanche said. "Has anyone tried to suborn the keeper's wife or daughters, assuming he has any?"

Lady Otley grimaced. "He has a wife, but she is no friend to us, and she keeps a close watch on her husband besides. As for the guards—well, you have seen for yourself what they are like. They'd not hesitate to take a bribe, but I do much doubt they'd keep any promise they made in return. Have you finished eating?"

Blanche looked down at her empty bowl. "I suppose I have, since there is nothing else to be had."

"Then it is time for us to pray once more."

Resigned, Blanche shifted until she was kneeling instead of sitting. The silent prayer she sent heavenward was heartfelt. She asked God for a speedy resolution to her quest. If she could determine who or what had caused Alison's death, she vowed never again to complain about the restrictions the Church of England placed on Sabbath day activities. She would even eliminate flesh and fowl from her Sunday diet and eat only fish.

Chapter Ten

I t was the middle of the night when Blanche woke. At first she thought she'd been roused from yet another bout of restless sleep by the cold. Her blanket and cloak and the heat from the braziers seemed to have done less than usual to dispel the chill that permeated the cavernous storeroom. She lay still in the dark, listening to the regular breathing of the women around her. And then she heard it—a muffled sob.

Slowly, stiff muscles protesting the movement, she rose first to a crouch and then to her knees. In the dull red glow given off by the charcoal, she could just make out a flicker of movement on the far side of the brazier. A form wrapped in an inadequate blanket lay there, curled up into a tight ball against the cold. Even at this distance, Blanche could see that her shoulders were shaking. It might only be the frigid air in their prison making her shiver, but Blanche did not think so. She suspected the woman was trying, most desperately, to contain great heaving sobs.

Wary of wakening the sleepers, she was careful where she stepped. Guided by the glow from the braziers and a sheen of moonlight, she made her way across the icy stone floor. Despite the near darkness, she felt certain that the one in distress was either Sarah Trott or her sister. The gently born prisoners slept closer to the warmth.

On this night, instead of huddling together, Sarah and Edith had bedded down on opposite sides of their betters. Blanche spoke softly as she reached out to touch the sobbing girl's shoulder.

"Hush, now. We will not be here forever."

The figure beneath the blanket shot upright in a panic, arms flailing.

Blanche had to dance backward to avoid being struck. Poised to retreat to an even safer distance, she watched Sarah Trott, waiting until the maidservant recognized her before moving close to her again.

"Mistress Wainfleet?" Sarah whispered.

"Even she."

Blanche looked over her shoulder. No one else had stirred. Even better, there was a small pocket of privacy around Sarah's makeshift pallet. Blanche settled herself on the floor beside the young woman and clasped one of her cold hands. Sarah's fingers felt like icicles, chilling Blanche's skin despite her gloves.

"I was dreaming," Sarah whispered, "but it seemed so real."

"If you wish to talk about it, I will listen. It may help you to forget if you tell me what you dreamed."

Sarah's response was a muffled sound that was half laugh and half sob. "Talking has done little to improve matters in the past."

Blanche studied her for a long moment, thinking that despite the trace of a rural accent she shared with Edith, she was well spoken for a country girl. Then again, Essex was one of the home counties. Many of its people, especially those who one day hoped to obtain a post in a wealthy household, learned early in life to ape the speech of their betters.

"Have you had this dream before?" she asked.

Sarah nodded. "All too often."

"Ever since you were locked up here?"

"Even before. Ever since Mistress Palmer—"

Despite the darkness that engulfed them, Blanche was close enough to see Sarah's entire body droop. She bowed her head in apparent despair.

"Since Alison Palmer was bewitched?" Blanche took great care to keep her voice low. The others might seem to be deeply asleep, but she could not afford to be careless.

Sarah nodded. She spoke in a tremulous whisper. "The priest drove the evil out of her, but then he began to question everyone at Otley Manor, seeking the witch who cast the spell. Edith had been in Lady Otley's service for some time, but I was newly come, and I was born and bred in Stisted."

57

Blanche stared at her in confusion. "I do not understand the significance of that place."

"Witches," Sarah whispered. "Joan Cony and her daughters, Avice and Margaret. They lived in Stisted. They were tried at Chelmsford nearly two years ago. Joan was hanged for a witch with two other women and Avice, like her mother, was found guilty of causing death by witchcraft and sentenced to die, but she pled her belly and when this was verified by a jury of matrons, her execution was delayed until after she gave birth. *Then* she was hanged."

Blanche knew nothing about this particular case, but she had heard similar stories and had read more than one pamphlet about the trial of a notorious witch. Then, too, since her sister Joanna lived in Essex, she also knew that there had been more witch trials in this county than in any other in England.

"What happened to the other Cony daughter?" she asked. "Margaret, was it?"

"She was found guilty on two counts of bewitchment and sentenced to one year in prison and six appearances in the stocks."

"And I suppose you knew them."

"Stisted is a small place. Everyone living there knew them. They were much talked of even before their arrest. Avice and Margaret each bore bastard sons and refused to identify their fathers."

Such children were a burden on the parish, which was the reason midwives were charged with asking unmarried women in the throes of childbirth to name a man who could be held responsible for the newborn's upkeep. Although Blanche had never had a child herself, she had witnessed births and she could not help but admire the fortitude of any woman who could endure that much pain and still keep her wits about her.

"Were those children still very young when their mothers were arrested?" That seemed likely, since Avice Cony had been great with another child at the time.

Sarah made a sound of derision. "No older than Jane Kenner is now. They should have been whipped. Both of them. They testified against their mothers and grandmother, telling outrageous tales about the familiar spirits

58

the women called up to do their bidding. Old Joan Cony needed no help from such creatures. She ill-wished Henry Finch's wife. She admitted it from the scaffold. She did so because Goodwife Finch refused to give Joan a drink when she was on her way to market. She caused terrible pains to afflict the goodwife's head and side. She was in most horrible agony for the space of a week before she died."

"If wishing misfortune on someone was effective, half the population of England would be halt or lame and the rest either on their deathbeds or about to be hanged because someone overheard them utter a short-tempered word against another."

Sarah's hand went to her neck. "That is what I dreamed of—being made to climb the ladder and put my head in the noose and jump to my death. Ever since the exorcism, I have been afraid I will be accused of bewitching Mistress Palmer."

"Simply because you were born in Stisted?" Sarah painted a grim picture, but Blanche failed to see why she should be so wracked by fear. "I can think of no sensible reason why you should share the grisly fate of Joan and Avice Cony. Did you quarrel with Mistress Palmer before she died?"

Sarah shook her head.

"Did you threaten her?"

"Never!"

"What of your sister?"

Sarah did not answer, but whether she was protecting Edith or simply did not know, Blanche was not able to tell.

"Edith was also born in Stisted," Blanche reminded her.

She was not certain why she was pursuing this point. She did not believe Alison had been the victim of witchcraft, nor did she think her sister had been possessed by a demon. There had to be a more rational explanation for her sudden death, but she doubted she would find one by questioning Sarah. The girl believed absolutely that a person could be bewitched to death.

"Edith left the village before Joan Cony and her daughters were accused," Sarah said.

"A trifling distinction. She must have known the family as well as you did." The agitation Blanche heard in the maidservant's voice warned her to proceed more slowly. "Tell me about your home. Where is Stisted? Did you need to travel far to find employment?"

Sarah's relief was palpable. Even though she was the one who had first introduced the subject of witches, it clearly upset her to talk about those accused of practicing that forbidden craft.

"Stisted is a market town on the banks of the river Blackwater in the hundred of Lexden. There was an abbey there once, but it is long gone now."

"Is it a goodly distance from Colchester?"

Sarah frowned. "I have heard my father say it is nigh unto fifteen miles as the crow flies, but I have never traveled here from there. Otley Manor is even farther away, but in another direction."

"And how did Edith come to be employed by Lady Otley?"

"She wanted to make something of herself, or so she said. She walked the entire distance from Stisted to Chelmsford—eighteen miles—for the May Day fair and offered herself up for service as a maid-of-all-work."

Blanche made an encouraging sound. This was a common practice. Servants hired at a fair were customarily taken on for a year at a time.

"She hoped to be trained as a tiring maid," Sarah continued. "To raise Lady Otley's opinion of her, she converted to Catholicism, and when Lady Otley had need of another maidservant, Edith persuaded her to send for me, but she never warned me I would have to become a Catholic, too. I do not like their papist ways."

Abruptly, Sarah's entire body went stiff and she clapped both hands over her mouth. Blanche knew what she must be thinking. Only that morning, she had heard Lady Otley promise to help Blanche enter a nunnery.

"Listen to me, Sarah." Blanche spoke close to the girl's ear. "Although I may appear eager to convert to Lady Otley's religion, it is all a ruse. You can trust me not to repeat anything you have told me."

Unlike the others with whom Blanche shared her imprisonment, Sarah had not yet learned to be mistrustful. After but a moment's hesitation, she took Blanche at her word.

"If Father had known he was sending me into a den of papists, he would never have allowed me to leave home."

"Why did you stay once you realized the truth?"

"I had no way to send word to my family. I can neither read nor write, nor can Mother or Father."

It was too dark to see the expression on Sarah's face, but Blanche heard the utter despair in her voice. Her gaze went to the motionless forms around the brazier. Were they truly asleep or could one among them be lying awake, listening to all they said? She watched, straining to see any telltale movement until, satisfied that no one would overhear her words, she once again turned her attention to Sarah.

"Once I am free of this prison, I will help you to leave Lady Otley's service."

It was a rash promise. Her own freedom was assured, but Blanche did not know if she would be able to take anyone else out of Colchester Castle with her.

Sarah made a gulping sound and then burst out with a wild laugh.

From the other side of the brazier someone grunted and another voice called out, "What's amiss?"

"A bad dream," Blanche answered, and put one hand on Sarah's arm to warn her to be silent.

After a few minutes, everything was quiet once more.

"Why did you laugh?"

"Because you think any of us will ever be free. You mean well, but you are as much a prisoner as I am. They will never let us go. We will all die here."

"Then you need not fear you will be hanged." Despite her sympathy for Sarah's plight, Blanche was out of patience with the girl.

Once again, Sarah's body began to shake with silent sobs. Blanche patted her hand, well aware of how feeble such consolation was but knowing there was nothing else she could do for the nonce. Why should Sarah believe her? She'd been taught her entire life to defer to the wishes of her betters. Defiance was as unnatural to her as attempting to fly. She saw Blanche as someone of higher station in life but still in a dependent position, powerless to escape herself, let alone rescue another.

"Sleep now," Blanche murmured. "When you have rested, things will not seem so desperate."

Sarah obeyed, as Blanche had expected she would, curling up in the cocoon of her blanket. She seemed to take comfort in Blanche's touch. After a time, she stopped sniffling. A few minutes later she was softly snoring.

Blanche was not so fortunate. She withdrew her hand from Sarah's lax grip and returned to her own bedding, but she did not sleep. She lay awake, staring at nothing, until the first faint fingers of sunlight pierced the darkness.

Chapter Eleven

The keeper's face wore a disgruntled look as he entered the vaulted storeroom. His beady eyes, dark and malevolent, put Blanche in mind of a carrion crow, one that had been driven away from its meal by the sudden approach of a rider.

Bustling forward to berate him, Lady Otley was at her most haughty. "These conditions are intolerable. If it is more money you want, send to my husband. Sir Stephen Otley will pay you well to assure my comfort."

Her threat—or mayhap it was her promise—caused his face to assume an even more morose expression. He cleared his throat before announcing, in a pained voice, that they were free to leave.

Instead of rejoicing, Lady Otley stared at him, eyes narrowed. "Is this some kind of trick?"

"Would that it were," the keeper muttered before proclaiming in a louder voice that they had all been pardoned. "The queen herself has ordered the release of all female prisoners now held in Colchester gaol."

These words washed away the last vestige of doubt. Mistress Kenner and Mistress Farleigh hugged each other. Little Jane began to cry for joy. Blanche alone felt dismay. Although it seemed as if she had been locked up for months, this was only the fifth day of her incarceration. As much as she hated being confined in Colchester gaol, imprisonment with these women had been her only real hope of discovering what happened to her sister.

A pardon? How had that come about? Surely Master Peyton, a mere country justice of the peace, was not influential enough to have the ear of the queen. Besides, the plan had been for her brother-in-law and his friend to come for her in a week's time. This was too soon.

Lost in a confusion of dark thoughts, Blanche gathered up her few possessions, put on her high-crowned hat, and followed the others up the stone steps, along the corridor, and out into a cold winter morning. The sky was overcast, but Blanche had grown so accustomed to the dim illumination in their underground prison that even this small increase in brightness made her eyes water. The brim of her hat did little to protect them. Blinking furiously, she tried to take in the tumultuous scene before her.

There were a great many horses about. She could hear and smell that much. By the time her vision cleared sufficiently to sort them out, she had already concluded that the families of the recusant women had been sent advance notice of their release.

A small sound made her look down. Jane Kenner stood beside her, a bleak expression on her pale face as she watched the milling men and horses.

"What is the matter, Jane?" Blanche asked.

"My father is not here. He sent servants to bring us home." Disappointment made her sulky.

"Then be of good cheer, for you will see him soon. Who is to have the litter?"

"That is for Mistress Farleigh and her aunt-by-marriage."

"Do you see Master Farleigh?"

"No. Sir Stephen did not come, either. That is his coach," she added, pointing at a very fine one just arriving on the scene.

Blanche turned to look just as Lady Otley realized that her husband had not accompanied the vehicle dispatched to convey her to her home. For an instant, her expression mirrored the child's.

"There. You see, Jane. None of the husbands came to fetch their wives. You should not feel slighted."

While the others sorted themselves out and said their farewells, Blanche stood a little apart. She hesitated to thrust herself forward, but if she held back, Lady Otley might forget all about her. Inspiration struck when she saw Edith Trott step aside to allow one of the menservants to assist their mistress into the coach.

64

"Edith," Blanche called out. "I am much obliged to you for your kindness."

The maid turned to stare at her, as well she might. They'd scarce spoken two words together since Blanche gave her a ribbon to replace the one Jane stole. Blanche reached up to touch her hair, a silent reminder that Edith had arranged it for her, although that "kindness" had not been repeated.

"And to you as well, Lady Otley," Blanche added, now that she'd caught the gentlewoman's attention.

She did not dare speak of nunneries in the Spanish Netherlands in the keeper's hearing, but she assumed what she hoped was a pious stance—hands folded as if in prayer—and strove for a facial expression that was both earnest and pleading.

Sir Stephen's wife leaned out of the coach. "Mistress Wainfleet, come hither."

Trying not to look too eager, Blanche approached.

"Get in. You will come with us to Otley Manor."

"You are most kind, madam, but—"

"Do not argue. You are ripe for further instruction in the true faith and since one of my maidservants shares your misfortune in being raised by heretics, you and Sarah can study together until you are ready to fully embrace Catholicism."

"You are most generous, Lady Otley." Blanche scrambled into the coach before her benefactress could change her mind.

Chapter Twelve

The journey to Otley Manor, situated just outside the village of Little Mabham, took most of the day. Blanche would much rather have ridden on horseback, even if she'd been relegated to sitting on a pillion behind one of the grooms. There were cushions on the hard board seats inside the coach, but they did little to keep the occupants from being jounced, battered, and bruised as they traveled over rough winter roads. It was as cold inside as out. Even provided with a heavy fur-lined robe to wrap around herself, she could not entirely ward off the chill.

Once they were under way, Lady Otley seemed to lose some of the starch that had kept her in command throughout her imprisonment. Blanche expected to be interrogated further, bombarded with a barrage of personal questions before she was fully accepted into the Otley household. There was the matter, too, of what place she would have there, but they had gone some considerable distance before Lady Otley spoke again.

"What are your skills, Mistress Wainfleet? Are you handy with a needle?"

Having already decided that her answers had best be a mixture of lies and truth, Blanche answered readily. "I can sew a straight hem, but I fear I have little talent for embroidery."

"Are you musical?"

"I have been taught to play the lute and the virginals." She did not claim to excel at either. That would become apparent soon enough.

"I already know that you can read. Can you write as well?" The two skills were taught separately and many a literate woman was unable to sign her own name.

"I can, and I am accounted to have excellent penmanship."

"You have a pleasant voice," Lady Otley allowed. "While others sew, perhaps you can read aloud to them from improving books."

Her heart sank at the prospect, but she said only, "Do you have many such?"

"A small selection. My husband has others, in French and in Latin, but I do not suppose you can translate those."

Blanche shook her head and told her first significant lie of the day. "I can only read English."

While it was true she was not fluent in any language but her own, Kit had taught her enough of several languages to help him with his business correspondence. She could acquit herself well, at least in writing, in French, Low Dutch, Spanish, and Italian, and she understood a smattering of Latin as well.

"You will do," Lady Otley declared. "If you want the post, I will take you on as my companion."

"I am most grateful," Blanche said, "and most humbly accept."

She had to struggle to hide her elation. Instead of ending her chance to find out what had happened to Alison, her release from prison would bring her closer to discovering the truth. She would enter Otley Manor in the very post Alison had once held.

Lady Otley next turned her attention to the Trott sisters. In such close quarters, they had heard every word she'd said to Blanche. Edith did not look pleased, but her ill-humor vanished when her mistress informed her that she would henceforth hold the position of tiring woman and be responsible for dressing both Lady Otley's person and her hair.

There was little conversation after that. The noise of the wheels and the constant lurching of the vehicle made conversation difficult. Although stealing a few hours of sleep proved impossible, Blanche did manage to doze. She started upright at the sound of shouted greetings. The coach swayed less noticeably as it began to slow.

Lifting the leather flap over the open window, she peered out. Her first glimpse of Otley Manor showed her a low brick gatehouse with a house beyond. The pale, late-afternoon sun hung low in the sky, signifying that it was nearly dusk, but there was still sufficient light to see that there was no other habitation nearby.

If they had passed through a village, they had done so without slowing down. This remote location, she supposed, made the manor an ideal gathering place for local recusants. Jesuit priests could come and go unseen, stopping only long enough to celebrate forbidden rituals.

On the outside, the dwelling was a modest brick and timber building. The interior was far more elaborate. The paneled walls and carved ceilings were exquisite. The hangings showed sylvan scenery, expertly stitched. Thanks to Kit's dealings as a merchant, Blanche had developed a keen eye for value and could tell at a glance that the Otleys had spent a fortune furnishing their home. They had purchased only the best and most expensive items.

On her mistress's orders, Sarah escorted Blanche to a middling sort of bedchamber. It was small but boasted its own fireplace where kindling had already been laid. The room was furnished with a chest for clothing and a comfortable-looking bed, its heavy foot posts carved to match the headboard. Both supported an elaborately embroidered tester. Gingerly, Blanche touched the coverlet, confirming that the blankets and sheets sat atop a featherbed. Under that would be a stuffed woolen mattress held up by interwoven strips of leather. Luxury indeed! The bed hangings, made of heavy green say, would be more than adequate to keep out the cold of a winter's night.

"With whom do I share?" she asked.

"No one." Sarah finished lighting the fire and stood. "This room will be yours alone, unless you acquire a maidservant."

An unexpected boon, Blanche thought, pleased by the thought that she would not have to spend every moment, waking and sleeping, playing her self-assigned role.

She found even more to be delighted about when two sturdy menservants carried in a wooden bathing tub and set it before the hearth. The room was already beginning to warm by the time the tub was lined with cloth and a tent had been erected around three sides of it. While a procession of

manservants carried in buckets of steaming water, Sarah disappeared, only
to return a short time later with her arms full of towels, a container of bay
leaves to add to the water, and a ball of sweet soap that smelled of lavender.

"Lady Otley expects you to bathe and wash away the grime of your
imprisonment before joining her to sup," Sarah said. "She is doing likewise
in her own chamber."

"The household boasts *two* bathing tubs? That is most remarkable."

"I am to assist you, and afterward use your bathwater to cleanse myself.
Edith will make use of Lady Otley's." She wrinkled her nose. "I warrant we
all stink, although I can no longer tell."

"Nor can I, but to anyone who was not locked up with us, we must smell
most offensive."

Blanche frowned, painfully aware that a bath alone would not render her
fit for respectable company. She regarded with intense dislike the bundle
that contained everything she had taken with her into prison. She had
changed her linen once during her incarceration, but she'd had no way to
wash the foul-smelling and filthy chemise after she'd removed it.

With Sarah's help, Blanche stripped off the kirtle and bodice she'd worn
throughout her imprisonment, clothing now fit only to be burnt. Her spare
garments were in little better condition. Dank, disgusting prison smells had
seeped through the thin layer of cloth to contaminate everything within.
Only frequent airings and a heavy application of perfume would render
those clothes wearable again, if they could be salvaged at all. Had she been
at home, Blanche would have discarded the lot.

Her mind still on the dilemma of what to wear once she had bathed, she
stepped into the gently steaming water and slowly lowered herself until she
was seated, her knees bent to fit the confines of the tub. Almost at once,
the water turned murky. Blanche sighed, and sent a guilty look in Sarah's
direction. By the time she was done, the maidservant would be hard pressed
to achieve any degree of cleanliness for herself. Still, it could not be helped.
Indeed, Sarah was fortunate to have been offered a turn in the bath at all.

"Shall I help you wash your hair?" the girl asked. "You can dry it by the
fire." On the open side of the tent, it was blazing nicely, heating the air

around them.

Had the tub been larger, like the one Blanche had at home, she would have invited Sarah to join her. That thought triggered memories of another bathing companion. She had to duck her head to hide the sudden warmth that swept into her cheeks at the memory. More than once, she and Kit had bathed together and retired afterward to a nearby bed. She hoped Sarah would attribute the hectic color in her face to the heat of the bathwater.

Blanche had done her best not to let her thoughts dwell on her husband during her time in gaol. Thinking about him, missing him, would have weakened her. But now that she was free, she found it increasingly difficult not to wonder how soon he would return from his voyage. What would he think if he arrived at Wainfleet House in Holborn and found her gone? She had told no one there where she was going. Only her sisters knew of the plan to discover what had caused Alison's death.

One worry at a time, she cautioned herself. If Kit did come home, it would occur to him sooner or later to write to Joanna or Philippa. Either of them would reassure him. They both believed in what she was doing. They would have done the same themselves, had they not had responsibilities at home to stop them, and they would understand her decision to stay at Otley Manor long enough to learn all there was to know about Alison's time as Lady Otley's companion.

Once she was as clean as one bath could make her, Blanche wrapped herself in a towel and let Sarah take her turn. Afterward, they combed each other's wet hair. There was something comforting about the process, and it allowed her to put off the unpleasant prospect of getting dressed again. Thinking of that, her gaze strayed to her bundle and she grimaced.

"What is it that concerns you so, Mistress Wainfleet?" Sarah asked, catching sight of Blanche's expression.

"I would give every penny that remains to me—pitifully few, as it happens—for clean clothing. All that I own—from bodice and kirtle to chemise and stockings—is as foul as our time in prison could make them."

Sarah's face fell. "You have been so kind to me. I would give you my own clothing if I could, but I own naught but that I must myself change into."

70

"It is no matter. If I must reappear in my filth, so be it. Mayhap, once I explain the difficulty, Lady Otley will find something for me to wear."

Of a sudden, Sarah sprang to her feet. "I know where there is clothing!"

As she watched, the girl went straight to the chest Blanche had noticed earlier, lifted the lid, and reached inside. She came up with her arms full of fabric, material that on closer inspection sorted itself out into kirtles and sleeves and bodices and, best of all, undergarments.

"Where did these come from?" Letting the still-damp hair she'd been attempting to twist into a bun fall loose again, Blanche rose to her feet to examine the bounty. The clothing was plain but of good quality.

"I hope you do not mind, but they were Mistress Palmer's. She has no further need of them."

Blanche felt tears prickle at the back of her eyes, but she could scarce refuse to wear her dead sister's clothing. She and Alison had been much of a size. Alison had been a bit thinner and a little shorter, but her garments would suffice.

"These will do very well," she said aloud. "Am I to take it that this was Mistress Palmer's chamber?"

Sarah nodded before turning away to root in the chest for more garments.

Blanche smiled to herself. All that her sister had left behind must be in this room. As soon as she was alone, she would search. She did not know what she expected to find, but even the smallest hint about what Alison had experienced during her time at Otley Manor might prove useful.

Discarding the towel, Blanche tugged a clean, sweet-smelling smock over her head. With Sarah's help, it did not take her long to dress and the girl made short work of pinning up her hair.

"It is a good thing you remembered that this clothing was here," Blanche said. "I should have hated to join Lady Otley at supper wearing the wrinkled and stinking garments in my bundle."

"I will see to it that those things are cleaned."

Blanche bit back the impulse to tell Sarah not to bother. She had to remind herself that here at Otley Manor she was not Mistress Wainfleet, wife of a wealthy merchant, but rather an unmarried outcast, penniless and completely dependent upon the good will of her newfound employer. Squaring her shoulders, she asked the way to the dining parlor.

Chapter Thirteen

T he table was an impressive one, made of solid oak and covered with a white cloth that hung to the floor. Such things were commonplace in Blanche's everyday life, but in light of her recent incarceration they struck her as surpassing luxurious. Brief as her stay in gaol had been, she had gained a new appreciation of the little things that made being wealthy so pleasurable.

She admired the spice boxes already set out—one each for mace, cloves, cinnamon, and ginger—and inhaled their wonderful scents. The smells emanating from platters of food awaiting them on side tables made her stomach growl in anticipation. Had she ever been properly grateful for well-prepared food? And light—the table was illuminated by wax candles set in iron supports suspended from the ceiling beams.

Even seeing Lady Otley in all her splendor could not dampen Blanche's high spirits. She supposed she should feel like a poor relation when she was wearing Alison's simple garments, especially when her hostess wore a gown of murrey velvet furred with sables and a kirtle of wrought velvet with a train, but she was too glad to be here, too glad to be free, to trouble herself about trivialities.

"Mistress Blanche Wainfleet is my new companion," Lady Otley said to her husband.

Blanche bobbed a perfunctory curtsey to Sir Stephen Otley before taking the chair Lady Otley indicated. He was a heavy-set man with a florid countenance. His jowly face did not lend itself well to the little tuft of a beard that grew from the point of his chin. This was darker than the hair on his head, which was liberally streaked with silver, suggesting that he was some years older than his wife. His pale, watery eyes fixed on Blanche only long enough to dismiss her as unimportant, but the fourth person at the table, Lady Otley's brother, showed considerably more interest in her.

Where his sister was stout, Joseph Yelverton was lean. He was younger than his sibling, although he had seen some thirty winters. His beardless face was undeniably appealing, with smooth, flawless skin and strong, sculpted features. He had a high forehead over dark, slightly arched eyebrows. His eyes were dark as well, and frankly admiring as he studied the newcomer. His lips were firm, his jaw was square, and his hair was the glossy black of a raven's wing. When he spoke, his voice was deep and melodious.

Blanche answered his words of welcome with a courteous reply, but it was all she could do to keep a smile on her face. This was the man who had lured Alison to Otley Manor. For his sake, she had abandoned both her family and her faith, and in the end she had lost her life. That he was toothsome, she could not deny, but if he had truly returned her sister's feelings, he would have married her. More importantly, he would have protected her when some fool of a priest claimed she needed to be exorcised.

Prayers preceded the meal, giving Blanche time to bring her emotions under control. She could not fault the others for being sincere in their beliefs. In truth, she had discovered little real difference between the prayers of Catholics and those of the Church of England. They all worshipped the same God.

Alison had found solace in the greater number of rituals. She had said as much to Philippa before following Joseph Yelverton to Otley Manor. How she had met him, Blanche and her sisters did not know, but Alison had sworn that she would have no other and would willingly accept his faith in order to win his heart. Once she'd left Philippa's home in Kent, no one in the family had heard a word from her until the arrival of that one disturbing letter. By the time Philippa had sent word from Kent to Joanna in Essex, and Joanna's husband Arthur was dispatched to fetch Alison home, Otley Manor had been raided. Arthur reached Colchester Castle only to discover that he was too late to do anything but claim Alison's body for burial.

It had been when they were gathered at Joanna's home after the funeral that Blanche and her sisters began to wonder if there was more to Alison's death than they knew. They found it hard to believe she could succumb so quickly to conditions in Colchester gaol and it had seemed most suspicious that *only* the woman who had doubts about her faith should fall ill and die. Blanche had been the one to devise a means to discover the truth, but Philippa and Joanna had encouraged her to pursue it, and Joanna had persuaded her husband to help implement the scheme.

So here she was, Blanche thought, as prayers came to an end, where Alison had lived during the final months of her life. She was wearing her sister's clothing and would be sleeping in her bed, performing the same duties she had performed, and praying the same prayers.

That she was little wiser than she had been a week earlier must change, and soon, before anyone began to doubt her sincerity. And yet, for the nonce, she must refrain from asking too many questions, lest she arouse suspicion. At first, she must do no more than observe and work hard to earn the trust of those who lived at Otley Manor.

Blanche ate heartily. It was a joyful experience to have such tasty dishes set before her. Lady Otley and her husband applied themselves to the meal with equal enthusiasm, although Blanche presumed Sir Stephen had eaten well throughout the time his wife was in prison. Yelverton was more abstemious. He sampled only a small portion of each course, but he kept up with the others when it came to imbibing Sir Stephen's fine Canary wine.

There was little conversation until their appetites were sated. Serving men moved silently, offering one course after another. One of them had the additional task of lowering the candles every half hour to trim the wicks, keeping the light strong and steady. As she watched them at their tasks, Blanche wondered how it happened that none of these stout fellows had been carried off to gaol when the women were arrested. Had they fled into the woods with the priest at the first hint of trouble?

Only after the cheese and fruit had been served did Sir Stephen broach the subject of his wife's ordeal. "I suppose we must be grateful to the queen for your release." Resentment underscored his words. "I did my best to persuade Lewknor to intervene, but he was not inclined to be reasonable."

"What can you expect of a fellow so radical in his beliefs?" Yelverton asked.

Lady Otley turned to Blanche. "My husband speaks of Sir Eustace Lewknor, the local magistrate, a man afflicted with the worst kind of reforming zeal. He does not wait for crimes to be reported to him but rather seeks out those he perceives to be evildoers. He seems to derive an unnatural pleasure from committing such offenders to gaol."

"I trust you were not too uncomfortable during your imprisonment, sister," Yelverton said.

Lady Otley glared at her brother. "Discomfort does not begin to describe it."

"A few days of rest will set you right." Sir Stephen used the sort of over-hearty voice some men mistakenly believe to be reassuring to women. He glanced at Blanche. "Your new companion, you said? What happened to the other one?"

"She died in gaol."

"Did she, by God!"

Eyes avid, Yelverton leaned toward his sister. "What caused her death?"

Blanche could scarce credit what she was hearing. Even if Yelverton had not wanted to marry Alison, it did not seem possible that he should be so lacking in feeling. Alison had been the beauty of the family, young and full of life, generous and giving and mad with love. Since Alison had believed with all her heart that Yelverton cared deeply for her, Blanche was certain they had been lovers. How could he be so unmoved by her death?

"She had not the strength of spirit to withstand the ordeal," Lady Otley answered.

"I am aware that she suffered a great affliction of the mind *before* she was imprisoned," Yelverton said in a bland voice, "but the wicked spirit that tempted her was cast out. She was fully herself again."

"That is a matter of opinion," Lady Otley said.

He fell silent under the weight of her repressive frown but the gleam in his eyes suggested that he would have enjoyed hearing the details of Alison's suffering. Although Blanche did not relish the prospect, she resolved to seek a closer acquaintance with Joseph Yelverton.

After supper, everyone in the house gathered for evening prayers in Lady Otley's withdrawing room, a large airy chamber directly above the great hall. Slitting her eyes open as Sir Stephen droned on in his schoolboy's Latin, Blanche took the opportunity to study the rest of the household.

There were a goodly number of servants, almost all of them men. She concluded that if one of them had been a Catholic priest in disguise, *he* would have been leading the prayers. Among the menials, the only individual who stood out was a ginger-haired stable boy. His red-rimmed eyes suggested he had recently shed copious tears. For Alison? She'd have to befriend the lad, Blanche decided, and find out.

Overall, the religious regimen at Otley Manor was nearly identical to the one Lady Otley had insisted upon in prison. Not for the first time, Blanche was struck by how little these lengthy prayer sessions differed from those she had been subjected to when she visited a friend who lived in an evangelical household. True, puritans would be appalled to hear prayers addressed to the Virgin Mary and an assortment of saints, and quick to confiscate the rosaries whose soft clicking underscored Sir Stephen's droning voice, but otherwise the two extremes of Christianity appeared to have a good deal in common.

Tomorrow, Blanche pledged, she would resume her search for answers. With that resolve firm in her mind, she bowed her head and closed her eyes in a silent prayer of her own.

Chapter Fourteen

The next morning Blanche was up early. She had slept soundly and well, but since she was accustomed to leave a window open at night—against accepted medical advice, which held that evil vapors crept inside with the darkness—she opened her eyes just before dawn to the sounds of servants going about their business in the kitchen yard below. As she came fully awake, pale streaks of winter sunlight crept into her east-facing chamber and slowly made their way toward the bed.

She smiled, but the expression quickly faded when she remembered where she was and why. Throwing her legs over the side of the high bed, she dropped to the floor. Since the fire in the hearth had gone out, it was ice cold beneath her bare feet. She lost no time scrambling into the same clothing she had worn the previous evening, glad that Alison's garments were simply made. It would have been impossible for her to assume more complicated clothes without assistance.

Sarah, as promised, had taken away Blanche's laundry. She had also applied a brush to her cloak and seen to it that Blanche's boots were cleaned after she retired for the night. Thankful for small favors, Blanche slid her stockinged feet into the latter and flung the former around her shoulders before creeping out of the chamber and into the passage. With the servants housed in the garrets, it was possible she had the entire floor to herself, but she could not be certain of that.

By rights, she should attend Lady Otley, who occupied a bedchamber on the floor below, but Blanche had other plans. Before everyone in the house was up and about, she wanted to reconnoiter. She could explore the interior of the manor easily enough at any time. Its immediate environs were another matter.

Based on the regimen Lady Otley had insisted upon while they were imprisoned and what she had observed the previous evening, Blanche expected her mistress to follow a similar daily routine at home. The gentlewoman had been accustomed to rise at dawn to meditate and engage in private prayers. That meant Blanche had at least an hour's grace before everyone else in the household was required to gather together for morning devotions. She intended to make good use of it.

If anyone questioned her, she would claim she'd wished to begin her day with a brisk constitutional. Surely there was nothing objectionable about taking healthful exercise in the crisp morning air? All the same, in the hope of avoiding the other residents of Otley Manor, she descended in stealth to the ground floor and let herself out of the house by way of the door that opened into the herb garden.

No one was in sight, either in the garden or in the meadow beyond. If someone looked out a window, they would see her, but by then it would be too late to stop her from exploring. Moving quickly past raised beds of plants that were dull and colorless at this time of year, she reached a gate and passed through it.

The winter had been wretchedly cold but there had been little snow. She walked over brown grass coated with rime, leaving faint footprints behind. Once she reached the meadow, she paused to look back at Otley Manor. As she'd half expected, there was a face at one of the windows, but she was too far away to identify the watcher.

Let them look, she thought. *I am doing nothing wrong.* She continued to ramble in a leisurely fashion until she came upon an ancient woman, stooped and gnarled, leading a cow on a length of rope.

The crone stopped in her tracks at the sight of a stranger and said in a belligerent voice, "This cow is mine."

Blanche blinked at her in surprise, wondering if the woman had all her wits about her. "I never said she was not."

Dropping the rope, the cow's owner flung her arms around its neck. "She is all I have in the world!"

"Then take good care of her, goodwife, and she will reward you with milk."

Blanche had already turned away when the woman released the animal and caught hold of her arm. The painfully tight grip brought Blanche up short. She turned, not yet alarmed but growing annoyed, and found her captor squinting at her.

"Have you the sight?"

"I can see you well enough."

Out of the corner of her eye, Blanche glimpsed a second figure approaching. She was glad of it, since she had no idea how to free herself from a person clearly fit for Bedlam. The woman saw the new arrival, too, but she did not loosen her hold.

"Good morrow to you, Goody Dunster," the man said in a cordial tone of voice.

Although he was simply dressed, as a husbandman might be, both his speech and his bearing proclaimed his gentle birth. Neither was there any disguising the intelligence in eyes that were the bright blue of a summer sea in sunlight. The hair beneath his tattered wool cap looked freshly washed and was as pale as new butter, very nearly as light in color as Blanche's.

This was no more a man who toiled in the fields than she was.

The old woman stared at him for a long moment, then released Blanche as abruptly as she had grabbed hold of her. Without a word, she reclaimed the cow, tugging on the rope to urge her bovine companion to greater speed. She almost appeared to be running away.

Blanche and the tall, slightly-built stranger watched until Goody Dunster disappeared into a copse of trees on the far side of the meadow. Blanche was intensely aware of it when his attention shifted to her.

"Poor thing," she said. "Her mind is addled."

"Your compassion speaks well of you, but you need not be concerned. She has kin to look after her."

"I am glad to hear it."

"Have you protectors, mistress? I have not seen you in these parts before."

"I am newly arrived." She sensed no threat in his question. Gesturing in the direction of Otley Manor, she added, "I am employed as Lady Otley's companion."

"I had heard she was pardoned, and that all those imprisoned with her had been freed. Were you one of them?"

In the ordinary way of things, Blanche would have been wary of confiding in a stranger, but this man exuded such an air of trustworthiness that she did not hesitate to confirm his guess. She even told him her name.

"I am Adam North and I am bound for Otley Manor myself." He offered her his arm. "May I escort you home?"

Blanche studied him from beneath her lashes as they retraced the route she had taken from the house, more curious about him than ever. Why would such a charming and well-mannered gentleman go about in disguise?

Her steps faltered as the obvious answer came to her. He was a priest. He'd arrived at Otley Manor to celebrate Mass for the recusant household. And not *just* a priest, she realized, but a Jesuit, mayhap even the one who had performed Alison's exorcism.

"Have a care for the slippery spots," North said, mistaking the reason for her near stumble.

Blanche cleared her throat. Could she be mistaken? Such thoughtfulness did not align with what she had always been told about the Jesuits. "Is Sir Stephen expecting you?"

"I have no doubt of my welcome," North said with an enigmatic smile. "I am an ...associate of Miles Mortimer and Hugh Chandler."

She had never heard either name before. At her obvious lack of recognition, North's brow furrowed. When his eyes narrowed a fraction, Blanche sensed that she had failed some kind of test, but his reaction made her more certain than ever that he was a priest.

Adam North's profession was confirmed the moment the first member of the Otley household caught sight of him. From the housekeeper to the boy who turned the spit in the kitchen, everyone recognized him, and everyone treated him with deference and respect. If Blanche had still entertained the slightest doubt, it would have been swept away by Lady Otley's effusive greeting.

"Welcome, Father North!" she called when he entered the great hall in Blanche's company. She all but ran the rest of the way down the staircase. "Will you hear confessions this morning? It has been far too long since I've been shriven. As for Mistress Wainfleet here, she has but newly embraced the true faith and is in dire need of your guidance."

Having had time enough to gather her wits, Blanche turned her best smile on the priest. "I presume that those names you mentioned—Mortimer and Chandler—are also Jesuits?"

Father North's expression was benign. "They are. As you have no doubt been told, most of us travel constantly to minister to our far flung flocks. Father Mortimer and Father Chandler have often preached at Otley Manor, but this is only my second visit."

"I ...I know very little of such things."

What she did know, in light of her first impression of Father North, left her in a state of considerable confusion.

Chapter Fifteen

Father North said Mass for the entire household in Lady Otley's withdrawing room. Blanche could not follow all of the Latin, although the priest spoke it far better than either of the Otleys. She doubted any of those listening understood more than she did. Since this was the first time she had done more than read about this Catholic ritual, she watched intently as Father North, now garbed in ceremonial robes, performed it. To her surprise, although the Mass was more elaborate than Sunday services in her parish church, it did not feel as alien as she had expected.

It was eleven of the clock when she sat down to dine with the Otleys, Joseph Yelverton, and the priest. Father North's opinion was much in demand. Master Yelverton in particular seemed to hang on his every word, although Blanche noticed that he did a fair amount of talking himself. When the two men entered into an intense, low-voiced discussion, she was unable to hear more than an occasional snippet, but it made her uneasy when they glanced up at the same time to stare directly at her. She turned quickly away, only to find Lady Otley's eyes were also upon her.

"Have you never met a Catholic priest before?" the gentlewoman asked.

Blanche shook her head. "He is not what I expected. Are all Jesuits so ...so ...?"

"Toothsome?" Lady Otley suggested, stifling a laugh. "Not that I have seen, although if they are to survive their dangerous mission to England, it is doubtless an advantage to be strong and fit."

Blanche seized the opportunity. "Has it been some time since Father North was here?"

"A year or more," Lady Otley said. "Why do you ask?"

Blanche fumbled for a reply, perplexed by how relieved she was to realize he could not have performed the exorcism. It would have been to her advantage to have that priest within reach.

"It is only that he seems to know everyone," she said after a moment, "and everyone knows who he is, even an old woman with a cow."

"He is memorable," Lady Otley said, "and he is devoted to his congregation. On his previous visit, he took the time to learn everyone's name."

"You speak as if that is a rare quality among visiting priests."

"Those who come here are alike in their faith, but not in all other ways. They make the rounds of country houses at great risk to themselves, as should be clear from what happened the last time Father Mortimer was here. Had he been taken, he'd have been executed."

Father Mortimer. Miles Mortimer. At last Blanche had a name for the man who had tortured her sister. She thought it a great pity that he had not been taken up by the searchers. Justice would have been served by his death.

"Will Father Mortimer return here, do you think? Given what happened the last time?"

"I expect he will be back ere long, especially since Father North is soon to leave Essex for London. He is a brave man. They all are."

At Lady Otley's request, Father North took Blanche aside as soon as they rose from the midday meal, keeping his promise to instruct her in the tenets of his faith. He began by questioning her about her religious beliefs. She thought she acquitted herself well, and when she did not sense any diminution in his friendly regard, she allowed herself to relax. He had a pleasing way about him, even when he was giving her instruction as to the manner in which a confession was conducted.

She had no difficulty thinking of sins to confess, but since most of them had to do with things she dared not confide to anyone at Otley Manor, let alone a Jesuit, she kept them to herself. Instead, she admitted to impure thoughts, to envy, and to a lack of proper gratitude for Lady Otley's many kindnesses.

"Subdue the earthly passions to which you have admitted," the priest advised, "and focus on Christ's Passion. Confront the devils of the world and the flesh with a heart surrendered to God."

"I will try," Blanche promised, and accepted the mild penance he gave her.

She was about to return to Lady Otley to take up her duties as companion—dull tasks but necessary if she was to remain in that gentlewoman's favor—when, on impulse, she turned back to the priest.

"I am glad you have come to Otley Manor. I am in need of instruction, but I fear that Lady Otley will grow impatient with me. She does not understand how difficult it is to change the habits of a lifetime."

His smile dazzled and made the unrepentantly secular side of her think what a waste it was that he was a priest sworn to remain celibate. How many of those he preached to, she wondered, fell in love with the man instead of the message?

"I feel certain that good lady does understand," Father North said. "Has she not been forced to stop crossing herself in public and telling her rosary beads for fear of being imprisoned?"

Blanche hung her head, pretending to be ashamed of her complaint. The feeling was not entirely feigned. "You have the right of it, Father."

"As for my continuing to instruct you, I will do my best to answer your questions as long as I am here, but I fear my stay will be a short one."

"You will not remain until the Sabbath?"

He shook his head. "I depart on Friday morning. There are other Catholic families in this part of Essex and I must minister to their needs as well. Besides, it is never safe to linger too long in any one house."

"Do you expect another raid?"

"That is always a possibility." His sea-blue eyes filled with ill-concealed merriment. "I will gladly die a martyr for my faith, but I would prefer to postpone that day for as long as possible."

Blanche did not find his words amusing. Her knowledge that the Crown executed Jesuits had never troubled her in the past, but now that she had met one and found herself liking him, she could no longer remain indifferent to the horror of such a fate.

"I fear for you," she admitted. "What if the searchers return to Otley Manor before you can get away?"

He did not appear to be at all worried. Indeed, her concern produced another twinkle. "I am safer in this house than in most. Has no one shown you the hides?"

She was not familiar with the term, but its meaning seemed clear enough. "Do you mean hiding places? Secret rooms?"

"Scarce that, but some hides are large enough to conceal a full-grown man until the danger is past."

That explained why no priest had been found when Lady Otley and her friends were arrested. Blanche had much to think about for the remainder of an otherwise uneventful day.

Evensong at three followed the same order as morning prayers, after which the servants tended to their chores and Lady Otley commanded her new companion to read to her from a book on the lives of the saints. Blanche was unfamiliar with the story of Saint Catherine of the Wheel and shocked by the ghastly punishment meted out to that lady when she was but eighteen years of age.

Lady Otley called it "a pleasant yet profitable tale." Hardly pleasant, Blanche thought, and she wondered where the profit was. The moral of the story seemed to be that even an intelligent, dedicated female—Catherine was renowned as a scholar as well as a martyr—could be destroyed by a powerful tyrant.

At six they sat down to sup. The meal was followed by a walk in the gallery for exercise. After that, there was time set aside for each member of the household to examine his or her conscience before evening prayers. By nine, Blanche was back in her bed, staring up at the tester and berating herself for letting the entire day pass without learning anything more about Alison's time at Otley Manor.

On the morrow, she vowed, she would do better.

Chapter Sixteen

On Thursday, Blanche once again woke early. The first thing that popped into her mind was the subject for that morning's meditation. She was supposed to think upon the last day of Judgment.

Her nose wrinkled as if she'd encountered a foul smell. She had no intention of dwelling upon such a grim matter. It was a wonder Catholics could enjoy life at all, given that the topics mandated for the rest of the days of the week were just as depressing. On Monday she was admonished to reflect upon her past sins. Tuesday was for present sins. Wednesday's meditation required her to contemplate death, and on Friday she was supposed to dwell upon the pains of Hell. Only Saturday brought relief. On that day she was permitted to meditate upon the joys of Heaven.

She much preferred the practice she followed at home. Before rising to face each day, she searched her heart and found her own words to use in a prayer. This was supposed to produce a more spiritual experience than repeating prayers by rote. Blanche feared she was lacking in true devotion, but she tried her best, and followed this exercise by reciting the prayer for the morning included in Mistress Anne Wheathill's little book, a collection of simple, conventional prayers to read and think upon when other inspiration failed. She whispered the plea with which it ended aloud: "Hear me, dear Father, and send thy Holy Ghost to direct me in all my doings. To thee, o glorious and blessed Trinity, the Father, the Son, and the Holy Ghost, be given all honor and praise, now and forevermore. Amen."

Blanche rose and dressed and quietly opened the door to the passage. She was, as she had suspected, the only inhabitant of this floor. The priest had been assigned to a chamber near the family rooms. Before the household gathered for morning prayers, she would have time enough to explore the part of the house she had not yet seen.

Two bedchambers besides her own opened off the same side of the passage. The corner room was slightly larger and had more windows, but in all other respects it was identical to the others. If there were hiding places within either, Blanche could not find them. She searched both as thoroughly as she had already gone through the room that had been Alison's and had as little to show for it when she was done.

Skirting the stairwell, Blanche next approached the solitary door on the opposite side of the passage. It opened into a small, unfurnished anteroom. She crossed it to open the door straight ahead of her and found herself in a nursery. Since the Otleys had no children, or at least none at home, it was unoccupied.

She made a brief inspection of the contents, pausing to examine one or two of the books. She smiled at the sight of a toy soldier. Perhaps the Otleys had a son. It would not be unusual to send a young boy off to another household to be educated. That was common practice among the gentry and nobility. Still, she wondered why no one had spoken of him.

Idly, she reached up to straighten a tapestry that was slightly askew. She was startled to discover another door behind it. Cautiously, she opened it and went through. In most houses, the room adjoining the nursery was assigned to a nursemaid, tutor, or governess. That was what Blanche expected to encounter. Instead she found a chamber furnished with tapestries depicting scenes from the Bible, a small desk fully equipped with paper and writing implements, and a single long bench with a low back, oddly positioned at the center of the chamber.

Aware of the fleeting nature of time, Blanche retraced her steps. She had one more room to explore. In common with the nursery, it was reached through the anteroom, but this door, unlike the others, boasted a stout lock. Seeing that the key had been left in it, Blanche hesitated only a moment before she turned it and lifted the latch.

The interior was dark. There were no windows. The only illumination came from the anteroom, but it was sufficient to reveal a small, unfurnished space. Blanche started to step inside for a better look but recoiled when a pungent smell made her nostrils flare. Retreating, she took a cautious sniff, but even at a distance the odor was strong enough to make her cough. Incense? She'd seen Father North use a censer but this did not strike her as being the same. The noisome miasma discouraged her from investigating any further.

She closed and locked the door and returned to the passage, wondering why no one had purified and purged the chamber by fumigation. It was not a difficult process. When her sister Philippa cleansed the unpleasant odors from the room where two of her children had lain sick, she took large green bunches of rosemary and marjoram, set fire to them, and waved them about. The wholesome, pleasantly-scented smoke drove away the foulness.

She supposed green boughs might be hard to come by at this time of year, but there were other ways to fumigate. Her mother had once set a pot of burning charcoal in the center of a polluted chamber and thrown handfuls of sweet herbs into the fire until the bad air was driven out by the good.

Blanche used what remained of the time before the household gathered in Lady Otley's withdrawing room for formal morning prayers to make a quick foray into the garret where the servants slept. The moment she reached the top of the narrow staircase, she realized she could not hope to examine the entire area before someone came looking for her. It would be a task requiring hours, not minutes. The low ceiling was only part of the challenge. Chimneys popped up everywhere, creating a maze of narrow paths containing many twists and turns.

She left further exploration for another day.

Chapter Seventeen

As Blanche drew near Lady Otley's rooms, the murmur of voices grew louder. It seemed to her that everyone else must have arrived ahead of her. Since it would call unwanted attention to herself if she came in last, she breathed a sigh of relief when Father North emerged from the passage directly under the one outside her bedchamber.

He smiled at her and once again offered his arm.

"I am surprised that there is no chapel in the house," she remarked just before they entered the withdrawing room.

"There is one on an upper floor, but it is too small to allow the entire household to attend Mass."

That explained the room behind the nursery.

Father North smiled down at her. "It does not matter where Mass is celebrated, so long as the priest has the proper tools."

"Are objects more important than words?"

"Mother Church requires that certain items be used—a missal, consecrated vessels for bread and wine, the priest's vestments, and an altar."

Blanche would have liked to ask Father North more questions, but too many people awaited him. She entered the room and knelt with the rest.

As soon the final amen had been said, the servants rose from their knees. They would have returned to their accustomed duties had not their mistress ordered them to remain where they were. She looked inordinately pleased with herself.

"Listen closely," she said. "I have devised a new plan to make certain we keep our priests and the trappings of our faith safe in the event of another

90

raid. We must practice what to do from the moment we hear searchers pounding on the door. Sir Stephen and I will greet them and delay them as long as possible. During that time, each of you will have a specific task to perform."

Two grooms were assigned to hide the slab of natural stone used as an altar. Edith Trott was made responsible for the missal. Other servants took charge of the vessels and vestments. Lady Otley continued to dole out tasks until only Blanche and Father North remained in her withdrawing room.

"Is there nothing I can do?" Blanche asked.

Lady Otley studied her for a long moment before coming to a decision. "You will be responsible for making certain the door to the smaller hide is secure."

Blanche's heart beat a little faster. She had hoped that, in time, all the secrets of Otley Manor would be revealed to her, but she had not expected Lady Otley to trust her with one of the most important ones this quickly.

"I do not know where it is," she said in a small, humble voice.

"That is a lack easy to remedy. Come along."

Uninvited, Father North accompanied them up to the garret. The hide was located in the roof space, between the slope of the gables and a vertical plaster partition that separated two sections of the attic. A triangular panel about four feet off the floor pivoted outward to reveal an open space large enough to hold the missal and the consecrated vessels. They had already been secreted there by the servants responsible for hiding them. In addition, the hide contained several other prohibited books and what Lady Otley identified as the family's most prized relic, a bone of St. Modwen of Burton set in gold.

"Watch carefully, Mistress Wainfleet," she said. "This door is closed with a spring-bolt. Do you see there, at the butt-end of that piece of wood, there is a second that is wedge shaped?"

Blanche nodded. It was also attached to the secret panel. The thin end pressed right up against the butt of the bolt.

"Now do you see this nail?"

Its point contained an eye. The piece of cord threaded through it also went through a hole pierced in the upright pivoting post, another hole in the timber studding, and a third hole in the butt of the bolt.

"When the trap is closed, the head of that nail appears to be nothing out of the ordinary, but there is no joist below. When the hide is shut, a wooden spring keeps the bolt in position. By pulling up on the head of the nail and moving it sideways, both cord and bolt are drawn back against the pressure of the bolt and the trapdoor opens."

Blanche studied the design. It was clever, yes, but she could see potential problems. For one thing, the wooden spring could easily snap off. For another, the cord might fray and break, leaving the bolt held shut by the spring. If that happened, she did not see any way the hide could be opened. Whatever was inside would remain there forever unless someone took an ax to the wall.

Lady Otley had Blanche practice opening and closing the hide. It took a half dozen repetitions of the process before she was satisfied that her companion could perform the task assigned to her with sufficient speed and skill.

"But what of Father North?" Blanche asked with a sideways glance at the priest. He was slender, but not small. "Surely he cannot squeeze inside a space this tiny?"

"There is a second hide in the house, one large enough to conceal a man."

"I know where it is," North said, as if to reassure her, "and how to climb into it by myself if it becomes necessary."

"But what if it is some other priest who is here when there is a raid? Will he know where to go?"

Seeing through her ruse, Father North laughed. "Our newest convert is curious, Lady Otley. With your permission, I will show her where the other hide is located."

When Lady Otley greeted this suggestion with a scowl, Blanche held her breath. Had she been too obvious in her interest?

"It will do no harm, I suppose," the gentlewoman said, and led the way to the second hide.

Blanche would never have found it on her own. A tread on a staircase landing lifted to reveal a ladder leading into a narrow space about nine feet deep and six feet square. On the underside of the trap door was the same kind of mechanism that worked the first hide, requiring someone on the outside to open it.

"This is a most secure place of concealment," Lady Otley boasted, "surrounded by solid stone. Moreover, it is warm, being next to the main chimney stack, and it has a spy-hole in one wall, so that the priest inside can better judge when the danger has passed."

"It does not look very comfortable," Blanche observed.

"There are worse places," Father North said. "Some houses have nothing more for *loca secretiora* than a nook in an attic or loft. I have myself been obliged to seek concealment in everything from a culvert to a hollow oak. Once I even had to hide inside a haystack to escape detection."

"Sir Stephen is a very forward-thinking householder. He ordered the construction of these purpose-built hiding places." Lady Otley beamed with pride.

"Would it not have been wise to provide a second secret door, one through which the priest could escape to the outside?" Blanche could not stop thinking of the hide as a trap. If everyone in the house was arrested, and the searchers did not find the hide, then the priest inside would likely die of slow starvation.

"An exterior door would only increase the risk of discovery by the authorities."

"And yet such devices are much talked of in Douai, where we Jesuits are trained," Father North interjected. "I have heard of one hide that is entered through a trapdoor between the floor of a garderobe and the roof of a bread oven. From there, a hole leads to a shaft of the same height as the house and at the bottom there is an opening into the moat."

"But how does the priest reach the lower opening if he starts out at the top of the house? Is there a ladder?"

"That is the clever part. This particular house already had a system of pulleys in place in the shaft. They had been installed decades earlier to work the spit in the fireplace in the adjoining kitchen. Using those, it is possible to lower one's self to the exit."

Lady Otley looked thoughtful. "A pity we did not think to install such a thing here."

For the rest of that day, Blanche played the part of devoted companion to perfection, listening to her mistress's complaints about domestic matters and even engaging in a few hours of needlework. The guidelines provided in *The Exercise of a Christian Life* helped her adapt to Catholic ritual and she took pride in the increasing ease with which she handled her rosary. Prayers and meals came at their appointed times and before she knew it, she was once in her chamber, preparing to go to bed.

Just as Blanche ignored suggestions for her morning meditations, she blithely disregarded the book's admonition to follow night-time prayers with a complete examination of her conscience. No one could see inside her head to read her thoughts, and since she had a bedchamber to herself, she did not have to worry that someone would notice if she failed to make the sign of the holy cross before climbing into bed.

That night, as she pulled the covers up to her chin, she was grateful that the Otleys had ignored at least one of that guidebook's teachings, the one about not loving too dainty and soft a bed. Fortunately, *The Exercise of a Christian Life* stopped short of suggesting that every good Catholic sleep on bare wood to prove they were devout.

Blanche rolled onto her side and plumped her pillow, expecting sleep would overtake her quickly. Instead, she found herself examining her conscience after all.

She had come to Otley Manor planning to spy upon and betray those who had taken her in. She had intended to report any priests, and their hiding places, to her brother-in-law's friend the justice of the peace. But that had been before she met Father North. He had been nothing but kind to her, and even though Lady Otley was opinionated and abrupt, Blanche did not question the sincerity of her beliefs. Whatever their faults, no matter how misguided they might be, most of the Catholics she had so far encountered seemed to be good people at heart. Did she really want to risk condemning them to death?

Alison, Blanche reminded herself.

Her sister was the reason she was at Otley Manor. Nothing else should concern her. She must not let herself become distracted from her quest.

She had not yet sought out the ginger-haired stable boy to ask him what he knew. Worse, she had avoided Joseph Yelverton, the one person who would surely be able to tell her more about her sister's time at Otley Manor.

Blanche shook her head to try to clear her thoughts. The only significant thing she had accomplished was to learn the name of the priest who had performed the exorcism—Miles Mortimer.

What had caused Alison's death? That was the question she must answer. Now that she had met those who had been with her sister at the end, Blanche could envision two possibilities.

One was that something done to Alison during the exorcism had weakened her, leading to her death after she was imprisoned. That put the blame on Father Mortimer. Blanche was determined to stay at Otley Manor until she could meet him and take his measure for herself.

The second possibility was the one Blanche, Philippa, and Joanna had already theorized, that someone in this household had learned that Alison had come to regret her conversion to Catholicism and planned to leave. What *Blanche* already knew about the Otleys and their circle was enough to make her a threat to them, should she decide to go to the authorities. *Alison* must have known much more.

How far would someone have gone to keep her from revealing their secrets?

Chapter Eighteen

ather North left Otley Manor when it was just past dawn on Friday morning. Blanche made a point of going into the stable yard to bid him farewell. She was unsurprised to find that he was disguised as a peddler. The Otleys had provided him with a cart, a donkey, and a traveling chest large enough to hold a small, flat altar stone and his eucharistic vestments. The alb, a long white linen robe, might easily be mistaken for a night gown. The dalmatic that went over it displayed a cross when it was worn, but when it was folded it appeared to be an ordinary quilt. The amice, stole, maniple, and chasuble were all likewise reversible, hiding their true purpose, while the chalice and paten were of tin instead of gold or silver, so that at first glance they did not in the least resemble consecrated vessels. To further allay suspicion, the chest contained numerous items a real peddler might carry—a selection of ribbons, hairnets, and points, a lady's bonnet, pins, needles, flat caps, and more.

After the priest climbed into the cart, he gifted Blanche with another of his warm smiles. "Bless you, my child. I wish you well in your studies. If, when you have learned all you can about the Church of Rome, you believe you have a true vocation, I will myself arrange for your transportation to St. Ursula's convent in Louvain. The prioress there is an Englishwoman. She will make you welcome."

Although Blanche put on a brave face, she felt a deep sense of foreboding as she watched him leave. He was a good man and a kind one. If he was arrested, as he was certain to be if he remained in England, he would be executed. Although she still thought some priests deserved that fate, this one most assuredly did not.

It was only when she turned to go back inside the manor house that she realized there had been another person present to watch Father North's departure. It was the ginger-haired stable boy, the one who had looked as if he might be crying after Lady Otley told the members of her household of Alison's death in prison.

"Good morrow, lad." He started to back away, but Blanche pursued him, following him inside a stable that smelled pleasantly of horses and leather and straw. "Wait, please. I only want to talk to you."

He stopped, swiped at his runny nose with his sleeve, and stared up at her through wary eyes. Belatedly realizing that they were indoors and she was gently born, he tugged off his cap.

"You need not fear me," Blanche said in a gentle voice. "I only wish to ask you a question. Do you remember Mistress Palmer?"

The look on his face gave her the answer she sought. He not only remembered Alison, he had worshipped her from afar. Blanche's sister had always had that effect on boys of a certain age. It had been more than her physical appearance that attracted them. She had possessed a beauty of spirit as well.

"Did she ever ask a favor of you?" Blanche asked.

At first she did not think the boy would answer. He kept his head down. His hands clenched and unclenched on the cap he held in front of him, mauling it until it was beyond redemption.

"Do you have a name?" Blanche asked. "I am Mistress Wainfleet."

"I know who you are, mistress. You took her place." The words sounded like an accusation.

"She was gone before I was sent to prison, and I am sorry for it. I should have liked to find her there alive and well."

The sullen expression on the boy's face did not alter, but when she asked, he told her that his name was Rafe.

"Well, then Rafe, I would be much obliged if you could answer a question for me. Did you ever perform a service for Mistress Palmer, mayhap something that she did not want the rest of the household to know about?"

"How did you—?" He broke off in alarm, realizing he'd already said too much.

"I will tell no one," Blanche promised, "but it is important that I know. Was it a letter?"

Shoulders slumped, eyes downcast, Rafe was a study in misery. "She gave me a penny to take it into Little Mabham and another to give it to the foot-post."

Blanche slid her hand through the slit in her cloak to the purse suspended from her waist and fished for a coin. At the sight of the tester, a silver coin worth sixpence, the boy's eyes grew big as crowns. If he'd thought two pennies a great windfall, this was treasure indeed.

Holding her finger to her lips, to signify that she was buying his silence, Blanche handed it over and watched it disappear inside the boy's leather jerkin. A moment later, the sound of footsteps crunching on the gravel path outside the stable sent him scurrying away with his prize.

Blanche regretted that she'd not had time to question him further, but in truth she knew she'd been fortunate they'd not been interrupted sooner. The grooms and several other servants might have business here, but she had none.

She gathered up her skirts, preparing to return to the house, but before she could turn around, she sensed a presence close behind her. She tried to tell herself it was only one of the Trott sisters, sent to tell her that their mistress wanted her, but as she turned, her heart pounding loudly in her ears, the faint scent of civet tickled her nose. She identified the wearer by smell an instant before sight confirmed his identity.

"Well met, Mistress Wainfleet," Joseph Yelverton said. "I have been hoping to speak with you."

The words sounded innocuous enough, but they alarmed her all the same. She did not care for the way Yelverton loomed, or for the intensity of his gaze when it was focused on her. Although she dearly wanted to know how he had managed to seduce her sister into abandoning both family and faith, she was wary of his sudden interest. Had he realized who she was? Or was he the sort of man to try to work his wiles on any woman he encountered?

"Your sister will be wanting me," Blanche said, but when she tried to step around him, he caught her arm in a punishing grip.

"Like the good priest, I only wish to help you learn the joys of embracing the true faith."

"I thank you, sir, but I must not linger." His touch made her skin crawl and she was acutely aware that they were alone in the stable now that Rafe had fled. "Lady Otley will be wroth with me if I do not go to her at once."

He tightened his grip still further and hauled her a few inches closer. "I need your assistance, Mistress Wainfleet, in order to save the soul of another."

Despite her desire to escape to the safety of Lady Otley's chamber, Blanche was struck by the odd note in Yelverton's voice. She fought down an urge to struggle.

"What is it you need, sir?"

"I ask that you be a shining example to young Sarah Trott."

"I do not understand."

"That foolish girl balks at embracing her conversion," Yelverton said. "Her sister tells me that she wants to leave here and go back to their parents' house."

For a moment, Blanche was unable to speak. What else had Sarah told Edith? Had she revealed Blanche's promise to help her leave Otley Manor and return to Stisted? Did Yelverton know that too?

"I do not see what I can do."

"Speak to her. Share the advice Father North gave you while he was here. Sarah Trott must not leave Otley Manor. Her going could endanger us all."

"Endanger?"

"If she tells what she knows, there will be another raid, this one more successful than the last."

"Why would she say anything? She can scarce wish to send her own sister back to prison. And in any case, none of us knows when the next Mass will be celebrated."

He ignored her objection. "You can convince her to embrace her conversion. I have faith in you." Yelverton's face was so close to hers that

99

Blanche could feel the warmth of his breath on her cheek.

"I will to do my best," she stammered. It was a promise she had no intention of keeping.

With disorienting abruptness, he released her. Blanche had to stagger to keep her balance. She felt his eyes bore into her back as she scurried away, a sensation that made her wish for a tub of hot water to wash away every trace of his touch.

How long, she wondered, had it taken her sister to look beneath Yelverton's pleasing outward appearance to see the casual cruelty of the man beneath?

Chapter Nineteen

S ome hours passed before Blanche created an opportunity to speak with Sarah alone. Lady Otley, suffering from a bilious attack, had sent the girl to the still room to fetch a tonic made from crushed agrimony. Blanche waited only until Sarah left before she suggested that a little catnip steeped in hot water would have the same effect without such a bitter aftertaste.

"I will most happily prepare the drink for you, madam," she offered.

Granted permission to do so, Blanche hurried through the house and out into the garden. The still room was a small, separate building on the far side of the herb beds. At the sound of raised voices, she slowed her steps. The words of the quarrel were indistinct but she caught one here and there, enough to tell her that Sarah was arguing with her sister.

Edith said "Stisted" and "trial."

Sarah said "familiars," the creatures—dogs, cats, even toads—said to help witches cast spells.

Blanche stepped closer and pressed her ear against the door.

"You were friends with her once, Edith."

"Never! Avice Cony was a wicked creature."

Blanche remembered the name. Avice Cony was one of the Stisted witches.

"No more wicked than you! What if you get with child, Edith? I fear for you."

"Keep out of my business, and say no more about Avice. That is dangerous talk. Do you want them to think I was the one who bewitched Mistress Palmer?"

101

"Did you?" When Edith failed to answer, Sarah's voice rose to a shout. "It is a good thing you left home before Avice was accused, else she would have named you along with the others."

"Have a care, sister! If I am as vile as you suppose, you should live in fear of what I will do to you."

"I will be wary, never fear. I know better than to take food from your hands. A pity Mistress Palmer was not so wise."

The sound of footfalls approaching the door sent Blanche scrambling to hide herself behind a tree before either of the sisters came outside. From that place of concealment, she watched first Sarah—empty handed—and then Edith leave the still room and stride toward the house.

It was in a deeply troubled state of mind that she prepared the infusion of catnip for Lady Otley. She had been inclined to place the blame for what happened to Alison on Father Mortimer's shoulders, or upon Joseph Yelverton's head because he had been the one her sister had so unwisely loved. Now, faced with Sarah's angry accusation, she had to wonder if Sarah truly believed her sister had played a role in Alison's death. Had Edith Trott *poisoned* Alison?

Chapter Twenty

For the rest of the day, Blanche struggled with this newest suspicion. She found no opportunity to question Sarah. Wroth with her servant for failing to return with the tonic of agrimony, Lady Otley banished the girl to the kitchen. The gentlewoman's sour mood continued for the remainder of the afternoon.

It was just dusk when they heard a commotion in the stable yard.

"Go and see what that racket is," she ordered Blanche.

Only too glad to leave her poorly executed embroidery behind, Blanche went straight to the nearest window, opened it to the crisp winter air, and leaned out. At first she saw nothing to alarm her. A small party on horseback had just arrived—a man, a woman, and several servants. The man, short and stocky, his dark hair liberally streaked with gray, dismounted to speak with one of Sir Stephen's grooms.

Blanche frowned. The fellow looked familiar. So, for that matter, did his horse, a bay gelding.

Comprehension swept over her like an icy wave, causing her hands to clench on the window frame. The horse was called Clyston. The rider was her sister Philippa's steward. That meant the still-mounted woman, heavily muffled against the cold, was Philippa herself. Blanche could think of only one reason why her oldest sister, a widow with five small children at home, would make the long journey from Kent to Otley Manor. She knew Blanche was here and had come in person to deliver news of the worst kind, that something dreadful had happened to Kit.

"Well?" Lady Otley demanded. "What is happening? Must we offer hospitality to some stranger?"

"I do not know who they are," Blanche lied, "but the party is well dressed and the horses are very fine." To her own ears, her voice sound high and unnatural.

Lady Otley did not appear to notice anything amiss. "Go down and greet them."

She was already bestirring herself to issue orders to the servants. It was the accepted custom for the owners of country manors to invite sojourners to stay the night. Gentry were asked to sup with the family while lesser persons were relegated to the servants' mess.

Praying there was some other reason for Philippa to have traveled all this way over bad roads in the bitter cold, Blanche obeyed. Her panic grew apace as she sped down the stairs and along the passage to arrive, breathless and disheveled, at the stable yard.

The frigid air struck her like a blow, a belated reminder that she had not taken the time to don her cloak. She did not go back for it. Instead she quickened her pace. How Philippa had learned she was now part of the Otley household she did not know, but it would be disastrous if her sister or one of the Riverton servants revealed that they knew Lady Otley's companion. Blanche had led everyone here to believe her only kin was the distant cousin whose husband had thrown her out of his house.

Philippa turned at the sound of approaching footsteps. She had dismounted and now stood holding the reins, waiting for Blanche to reach her side.

"Good day to you, young woman," she called. "I am Lady Gallantree. Will you be so kind as to take me to your mistress?"

The manner of her greeting at once relieved Blanche's mind. She should have known her sister would be circumspect. Philippa knew full well why Blanche had arranged to have herself be imprisoned with the women arrested in the raid on Otley Manor.

Skidding to a stop just inches from the horse, a gentle palfrey called Princess, Blanche was close enough to Philippa to speak to her without being overheard. She blurted out the question foremost in her mind.

"Kit—is he?"

"Your husband is still in France, or so I presume," Philippa whispered back. "I bring no ill tidings."

At once Blanche's heart felt lighter.

Philippa raised a voice geared to sound apologetic. "I regret that we must impose ourselves upon you, but one of the horses came up lame and the light is fading."

"You are most welcome to the hospitality of the house, Lady …Gallantree." Blanche had no idea where that surname had come from. Born a Palmer like her sisters, by her marriage Philippa had become Lady Riverton.

She turned to Sir Stephen's groom and informed him that Lady Otley wished their guests to be shown every courtesy. Out of the corner of her eye, she caught sight of Rafe's ginger-colored hair. His presence worried her until she remembered that he would not recognize the name Philippa had assumed. Perhaps he'd not even have recognized the surname Riverton, since it was unlikely he could read. The direction written on the outside of the folded and sealed missive Alison had asked him to smuggle out of Otley Manor would have meant nothing to him.

"It is too cold to stand about." Philippa gave Blanche's inadequate attire a disapproving look before setting off toward the nearest door.

She moved at a rapid pace, leaving Blanche to scurry after her. They would have only a few moments of privacy before they had to enter the house.

"What are you doing here, Philippa?"

"I grew concerned for your safety when I heard about the pardon. Joanna expected you to return to them. When you did not, and neither of us had received any message from you, we feared—" She broke off and took a moment to compose herself before stopping to face Blanche with a wry smile on her face. "Let us just say that I understand why you asked first about Kit's safety."

"It never occurred to me that you would think I had come to harm."

If she'd considered the matter at all, she'd have assumed they wouldn't know about the pardon until Arthur arrived at Colchester gaol with the order for her release, and that they'd have been told then that she'd been in good health when she left.

She pictured the keeper, Luke Fludd, as she'd last seen him. Perhaps not.

"I did not mean to worry you. I seized the opportunity to remain with Lady Otley."

Philippa sighed. "I expected no less, but I had to see for myself that you were not being kept here against your will."

"I have much to tell you," Blanche said, "but there is no time for that now. We cannot risk being overheard. Between the family and the servants, there are ears everywhere."

"You are right to trust no one," Philippa said. "When can we meet?"

"Not until after everyone else is safely abed." She thought quickly. "The only chamber Lady Otley has to offer you is hard by the one assigned to me. Come to my bedchamber tonight and we will talk."

Philippa pressed her hand to signal her agreement. Without further delay, Blanche took "Lady Gallantree" in to meet Lady Otley.

Chapter Twenty-One

B lanche heard Philippa pause outside the bedchamber door and draw in a strengthening breath before she lifted the latch. That faint click sounded abnormally loud in the silence of the house.

The moon was at the full on this clear and cloudless night. Silvery beams shining through the window provided sufficient illumination to do without a candle. Blanche could see that Philippa had pulled back her light brown hair and braided it for the night. Her face was a perfect, pale oval above a night gown of dark-colored velvet. The scent of rosewater proceeded her as she walked briskly toward her youngest surviving sibling.

Blanche spoke first from her place by the hearth, where the fire had been banked but still gave off a modicum of warmth. "There was no need for you to come to Otley Manor."

"There was every need. I had to see for myself that you had not been harmed." Philippa held out her arms and Blanche went into them. They held each other tight, not speaking until Philippa stepped back, blinking away her tears. "I have heard too many stories about the horrendous conditions in prisons to take your disappearance lightly. Prisoners die even in the most luxurious accommodations in the Tower of London."

"More often just *after* they have been removed from those lodgings."

Blanche's quip drew a repressive glare from her sister, but there were unshed tears glistening in Philippa's eyes as they settled themselves side-by-side on the bed. She took her sister's hands in hers.

"How much longer must you remain in this household? Is there any possibility I can persuade you to come home with me?"

Philippa was the oldest of the sisters, eight years Blanche's senior. She had always been the most serene of the four of them, and the most nurturing. There was nothing Blanche would have liked better than to let Philippa take her under her wing and coddle her, but she shook her head.

"There is more for me to discover here, and a certain man I need to meet face-to-face. A priest."

"Have you been able to learn how Alison died?"

"She fell sick, quite suddenly, shortly before the raid."

Philippa drew in a sharp breath. "So she *was* carried off by some contagion, a fever or a catarrh?"

Blanche shook her head. "Even if that is true, there is more to it than the natural progression of illness into death. Her symptoms, even the earliest of them, may have been brought on by poison. Whatever ailed her, it was made worse by a misguided belief that she was bewitched. To rid her of the demon they claim possessed her, she was subjected to an exorcism."

In silence, but showing signs of increasing agitation with every word Blanche spoke, Philippa listened to her sister recount everything she had learned during her confinement in Colchester Castle. When she paused to draw breath, Philippa could no longer contain her anger.

"Have these people no sense? If they truly believed Alison was bewitched, then they should have looked for the person who cursed her and threatened her until she removed the spell. At the least they should have hired a local cunning woman to unwitch her. There was no need to involve a priest."

Blanche stared at her sister. "You sound as if you believe she could have been possessed."

"I think *Alison* must have believed it. She was always easily influenced by the opinions of others. You know that, Blanche. Much as we both loved our youngest sister, she did not have a great deal of common sense." Philippa wrinkled her nose. "Why else would she have been such a fool as to fall in love with that man?"

She had met Joseph Yelverton at supper. He had tried his best to charm her, but to no avail.

"She was indeed foolish," Blanche agreed, "and stubborn, but no one has ever said Alison thought herself to be under a spell. That was the verdict of those who witnessed her behavior. What do you make of her symptoms?"

As the mistress of a rural household, Philippa was far more knowledgeable when it came to treating illnesses than Blanche would ever be. She owned several herbals and knew dozens of remedies for all the most common ailments.

"Uncontrollable sneezing and flailing limbs are not suspicious in themselves. Why anyone would think they were the result of possession by a demon I cannot imagine."

"Could Alison have been poisoned?"

Philippa took a moment to consider the question before she spoke. "It is possible. There are herbs that can cause the symptoms you have described. But that is all the more reason to wonder why they leapt at once to the conclusion she had been bewitched, and to exorcism as a cure. These papists hold strange beliefs."

"To be fair, some puritans also believe a person can be saved of possession by the prayers and rituals."

Philippa ignored this. "You said that some symptoms manifested themselves at a later time, after Alison was in prison. Convulsions and blisters on her hands?"

"Lady Otley spoke of convulsions. Only young Jane Kenner mentioned the blisters and it is possible she was exaggerating to call attention to herself. When I tried to question her, she made it seem as if she knew more, but she also revealed herself to be both sly and dishonest." She told Philippa about ribbon Jane had stolen from Edith.

"And you were not able to speak with her again?"

Blanche shook her head. "I do not think she could tell me much, even if she would, but there is more to be learned here at Otley Manor." She hesitated, then asked, "Could Alison have been genuinely ill and poisoned in an attempt to cure her?"

"Sadly, yes. Many of the plants that heal are lethal if they are administered in the wrong dosage, but if Lady Otley miscalculated, why would there have been a brief period of remission following the exorcism?"

"A second dose of poison, given to her after they were in gaol?"

"What are you saying? With the best of intentions, she may have been given something that led not to recovery but to death."

"Not everyone here is well-meaning. There is Lady Otley's brother, and the priest, Father Mortimer. And do not forget our original fear, that Alison was silenced to prevent her from betraying everyone in the household."

"Do *you* think someone deliberately poisoned our sister?"

"I do not *know*, and that is what torments me. Only this morning, I overheard something new to make me wonder if Alison was murdered." She recounted all she could recall of the quarrel between Sarah Trott and her sister.

A rueful half smile flitted across Philippa's face. "Sisters have been known to say outrageous things in anger. Why would this Edith have wanted Alison dead?"

"I do not know," Blanche said again. "She might have acted on Lady Otley's orders." Frustration had her clenching her hands into fists. "Or mayhap she was only trying to ease Alison's suffering, but I cannot escape the feeling that *something* untoward befell our sister, and I cannot in good conscience leave this place until I have discovered everything that happened to her while she was here."

"A feeling?"

"Yelverton behaves strangely when people speak of Alison."

"In what way?"

"I cannot describe it, but it is not in the manner of a man remembering his lost love and I cannot help but think it is in some way connected to the exorcism. When Father Mortimer arrives, I hope to learn more."

The sound Philippa made was as brief as it was soft, but it conveyed, unmistakably, her disapproval of Blanche's plans. "Do you truly believe this priest will confide in you simply because you ask him nicely? More likely, your questions will make him suspicious, and if he was in any way responsible for Alison's death, it will scarce trouble him to get rid of you, too."

"Lady Otley accepts that I am sincere in my desire to convert. So long as I continue to be careful not to press too hard for details, I am certain I can learn more about what happened to Alison while she was here. As for the priest …." Her voice trailed off.

"Leave with me on the morrow." Philippa's voice was urgent. "We will go straight to the local justice of the peace. Surely you know enough to convince him to make another raid. Let the law deal with all of them."

"Would you send innocent women and children back to prison?"

"Not so innocent," Philippa grumbled.

"And not yet proven guilty, either."

Two weeks earlier, Blanche would have agreed to her sister's proposal. With everything she had learned about recusant women since entering Colchester gaol, she could no longer tar all of them with one brush, nor was she entirely sure anyone at Otley Manor *had* meant Alison to die. She had to be certain before she took action.

"The local justice is a man named Sir Eustace Lewknor. There is no love lost between him and the Otleys. If I tell him where certain forbidden relics and books are hidden, he may not wait until there is a priest in residence to conduct a raid. Possession of those things alone would send Sir Stephen and his wife to gaol, and mayhap to the gallows, but Yelverton could weasel out of punishment because this is not his house. No, Philippa. At the least, I must stay here until Father Mortimer arrives and I can take his measure for myself."

"Your sudden sympathy for these papists astonishes me."

"They are not all traitors, not even the Jesuits. Father North, the one priest I have met, is a good man, for all that he puts the pope's authority over the queen's. Father Mortimer could be another like him."

Philippa grasped Blanche's shoulders and shook her. "Do you hear yourself? Have these papists infected you with their beliefs, as they did Alison? Jesuits have no purpose in England save to sow discord. They plot to replace Queen Elizabeth with a foreign, Catholic monarch. They foment rebellion and preach sedition."

"Not all of them." Blanche clasped her hands over her sister's. "I do not want to condemn the wrong person. What if Father Mortimer truly believed he was helping Alison? If he never intended to harm her, how can I betray him when betrayal would mean his death?"

Philippa broke the hold and drew away from her sister. "You are too trusting."

"I am not." She gave a self-deprecating laugh. "In truth, it is your fault that I now have doubts about my purpose here. Telling you what I have learned, what I have seen, remembering more than I have said, has made me realize how little I can be certain of anything. Can you not see? I have no choice but to remain here until I know exactly what happened to Alison in her final days at Otley Manor."

Philippa released a gusty sigh. "Are you sure it is safe to stay?"

"No one doubts the sincerity of my desire to convert. Even Yelverton holds me up as a shining example for young Sarah Trott to follow. And both Lady Otley and Father North have offered to help me leave England and enter a nunnery, if that is my desire."

Philippa snorted. "I cannot imagine a more unlikely candidate for a chaste, contemplative life." She slid an arm around her sister's shoulders. "You frighten me, Blanche. I know your nature too well. Like Alison, once you are set on a purpose, it is difficult, if not impossible, to dissuade you from it. Joanna and I supported the plan whereby you entered Colchester goal to search for answers, but that was to be for a week's time. What you are asking now is to remain indefinitely in this nest of vipers."

"They are not that bad."

"You deceive yourself if you think you can believe what you are told by anyone living here. If someone in this house caused Alison harm, that person will not be pleased to discover that you have been meddling in the matter."

"I *can* be subtle."

Philippa stifled a laugh. "Not with your temper."

"I can control it." She was glad she had not told Philippa about the incident with the guards in Colchester gaol.

"If you insist upon remaining here, I beg you to be discreet, but also be *careful*. Do not eat or drink anything others have not also consumed. Do not confide in anyone, not even this girl you want to help."

"I will come to no harm. No one here has reason to think I am anything but what I claim to be."

Her sister released a pent-up sigh. "I can see that your mind is made up, so I will not lecture you further, but the admiration I heard in your voice when you spoke of this Father North alarms me. Promise me you are not in the least tempted to convert."

"You need not fear on that account, but is it so wrong to wish to avoid causing trouble for good people like the Farleighs and Mistress Kenner? Is it truly evil to cling to an outlawed faith?"

"I have a certain sympathy for anyone who is true to their beliefs," Philippa admitted. "If I did not, I should have arrived with a troop of retainers and carried you home with me whether you wished to leave or not. But religious dissention threatens the stability of the realm and you know that what I said before is true. Jesuits are trained to preach the overthrow of the queen. That is why persons caught hearing Mass are arrested."

Blanche sent her sister a wary look. "Promise me that you will not go to Sir Eustace on your own."

"What would I tell him? Besides, I do not want *you* to be arrested."

"All will be well. You must not worry."

"Well, I cannot say I did not expect this outcome." Philippa untied the strip of fabric that belted her night robe and pressed it into Blanche's hands. "When you are ready to leave this place, you will need the coins sewn inside this cloth. God grant they are sufficient to bring you safely home."

They were both fighting tears when they embraced.

Blanche watched her sister leave the chamber with an ache in her heart and a mind filled with doubt. Philippa was right about one thing. If her decision to remain behind was the wrong one, she might well pay for it with her life.

Chapter Twenty-Two

Considerable speculation followed Philippa's departure the next morning. Joseph Yelverton wondered aloud if the travelers had been sent to spy on those living at Otley Manor. Lady Otley dismissed the notion as unlikely, but Sir Stephen found it suspicious that the "lame" horse had made such a speedy recovery. Blanche said nothing, reluctant to draw attention to herself.

When a stranger joined them for supper that evening, she understood why Philippa's visit had made Yelverton so nervous. His deferential behavior toward the man suggested that he was a priest even before Lady Otley addressed him as Father Mortimer.

He was older than Father North, balding and with a decided paunch, and he displayed none of the younger man's civility. He barked his words, making everything he said sound like a command. His perpetually sour expression made Blanche wonder if he suffered from sore feet or mayhap a toothache. Her instinctive dislike of the priest produced in her a strong desire to confront him and demand the truth, but she was not so foolish as to approach him directly.

As soon as the meal was finished, Father Mortimer announced that he would hear confessions in the chapel behind the nursery. Lady Otley, Sir Stephen, and Lady Otley's brother were first in line. The two gentlemen waited in the nursery while Lady Otley was with the priest, leaving lesser mortals to cool their heels in the passage. The moment their betters were safely behind a closed door, a low murmur began among the servants.

Blanche stood still, hands clasped in front of her, listening to the others with only part of her attention. She was preoccupied with thoughts of the ordeal ahead. Could she remain calm? Could she hide her suspicions well enough, be subtle enough, to risk a question or two?

She did not look forward to being alone with the priest, but at least she did not have to worry that he would disbelieve her list of minor sins. After her first experience with Father North, she had prepared for the next. She would admit to envy, sloth, and gluttony, the latter because she had eaten too many comfits while she and Lady Otley sat and wrought.

As the wait lengthened, Blanche slowly became more attuned to the conversations around her. When she realized that two of the servants, the horse master and the undercook, were talking about Father Mortimer, she listened more intently. Her eyes widened at what she heard.

The priest had spent time in prison. He had been tortured. His hands were terribly scarred. That was why he never removed the thin leather gloves he wore, not even at table.

Blanche thought back to the meal they'd just shared. Had he kept his gloves on? She hadn't noticed. She'd been trying her best *not* to stare at the priest while he ate.

At last it was her turn to confess. Father Mortimer waited for her in the dimly-lit chamber and gestured for her to seat herself on the opposite end of the bench he already occupied. She thought that an odd confessional, but then this room made a strange sort of chapel.

Even when he was seated with his head bowed, the priest was intimidating. Beset by the sweat-producing anxiety that he would somehow see straight into her heart and denounce her for the fraud she was, Blanche was grateful she had a ritual to follow. She choked out the opening phrase—"Forgive me, Father, for I have sinned."

After that, the words came more easily, but Father Mortimer did not seem greatly interested in the minor infractions she listed. In a perfunctory way, he assigned the prayers she must recite for penance.

Absolved of sin, Blanche sprang to her feet, abandoning all thought of interrogating the priest. She wanted only to escape and started violently when he barked a question at her.

"Upon what subjects do you meditate?"

Blanche froze, her mind momentarily blank. She remained on her feet, her head bowed, while she struggled to remember the list she had memorized from *The Exercise of a Christian Life*. She felt a surge of relief when it came back to her and she was able to rattle off each day's subject.

"Give more thought to eternal damnation," the priest instructed. "Young women are prone to sin."

She fought to quell a flash of temper. She wanted to challenge his absurd statement. Young *men* were far more likely to follow that path. Reduced to silence by the long, hard stare the priest leveled at her, she held her tongue.

Apparently satisfied that she was properly cowed, he waved her away. "Go with God."

The words sounded more like an order than a blessing, but Blanche was glad to obey.

Once everyone in the household had been to confession, they were obliged to attend evening prayers. Father Mortimer's Latin was better than Lady Otley's but he droned on just as interminably. Blanche spent the time berating herself for cowardice. She had lost a heaven-sent opportunity, failing to realize until it was too late that if she had asked Father Mortimer to elaborate on the sins of young women, he might well have cited Alison as an example.

Sleep was long in coming that night, at least in part because the next day was the Sabbath. Sundays and feast days started earlier than other days. Blanche would be expected to engage in a greater number of devotions and each period of prayer or meditation would be longer than usual. Worse, when Mass was celebrated, she would be expected to take holy Communion. She had been excused when Father North presided, on the grounds that she was not yet fully instructed in the true faith, but there would be no avoiding it this time.

She told herself the ritual was no different when presided over by a Catholic priest than it was in her own parish church of St. Andrew Holborn, but doubts lingered. The next morning, she was visibly shaking when she sipped from the cup.

Her relief was palpable when she tasted the contents on her tongue. The wine was of a good vintage, but it was still wine. Even better, no lightning bolt had come down from above to smite her for participating in a forbidden papist rite.

Father Mortimer sent her a sour smile. She supposed that passed for approval from a man like him. If he'd noticed how nervous she was, he must have attributed it to her sinful woman's nature.

Blanche's meditations that day strayed far from the topics approved by the church of Rome. She briefly entertained the heretical idea that God might not care how He was worshiped. Then her thoughts moved on to consider how, during the time Father Mortimer remained at Otley Manor, she was to discover what he had done to Alison during her exorcism. She knew she must not let another opportunity slip away from her. If this priest followed the same pattern as Father North, he would leave again within a day or two.

Chapter Twenty-Three

B lanche put on her cloak and went out into the garden, forging a path through an inch or two of newly-fallen snow. Lady Otley took her exercise in the great hall, attended by Edith and Sarah, but Blanche had begged permission to seek fresh air.

It was the first day of February. The temperature was warm enough to make outdoor activity pleasant and Blanche looked forward to being alone with her thoughts. She hoped to formulate a plan whereby, without seeming to take too great an interest in a woman she had never met, she could persuade the priest to reveal the details of Alison's ordeal.

She had been outside no more than a quarter of an hour when she heard the loud crunching noise of heavy boots breaking through a crusty surface. Someone was behind her on the snow-covered gravel path that ran between two of the raised flower beds.

On her guard, she turned, unsure whether to be relieved or alarmed when she recognized Joseph Yelverton bearing down on her. His first words took her aback.

"I am told, Mistress Wainfleet, that you have a talent for finding things that are lost."

Something about the avid look in his eyes made her uneasy. He was examining her in the same way a small boy might look at an injured animal he was about to poke with a stick.

Blanche was careful to keep her voice noncommittal as she told an outright lie. "I suppose someone repeated the careless words I spoke in Colchester gaol. It was pure good fortune that I found the ribbon Edith lost. When I deliberately try to find misplaced items, I fail far more often than I succeed."

Yelverton looked disappointed, but his words conveyed the opposite impression. "I am glad to hear it. It is an unnatural thing to be able to locate what others cannot."

When he offered Blanche his arm, she had no choice but to take it. "It is always a matter of chance, I do assure you."

"Have you ever kept a cat?"

Blanche answered this unexpected question with a partial truth. "My father made use of an old tom to keep vermin from infesting his warehouse. Cats are most excellent hunters."

Had she seen a single feline since coming to Otley Manor? She could not recall catching so much as a glimpse of one.

"True," Yelverton said. "Very true. But would you not say it is unnatural for a cat to follow a person like a dog?"

"I suppose that any animal may be trained to do tricks," Blanche said carefully, "and cats appear to be clever creatures." They could do many things on their own, if they were so inclined.

"For someone who does not keep a cat, you seem passing *familiar* with the ways of the species."

Blanche felt as if a great chasm had just opened up under her feet. There was that word again. Familiar. The term used to describe animals who obeyed the commands of a witch.

"I do not understand you, sir."

Although she feigned ignorance, she could guess where Yelverton's questions were leading. She had a vague memory of hearing about a trial for witchcraft, perhaps ten years earlier, that had a involved a witch with familiars named Titty and Jack—two cats.

"There was a young woman here not long ago," Yelverton said, "who was over-fond of cats. I cannot abide the creatures myself, and for good reason. Alison Palmer made the fatal mistake of befriending one such beast and it was the means through which she was bewitched."

Alison *had* always had a great affection for cats. More than once, one had followed her home and been adopted into the family as a pet. Those who had not proven their worth in keeping down the population of mice and rats had stayed on anyway, for they were passing good company.

Aloud, Blanche said only, "I have heard others speak of this Mistress Palmer, but I do not understand why you should think she was cursed by supernatural means."

"She was possessed by a demon," Yelverton corrected her. "The signs are clear when they manifest themselves. Crying. Gnashing of the teeth. Foaming at the mouth. The inability to hear or speak."

Blanche turned her head to stare up at him in astonishment. The symptoms he'd listed were not the same as the ones she'd previously heard.

"How terrible," she murmured. "Do you mean to tell me that the poor woman suffered all those afflictions?"

"She would have, had we let the demon remain to torment her, but she did sneeze very loudly and heavily for periods of an hour and more."

Pity anyone who fell ill of a catarrh in this house, Blanche thought. No doubt bouts of coughing would also be seen as proof of evil manifestations.

"She would shake one leg," Yelverton continued, "and then the other and make jerking motions with her arms and head." He leaned closer, until Blanche nearly choked on the scent of the civet he used to perfume his clothing. "It was the devil inside her who made her behave in such an obscene manner."

Blanche stopped walking. Her hands had curled into fists at her sides. She wanted most urgently to strike Joseph Yelverton, but she could not, nor could she shout at him to stop being a credulous fool. Any number of physical ailments might have accounted for Alison's symptoms. More than one illness caused its sufferer to have fits. Possession by a demon should have been the last thing anyone thought of.

"Was a physician sent for?" she asked through clenched teeth.

"A doctor would have been of no help."

"The local cunning woman, then?"

"She was suspected of causing of Alison's possession."

They had completed one circuit of the garden. Yelverton's gaze fixed on the tracks they had left in the snow. "The Devil and his minions are ever but a footfall away. Our intercession saved Alison Palmer's soul."

He left her then, continuing on into the stable yard. Blanche stared after him, struck dumb by his parting words. The way he had said "our intercession" left her in no doubt. Father Mortimer had not acted alone in performing Alison's exorcism. Joseph Yelverton had assisted him ...and he had relished every moment of the experience.

Chapter Twenty-Four

I t was later that same day, during the part of the afternoon when everyone was given leave to meditate in private, that Blanche chanced upon Sarah Trott. She was sitting on the floor of the passage that led to Blanche's bedchamber, sobbing as if her heart would break. Finding the pitiful sound impossible to ignore, Blanche knelt beside the younger woman and placed a gentle hand on her forearm.

"Hush, Sarah. Whatever troubles you cannot be so bad as all that."

"Do you believe in Purgatory, Mistress Wainfleet?"

Blanche blinked at her, momentarily uncertain how to answer. "I have not thought much about it."

"Father Mortimer says that even if I escape going to Hell, I will surely spend eternity in that terrible halfway place."

When Sarah began to cry even harder, Blanche settled herself tailor fashion on the floor beside her and awkwardly patted first Sarah's arm and then her back. It did little good, but at length the sobbing ebbed sufficiently for Blanche to ask a question.

"Why does the priest say you are condemned to Purgatory?"

"It is because I am a heretic," Sarah whispered. "He told me that I am doomed to eternal torment unless I make a sincere conversion to the true faith."

"I dare say the vicar of your village church has a different opinion."

The faintest of smiles played about Sarah's lips, but she did not seem much comforted. "I will never see Stisted again. They will never let me leave here." She hesitated. "I do not think they will let you go, either."

"I must remain a little longer in any case, so if I am to take you away with me when I go, you must stay, too. Can you bring yourself to pretend to embrace their beliefs?"

Sarah sent her an odd look. "Is that what you do?"

Blanche nodded.

"But everyone says you want to be a nun."

Blanche warned herself to be careful how much she confided in Sarah, lest she let something slip to her sister. Edith Trott had a sly way about her, and there was still the possibility that she had given Alison a potion that had made her even sicker.

"It is a ruse, Sarah. I cannot say more, but believe me when I say I am your friend and that I will help you all I can."

"Father Mortimer frightens me." Sarah's voice shook.

"He will be gone from here soon."

"He is the priest who performed Mistress Palmer's exorcism. He would like to discover the one who bewitched her."

"Do you still fear that he will suspect you of being a witch?"

"It is worse than that," Sarah whispered. "He said I had evil *in* me, evil that must be removed. What if he decides that I must be exorcised?"

Blanche did not at once reply. Her mind was racing. Like Sarah, Alison had experienced doubts about changing her faith. Like Sarah, she had joined this household at the urging of someone she loved, but at least Alison had known before she arrived that the Otleys were recusants. Edith had not bothered to warn her sister that she would be expected to convert.

"I am not a witch." Sarah's voice was a little stronger but no less panicked. "And I have not been bewitched."

Blanche caught her shoulders with both hands and waited until Sarah met her eyes before she spoke. "I believe you, but you are right to be afraid. You must take precautions. Tell me again about Mistress Palmer's symptoms."

"At first we thought she had caught an ague. She was coughing and sneezing and her forehead was hot to the touch. Then the twitching started."

"What convinced Father Mortimer that she was bewitched?"

"Sick as she was, she came to Mass with the rest of the household, but at the sight of the consecrated host she began to scream and would not stop."

"What you have described, even the screaming, was likely the result of her fever. She was delirious, not possessed." Blanche released her grip on Sarah's shoulders.

"Lady Otley tried treating her with herbal remedies, but none of them did any good."

Blanche hesitated before asking her next question. She did not want to frighten Sarah more than she was already, but they could not ignore the fact that both Father Mortimer and Joseph Yelverton seemed focused on the subject of witchcraft.

"Tell me more about the witches of Stisted."

Sarah started to refuse, but Blanche fixed her with a stern look. The girl darted a frightened glance over her shoulder, as if she expected the priest to leap out at them.

"We are as private here as anyone can be in a house full of people," Blanche said, "and I believe I need to know this if I am to help you."

Sarah choked back a sob. "It was years ago when it began. I was a mere child."

"Children hear and see more than adults realize." She thought again of Jane Kenner and wondered why the girl and her mother had not come to Otley Manor to hear Father Mortimer say Mass. Had they feared the raiders would come again?

"I told you about Joan Cony and her daughters," Sarah reminded her.

"But you have not, I think, told me everything."

Only with great reluctance did Sarah oblige her. "Joan Cony was taught witchcraft by another woman of Stisted. Old Mother Humfrye showed her how to draw circles on the ground to call Satan. Because Joan worshipped him, the devil gave her two familiars in the shape of black frogs. One had the power to kill men and the other could kill women. Some people were able to repel them by the force of their belief in God, but others were harmed."

"How do you know this?"

"Joan confessed to it all at her trial, and to more, too, even that she trained up her daughters to be witches."

CHAPTER TWENTY-FOUR

"But not her grandsons?"

"No. I told you. They gave evidence against her, and against their own mothers."

"Why? Did a witch finder persuade them to it?" It seemed possible to Blanche that young boys might have made up stories at the urging of such a man.

Sarah's head was bowed, her voice faint. "My parents' house is hard by that of Joan Cony. My youngest brother was wont to sneak off and play with Margaret's son, since they were of an age. The boy told him that once, when he and his grandmother were in a field, she called upon one of her familiars to knock down an oak tree, and at her command it toppled over."

"The wind—"

"There was no wind that day."

Blanche let that pass. "Were other people charged with witchcraft at the same time?" The trials she had read about in pamphlets printed afterward tended to involve a dozen or more indictments.

"In all, nine women and one man were tried for witchcraft. The Conys accused the others. Joan Upney and Joan Prentis were hanged along with Joan Cony, and you know already the fate Avice Cony met. Three others were found not guilty and the rest were imprisoned, including Margaret Cony."

"Did they all make use of familiars?"

"Joan Prentis said the Devil appeared to her as Bidd, a dun colored ferret with fiery eyes. When it asked for her soul, she told it that her soul belonged to Jesus, but she offered it blood from her finger instead. Then Bidd killed a young girl for her, because the child's mother had refused to give her alms."

Cats, frogs, and now a ferret. "What familiar helped Joan Upney?"

"She used toads to murder the wives of two men who had accused her of being a witch." Sarah paused and said, her voice thoughtful, "In truth, I do not think Goody Upney was anything more than a cunning woman. She had knowledge of herbs and was said to excel at finding lost property and at unwitching."

Blanche winced at the reference to finding what was lost, but it was the other activity Sarah had cited that prompted her next question. "What means did she use to unwitch those who had been bewitched? Was she an exorcist?"

Sarah made a choked sound. "She would never have done anything as horrible as what that priest did to Mistress Palmer."

Blanche wanted to press for those details, but she warned herself to be patient. Besides, she was curious. "What *did* she do, then?"

"I only know what my mother told me. She said that Goodwife Upney recommended steeping three leaves each of sage and St. John's wort in ale and drinking it all down at once to resist bewitchment."

That sounded harmless enough. Blanche wanted more than anything to ask about the exorcism, but if Sarah dissolved again into tears, she would get no answers of any kind. Other questions had been plaguing her nearly as badly.

"I overheard you quarreling with your sister in the still room," she said. "It sounded as if you thought Edith might have harmed Alison Palmer."

Eyes wide and frightened, Sarah opened her mouth but no words came out.

"Did you see her give Alison something to eat or drink before she fell ill?"

"I ...I." Sarah shook herself, and then she shook her head.

"No?" Blanche was certain she'd heard Sarah make that accusation. "Was Edith friendly with the Conys when she lived in Stisted?"

Once again, Sarah shook her head in denial, and this time Blanche knew she was lying.

"You deny it now, but in the stillroom that day, you spoke of her friendship with Avice Cony and you sounded very certain that Mistress Palmer had been a fool to take food or drink from Edith's hand. Why did you suspect your sister of involvement in what happened to Alison?"

"It was the way she flinched," Sarah blurted.

Blanche waited.

"When it was first suggested that Mistress Palmer might have been bewitched, when Father Mortimer was last at Otley Manor, old Mistress Farleigh said she should use a counter spell to find the witch. No one else noticed, but I saw Edith's face when she said that. Edith was afraid."

"Old Mistress Farleigh? The former nun?"

Sarah nodded.

"She said that scratching the witch who had cast the spell on Mistress Palmer and drawing blood was a sure way to end her bewitchment. She said we must find the witch, tether her to a stake, and persuade Mistress Palmer to attack her."

"But no one knew who had bewitched her." Hearing her own words, Blanche grimaced. She sounded for all the world as if she *did* believe in witchcraft.

"No one favored the suggestion, even if we could have discovered who she was. Lady Otley worried that a counter spell could incite the witch to greater malice, and Father Mortimer claimed that such an attack would turn Mistress Palmer herself into a witch. He insisted that the only way to save her was an exorcism and that he would conduct it. And now he thinks I have evil in me, too," Sarah added in a small voice. "I am afraid to stay here any longer, Mistress Wainfleet. I do not want them to do to me what they did to her."

Blanche could scarce blame her for desiring to get away from this place, but if Sarah ran, she was not likely to get very far. She took both the girl's hands in hers.

"Listen to me, Sarah. If you leave here, you will be hunted down and forced to return. You hired yourself out to Lady Otley for a year, did you not?"

That was the customary length of time for those who entered domestic service. At Sarah's nod, Blanche continued.

"It requires a hearing before two justices to break such a contract. Anyone unduly departing her master's house is subject to arrest. You could be sent to prison, but more likely you would be sentenced to return here to serve out the remainder of your term. During that time you would be treated little better than a slave."

Sarah looked as if she would burst into tears again at any moment.

Blanche spoke sharply to stay the deluge. "I swear to you that I will take you with me when I leave, and that I will find a way to keep you safe from the authorities, but we cannot go yet."

Sarah's expression changed to one of bewilderment. "If you mean to go, why not now? Why must we stay?"

"I cannot tell you that. I can only ask you to trust me."

Sarah worried her lower lip with her teeth. "Is it true that an employer who hires a runaway servant is liable for a fine of five pounds."

Blanche sighed. "I do not intend to employ you, Sarah. I intend to see you safely back to Stisted, but it is crucial that we choose the right moment to depart."

"I do not see why we must wait." She sounded sulky, reminding Blanche of just how young she was.

"I cannot explain. Not yet. Now, go you to your duties. Be of good cheer, but do not share what I have said to you with no one, not even Edith." *Especially not with Edith.*

Once the girl had scurried down the stairs, Blanche rose more slowly and made her way to her bedchamber. Instead of meditating, she prayed, humbly asking God for the strength to persevere, and that He grant Sarah sufficient courage to stay the course.

Chapter Twenty-Five

A great commotion greeted Blanche as she descended the stairs the next morning. She followed the sounds of a loud argument to the dining parlor adjacent to the great hall. Nearly the entire household appeared to have done likewise, although most of the servants were quick to slink away again when they caught sight of Sarah Trott. Half-conscious, her hair and clothing in disarray, she was held upright by Joseph Yelverton on one side and Father Mortimer on the other.

Blanche did not flee, but her heart raced as she crept closer to watch and listen. It did not take her long to work out what had happened. Sarah had run away in the wee hours of the morning. Alerted, men were sent in pursuit. When they caught her, she had been frantic with fear, striking out at those who tried to return her to Otley Manor. Since she was smaller and weaker, she was much the worse for her attempt at escape.

"She was lured into leaving by the Devil." For once, Father Mortimer did not look as if he had just bitten into sour fruit. His color was high and there was a gleam in his protuberant eyes, as if he derived physical pleasure from the prospect of doing battle with Satan. "She must be cleansed."

"No!"

Everyone turned to look at Edith, as surprised as if a stone statue in the garden had come to life. It was the first time Blanche could remember the older sister taking her younger sibling's part.

Edith quailed before the priest's intense scrutiny, clapping both hands over her mouth.

Father Mortimer's thin lips twisted into a mockery of a smile. "Do you

129

think I am mistaken?"

Edith face was easy to read. Trapped, she considered lying, but in the end she told the truth. "My sister is a God-fearing Christian. She has naught to do with the Devil."

"I did not say this congress was her doing." Father Mortimer's voice was less harsh than usual but a far cry from soothing. "She is bewitched, just as that other young woman was. A demon has taken possession of her through some evil enchantment."

Edith's denial was vigorous, if silent, but no one except Blanche saw her shake her head. Everyone else's attention was fixed upon the priest.

"You must rid Sarah of this demon," Lady Otley said.

"At once," Sir Stephen agreed.

But it was Joseph Yelverton's enthusiasm for another exorcism that made Blanche's stomach clench. The anticipation she saw on his face, a slavering excitement she could only equate with extreme lechery, surpassed even Father Mortimer's. Eyes alight, Yelverton released Sarah's arm and made a grab for Edith. "The evil has infected them both. Both must be purified."

Realizing her imminent peril, Edith tried to flee. Sir Stephen blocked her way. When he seized hold of her, she shrank into herself, as if she had lost all will to resist. While Blanche looked on in shock, Edith and Sarah, who had regained some control over her limbs, were marched upstairs and thrust into the small, interior room Blanche had discovered when she first explored the house. The unpleasant smell she remembered still lingered within.

"That such a thing should happen here again," Lady Otley fretted when Father Mortimer had locked them inside. "Who is causing it? How can we stop it?"

Blanche had to bite her lip to keep from answering. The only ones to blame were Lady Otley's brother and the Jesuit. The way to stop it was to set the Trott sisters free and expel these two evil men from Otley Manor.

She dared not speak the truth, or do anything to suggest she was in sympathy with the prisoners. She would be of no use to Sarah and Edith if she was also accused of being possessed. She'd be locked up right along with them.

As the day progressed, normal in every other way, Blanche's sense of helplessness grew. There was no safe way to rescue the two maidservants and escape with them from Otley Manor and she could think of no way to stop the exorcism.

They were in good health, she assured herself as the afternoon wore on. Unlike poor Alison. They would not suffer any permanent damage. The purpose of the exorcism was to save them, not to do them harm. Since she had no way to prevent the ritual from taking place, she could only bear witness to what was done to them and afterward, when Sarah and Edith were declared free of demons, do everything in her power to get Sarah, and herself, far away from this place.

Lady Otley was as distracted as her companion, but her concern was somewhat different. She lamented her inability to identify the witch who had cursed members of her household.

"First Alison and now Sarah and Edith," she said, for what seemed like the hundredth time. "I cannot understand it. We get on well with all our neighbors. We pay our debts. We refuse charity to none. No one has any cause to hate us, not even those who despise our faith." Her lips compressed and her voice took on a bitter edge. "They have no need to resort to witchcraft. If they wished to torment us, they have the legal means to do so."

"I thought Sir Stephen and Sir Eustace were bitter enemies," Blanche said, remembering what the Otleys had said about the local magistrate.

Lady Otley made a sound of derision. "They get on well enough for the most part, so long as my husband regularly attends the parish church and pays my fines for recusing myself. Even so, Sir Eustace would dearly love to catch himself a priest."

"How does he feel about witches?"

"There, I suspect, we may be in agreement. But who is there to accuse?"

Blanche opened her mouth to suggest the old woman with the cow, the one with half her wits lacking, but she closed it again without speaking. Mother Dunster had been rude to her, and might well be mad, but she had

131

done nothing to warrant being hanged for witchcraft. The same prohibition applied to suggesting that the local cunning woman, whoever she was, might be to blame. She wondered if Sir Eustace had a wife.

At supper, Father Mortimer wore a self-satisfied smile as he helped himself to generous portions of every dish. When Lady Otley asked about sending food to the prisoners, he gleefully reminded her that forcing them to fast was part of the preparation for their exorcism.

Blanche's disgust grew with every word he spoke. This was not how a priest should behave. Father North had been sincere and devout and kind, despite his desire to return England to the Church of Rome, but Mortimer seemed to take a perverse pleasure in the prospect of torturing innocents.

She considered ways in which she might secret food about her person and take it to Sarah and Edith during the night, but she soon realized how impractical this plan was. Not only had two of Sir Stephen's grooms been assigned to guard the door to the little room, but Father Mortimer had taken away the key.

Schooling her facial features to express morbid curiosity with a touch of admiration—eyes wide, nose wrinkled, and mouth slightly agape—she turned to the priest and asked a direct question: "How do you know what to do? Are all priests trained to exorcise demons?"

"Only a select few."

Puffed up with pride, he waxed eloquent on the subject. Blanche listened closely, even though some of what he said, and the way he said it, made her skin crawl.

"Both the recently published manual on exorcism written by Petrus Thyraeus, a Jesuit, and another by a Franciscan, Girolamo Menghi, contain precise directions for combining certain substances that can then be administered by mouth or through the nose to drive out demons. These ingredients are naturally strengthening to the patient, or naturally repulsive to the demon, or both."

"Ingredients?" The word struck Blanche as far too benign.

"Each one is blessed before it is used," Mortimer informed her in a pious tone of voice.

"What were the herbs we used on that other girl?" The salacious look on Yelverton's face suggested that he was savoring the memory of Alison's reaction to them.

"A dram of choice rhubarb combined with the roots of elecampane, artemisia, some lesser centaury, and aquatic mint."

"It was my task to boil everything except the artemisia in wine," Lady Otley put in with a hint of pride. "I cooked that in a pot of water."

"I fear there may have been a mistake made in the preparation." Mortimer gave every outward appearance of regret, but his true feelings were betrayed by the calculating gleam in his eyes.

Lady Otley looked stricken, taking it for granted that any error must have been hers. Jesuits, it seemed, were supposed to be as infallible as the Pope.

"You will recall," Mortimer continued, "that the instructions called for a poor but pious man to stir the mixture, all the while reciting the Lord's Prayer and then saying the Hail Mary five times. Your choice of the man must have been flawed. How else can we explain that the demon was not expelled, but only became dormant?"

Lady Otley's eyes narrowed, making Blanche wonder it had been Father Mortimer who selected the fellow. At the least, he must have approved the choice she'd made.

"You will do better this time," the priest said.

Pompous ass, Blanche thought, and Yelverton was just as bad. Indeed, he was likely worse, and he might yet prove to be the more dangerous of the two. She did not like the way he kept glancing toward her as the discussion continued.

Wary of his interest, she asked no further questions. She listened closely as the others talked of a variety of recipes used in exorcisms, but she did not learn anything new about what to expect on the morrow.

She went to bed that night half-convinced that exorcisms were no more than conjurer's tricks. Those who conducted them wished to make themselves look important and at the same time strike fear into the hearts of every woman in the household.

Chapter Twenty-Six

After a hearty breakfast, Lady Otley, her husband, her brother, and her priest adjourned to the locked room. Blanche trailed after them, sickened by the air of repressed excitement bubbling up from all four of them.

The door opened to reveal the two sisters huddled together in a corner. Their tear-stained cheeks and hollow eyes gave proof of a sleepless, dread-filled night. Having borne witness to Alison's exorcism, they knew far better than Blanche did what was about to happen. Their dread communicated itself to her, making her painfully aware that she had been lying to herself. There would be much more to this ritual than drinking herbal potions and saying prayers.

Forcibly separated from Edith, Sarah was dragged to the center of the room and made to lie on her back on the bare floor. Father Mortimer, wearing richly embroidered vestments, sat on her legs and allowed Yelverton to pour a small amount of vinegar into his mouth. In the next instant, the priest leaned over Sarah's body, grabbed hold of her wrists, and spat the vinegar straight up her nose.

When Sarah cried out in pain, Blanche made a strangled sound of protest and took a step toward them. She wanted to intervene but dared not. It was only vinegar, she told herself. It would have caused a stinging, burning pain, but it would have done Sarah no permanent harm.

Prayers followed, after which Father Mortimer inflicted the same treatment on Edith.

Tears streaming down her face, she looked up at him and spoke in a voice so hoarse that it was almost unrecognizable. "The Devil has gone. I felt it leave my body."

No one believed her.

With the flair of players giving a performance on a stage, Father Mortimer and Master Yelverton proceeded to tie both women to chairs. This time they focused their attention on Edith first. She was made to drink holy water. When she recoiled—no doubt, Blanche thought, because of the salty taste—a triumphant smile appeared on Father Mortimer's face.

"It has been rejected by the demon inside her."

Although by now Blanche was silently praying that this success would mark the end of the exorcism, the play was only in its first act. Father Mortimer delivered a little lecture as he moved on to the next scene, eager to show off his self-proclaimed expertise.

"You will have heard," he said, "that medicinal suffumigation may be used to relieve symptoms of a stuffed up head."

Her sister, Philippa, Blanche remembered, recommended burning rinds of rosemary for that purpose, but what Father Mortimer did was far different. The smoke from his "hallowed" substances created a great stink and she understood at last why such a stomach-turning stench had lingered in this room.

Sarah was forced to inhale sanctified smoke from burning feathers. Then, after rue, brimstone, and asafetida were added to the brazier, the priest pushed her head so close to the heat that, fearing to be burnt, she cried out and began to struggle. He would not release her, or permit her to rise, until her strength failed her and she very nearly fell into the fire. When he finally jerked her upright, her face was as blackened as a chimney sweep's.

"She swoons," Yelverton sounded disappointed.

"It is a reaction to the holy smoke—the Devil grows quiet."

The priest gestured for Yelverton to move Sarah's limp form out of the way while he turned his attention to Edith. He burned different herbs for her to inhale, enumerating them as he added each one to the coals.

"Cinquefoil. Verbena. Valerian. Betony. Dried bryony root. Alyssum."

A prickle of alarm raised goosebumps on Blanche's arms. She was no

135

herbist, but she did know that some kinds of bryony were poisonous. She had learned that much as a child, on a long-ago visit to an apothecary's shop with her mother. The apothecary, seizing the opportunity to educate a future customer, had told her all about white bryony.

It was sold as a dry root in circular, brittle pieces a quarter to a third of an inch thick and two inches in diameter. It had a thin, greyish-brown bark, rough and longitudinally wrinkled. Although it had no odor, it did have a nauseatingly bitter taste, and its juice had a purgative effect. In small pieces it resembled horseradish root, except that horseradish was smooth. Apothecaries, he'd told her, always used gloves when they handled bryony, even when they did no more than crush the juice out of the stems with a mortar and pestle. Every part of the plant caused blisters to form on the skin.

Jane Kenner had spoken of blisters on Alison's hands. Was it possible ...?

Blanche frowned. What she was thinking made no sense. Alison's blisters had not appeared while she was at Otley Manor. They had surfaced only after she was imprisoned in Colchester gaol.

A high, keening cry jerked Blanche's thoughts back to the present. Father Mortimer had set aside the brazier and was tearing at Edith's clothing. Enthusiastically aided and abetted by Yelverton, he soon had the helpless woman down to her shift, and then that, too, was stripped away. Not a word of protest came from the Otleys. Blanche herself was too shocked by what she was seeing to do anything more than stare.

Mortimer flung the clothing aside. "These garments are full of evil spirits!"

Blanche opened her mouth to protest when he began to run his hands over Edith's naked body, but Lady Otley took a firm grip on her arm.

"Be silent," she hissed.

"This is indecent."

Blanche's horrified whisper failed to move the gentlewoman. She shook her head and indicated with a gesture of her free hand that Blanche should pay heed to the proceedings and not interfere.

"Father Mortimer is hunting the Devil out of her. He is able to locate demons by touch. In a moment he will use sanctified oil to anoint the places where they dwell."

Stomach roiling, Blanche watched. Had Alison suffered these same indignities? The priest touched the oil to Edith's eyes, ears, mouth, hands, feet, and breasts. That done, he took off his stole and used it to strike her repeatedly across the face and body.

Again and again she cried out.

Again and again he struck her.

By the time he stopped, she was curled into a ball on the floor and silently weeping.

Mortimer wiped the sweat from his brow, a satisfied smirk on his face. Then he picked up the holy relic Blanche had last seen in the hide—the bone of St. Modwen of Burton set in gold. Seizing Edith by the hair, he pulled her head back and forced the small, sharp shard into her mouth.

A scream rent the air, but it had not come from Edith. Recovering from her swoon, Sarah had opened her eyes in time to what was being done to her naked and helpless sister.

Slowly, Father Mortimer turned her way. His countenance was flushed and there was an eager look in his eyes.

At first Sarah stared back at him, as if struck dumb by terror. Then a travesty of a smile overspread her features. "Look!" she cried, pointing to where her sister lay. "The demon has left her!"

Yelverton, who was standing closer to Edith, bent down to examine the maidservant. "She has but fainted."

Mortimer shoved him aside and retrieved the relic. Setting the bone aside, he knelt beside Edith and used both hands to force open her mouth. He examined the interior with less care than he would have taken in checking the teeth of a horse he contemplated buying.

"I see no damage. There are no burns." The priest stood before announcing, in ringing tones, "She is cured!"

She was still unconscious, but that did not seem to bother him. He returned his attention to Sarah. Her face was still frozen in the same grotesque expression and her body was rigid.

"Shall we remove her clothing?" Yelverton's eagerness was so blatant, his licentiousness so obvious, that even Father Mortimer could not pretend to believe he was driven by religious zeal alone.

"That is a smile of holy ecstasy," the priest declared. "She, too, is free of demons."

Just that abruptly, the exorcism was over. The sisters were put to bed to recover and the rest of the household went about its daily routine as if nothing out of the ordinary had occurred.

Chapter Twenty-Seven

T he next morning, Blanche was ripped from sleep by a series of piercing screams. She sat bolt upright in bed, hands clenched on the coverlet and heart pounding. She was so frightened that she did not at first comprehend that the sound had come from the garret where the servants slept. When she did understand, she delayed only long enough to fling her cloak around her for decency. She ran out into the passage and raced along it toward the stairwell.

It was not yet dawn, but Blanche knew most of the servants who slept in the attics would already be at work in the rooms below. Their days started early. She caught only a glimpse of someone on the landing below as she started upward.

The screaming had stopped, but she followed a faint whimpering sound to find Sarah Trott standing beside the bed she shared with her sister. A look of horror disfigured her face.

Edith had not yet risen. It did not seem likely she ever would. She was not sleeping. By the light of the single candle Sarah had lit, Blanche beheld a pale, stiff body lying atop the coverlet.

Slowly, reluctantly, she moved closer, her nose wrinkling as she encountered an unpleasant stench. It was more than the natural voiding of a body upon death. Edith had been violently sick before she died.

Moving more briskly, Blanche seized Sarah by one arm and tugged her away from her sister. The girl gave a wail of distress and turned to burrow her face in Blanche's shoulder. Blanche patted her on the back, giving what comfort she could while Sarah wept, but she dared not let her grieve for long.

"What happened, Sarah?"

"She was lying dead beside me and I never knew it." Sarah choked out the words between sobs. "How could I not know? If I'd waked, I might have saved her."

Blanche doubted it.

Narrowing her eyes, she stared past Sarah at the dead woman's lips and thought she saw blisters. Before she could confirm this, or examine the body further, she heard the sound of approaching footsteps. Everyone at Otley Manor had likely heard Sarah's screams. It had just taken them longer to locate the source of the trouble.

Sir Stephen Otley pushed Blanche aside to enter the small attic chamber. Joseph Yelverton was hard on his heels. Keeping hold of Sarah, Blanche shrank back against the nearest wall. Father Mortimer arrived moments later. Stalking straight to the bedside, he began to mumble in Latin.

Blanche scarce heard his words. All her attention was fixed on his hands. Unlike the others, he was fully dressed and wore, as he always did, an expensive pair of thin leather gloves. They might hide scars, as he claimed, but Blanche found herself wondering if they also protected him from the harmful effects of white bryony. Mayhap the scars themselves had come from handling that caustic herb. It was a horrifying notion, that a man of the cloth would deliberately poison young women, but Blanche had already seen ample evidence of his cruel nature. He took joy in inflicting pain on others. Did he find some perverse satisfaction in killing them, too?

Sir Stephen's clerk and two of the household's manservants crowded into the space around the bed, gawking and pointing and whispering among themselves. Lady Otley arrived, a gown hastily assumed over her night rail. Her thinning, dun-colored hair was still in its braid. She wrung her hands and made small, inarticulate mewling sounds in her distress. Blanche half expected her to begin reciting Latin prayers of her own. Instead she plucked at her husband's sleeve.

"What are we to do? This is no natural death."

It was the clerk who answered, a dour-faced individual who rarely ventured out of his counting house. "The coroner will advise you, m'lady."

At the mention of this official, Yelverton's face drained of color. Without it, he lost much of his masculine beauty. The ugliness beneath shone through.

Lady Otley gave a little shriek of distress. "Must he be brought into this?"

The clerk took a step back. His gaze darted to the bed and away again. "It cannot be helped. Ellen, the scullery maid, was late coming down and when Sarah screamed she looked in and saw Edith's body. As soon as she told the cook, he sent a boy to inform the bailiff, and the bailiff will go straight away to fetch the constable, and the constable will perforce send for the coroner."

"You fool!" Lady Otley berated him. "Why did you let the lad go? We do not want the authorities coming here."

The clerk, his demeanor cowed, mumbled an apology, but there was nothing to be done. It was too late to undo the damage.

Sir Stephen spoke first to the priest, urging him to make haste to depart. Once Father Mortimer had gone, Sir Stephen glowered at everyone else until the servants scattered, leaving behind only Sarah, still huddled beside Blanche, Lady Otley, and Joseph Yelverton.

Sir Stephen regarded Sarah and Blanche with extreme disfavor. "When you have dressed, come at once to my wife's withdrawing room."

He took their agreement for granted and left the garret, quickly followed by his wife and her brother. They would be distracted for the next little while, Blanche thought. Before either constable or coroner arrived, they would have to hide all evidence that a forbidden religion had ever been practiced in this house.

She seized the opportunity to approach the body. Those *were* blisters on the dead woman's lips. Blanche did not risk opening Edith's mouth, but she suspected that her tongue and palate were similarly afflicted.

Edith had been poisoned. She was sure of it. But she was equally certain that the poison had not been administered during the exorcism. After a terrifying night as a prisoner, the young woman had been abused and subjected to suffumigation, drugged by toxic fumes. By the time she was freed from that torture chamber, she had been close to collapse. Had she still been too weak during the night that followed to resist when someone forced her to drink the juice of bryony?

Blanche peered more closely at Edith's chin and cheeks. The light in the room was poor, but she thought she could make out faint bruises, perhaps the marks left by fingers clamping down on Edith's jaw to hold her mouth closed.

She glanced at Sarah. The girl stood propped up against the wall, her shoulders slumped and her head bowed. Silent tears coursed down her pale cheeks. She had been subjected to the same ordeal as Edith, with the same results—complete exhaustion. To Blanche's mind, that explained why Sarah had slept so soundly, not even waking when someone crept into the garret and murdered her sister.

Chapter Twenty-Eight

A quarter of an hour later, Blanche had helped Sarah into her clothing and had dressed herself in garments that once belonged to Alison. Descending the stairs, Sarah moved like a sleepwalker, eyes open but unfocused and with no clear understanding of where she went or why.

Lady Otley waited for them in her withdrawing room. She had not dressed and her hair was still undone.

"My husband and I have conferred," she announced. "Listen well. Here is how we will proceed. When the constable arrives, we will tell him that we have all been ill. It was a matter of the cook picking the wrong herb. Everyone ate of the same dish and suffered from belly gripes and other discomforts throughout the night. Edith Trott, being frail to begin with, did not recover."

"Will the constable believe this tale?" Blanche asked.

"He is a simple fellow. He will give us no trouble. It is Sir Eustace who may create problems. Waverley House is but two miles distant. He is bound to hear what happened here, even if the coroner is not summoned."

Sir Stephen spoke from the doorway. "If he does, he is sure to be amused by the news that I was laid low by my supper. So long as he has no cause to investigate further, I will gladly endure whatever taunts he flings my way. I have told the servants what to say and warned them not to speculate among themselves."

"Excellent, my dear." She turned to Blanche. "Take Sarah to your bedchamber and make certain she understands what is expected of her. I mean to return to my bed. You will support my claim that I was too ill to rise from it this morning."

She went at once into the adjoining bedchamber and Sir Stephen likewise departed, leaving Blanche alone with Sarah in the withdrawing room. The girl stood like a statue, staring at nothing, her face expressionless, but she jumped when Blanche touched her arm.

"Do you understand what you must say to the constable?"

Abruptly, Sarah came to life. "I will not lie. I will tell him the truth, that they killed her with their wicked Catholic rites."

"That would not be true. Neither would it be wise. No one will believe you. No constable, coroner, or magistrate would ever take the word of a mere servant over that of a landed knight and his lady wife. They will conclude that you killed your sister and invented a story to cover up your crime."

"It must have been the exorcism that killed her. It must have been. And I think …I think that must be what killed Mistress Palmer, too."

"In that case, you would also be dead."

"You cannot think Edith's death was natural!"

"No. Nor Mistress Palmer's, either."

"Then how—?"

"Think, Sarah. All of you survived the ritual. What was done to you in that windowless room was unspeakable, but not fatal. Edith was killed later, while you slept. One of the herbs the priest used in the exorcism is a deadly poison, relatively harmless as he used it, but when Edith was forced to swallow another dose of it, undiluted, it killed her."

Sarah's eyes went wide. "Poison?"

"I saw the signs of it with my own eyes."

"Then we *must* tell the constable. It is his duty to take us away from here, to keep us safe."

Blanche took hold of Sarah's upper arms and gave her a little shake. "Did you not hear what I said? He will not believe either of us if everyone else in this house tells a different tale. Recusants or not, the Otleys are gentry. Sir Stephen has influence you and I lack."

"You can convince the constable. I know you can. You would not have promised to take me away with you if you did not have some plan of escape."

A faint sound from the doorway behind her made Blanche whip her head around. She saw no one and the noise was not repeated, but a great uneasiness came over her. "Did you hear something just now? See anyone pass by the door?"

Sarah shook her head. Although she had been facing in that direction, her full attention had been focused on Blanche.

It was just the creaking of an old house, Blanche told herself. *Nothing to worry about.*

All the same, she thought it best to say no more until she and Sarah had followed Lady Otley's orders. "We will continue this discussion when we are safe in my bedchamber."

They returned with all speed to the upper floor. Blanche saw no one else, but she continued to feel uneasy. The moment she closed the door to her bedchamber, she retrieved the cloth belt Philippa had given her and tied it in place beneath her kirtle. Half of the money was still sewn inside it. The rest she had secured in the lining of her cloak. Having the wherewithal to pay their way would do much to assure their safe passage through Essex to London.

"Edith is dead because of me." Bitterness and self-loathing underscored Sarah's words and made Blanche's heart ache for her. "I should have listened to you. If I had not tried to leave on my own, none of this would have happened. I was not possessed by anything but hatred for my tormenters and Edith knew it. She tried to protect me. That is why she died."

"You cannot be certain you'd have been spared, even if you had not run away. Those men—the priest and Master Yelverton—would have found some other reason to perform the ritual. They were only looking for an excuse, no matter how paltry."

Sarah's pale face lost even more of its color. "If the constable will not believe me, what am I to do? I cannot stay here. What if they decide I must be exorcised again?"

Blanche took the girl into her arms, hoping to soothe her fears. "Be brave for just a little longer, Sarah. We will leave Otley Manor very soon, but we cannot attempt it until after the constable has been and gone."

"Can we leave as soon as he questions us?" Sarah asked in a small voice.

"Much as I would like to, it will be best if we do not undertake the first part of our journey until after nightfall. We will go then, on foot, taking great care to avoid the mistakes you made when you attempted to flee on your own. Then tomorrow, in the first village we come to, I will hire horses. After that we will make good speed all the way to London."

In two days' time, mayhap less, she would be safely back in her own house in Holborn. Even if someone from Otley Manor succeeded in following them there—a most remote possibility—they would be hard put to convince anyone that Blanche had stolen away a serving maid before the end of her contract. In London, the word of Kit Wainfleet's wife would carry more weight than that of Sir Stephen or Master Joseph Yelverton, and Father Mortimer would never dare risk his own neck by coming forward to accuse her.

Chapter Twenty-Nine

A scant half hour after Blanche and Sarah retreated to Blanche's bedchamber, the girl was summoned to speak with the constable. The same servant sent to fetch her gave Blanche a message from Lady Otley. She was to remain where she was until someone came for her. Shortly after that, she thought she heard the clomp of boots on the stairs, but her bedchamber was some distance away along the passage and she could not be certain.

Many hours later, Blanche stood at her window, staring out at the bleak winter landscape and attempting to ignore both the hollow feeling in her belly and the nagging suspicion that all was not well. It was nearly time for supper and she had not had a bite to eat or so much as a sip of barley water all that long day. The last food she'd consumed had been at supper the previous evening and she'd taken precious little nourishment then. She had not had much appetite after bearing witness to the exorcism. To add to her misery, the fire had gone out and she had no more fuel to kindle another. To keep warm, she'd wrapped herself in her cloak.

Had she been forgotten? Such a thing was not impossible, she supposed. Sir Stephen and Lady Otley must have a great deal on their minds. Still, it seemed odd to her that the constable had not wanted to speak to her. Save for the scullery maid, she had been the first to respond to Sarah's screams. And where was Sarah? Surely she remembered that Blanche had been told to remain in her chamber.

Blanche could not see the stable yard from her window, not even if she leaned out as far as she could without falling. Had the constable left? Had the coroner arrived? She had no way of knowing. Not for the first time, she began to pace. She was worried about Sarah, afraid that the girl had lost all common sense and said more than she should have. Had she been taken away, accused of killing her sister? Or had everyone in the house been arrested for hearing Mass and owning forbidden Catholic books and relics? From time to time she had opened her door and listened, hoping to hear voices, but not a sound had reached her.

Shaking her head, she rejected the notion that the house stood empty. It was absurd to imagine that everyone except herself had been taken away to gaol. If another raid had been staged, the searchers would have looked everywhere for the priest, including her bedchamber. A more reasonable explanation was that Sir Stephen's lie had convinced the constable he had no need to call in the coroner. That meant her earlier suspicion was correct—no one had sent for her because they'd forgotten she was waiting for a summons. In all likelihood, Lady Otley had taken a dose of poppy juice for her nerves and had fallen asleep. She might be sleeping still.

Blanche told herself she should leave this room and go downstairs. No doubt Sir Stephen and his brother-in-law, and mayhap the priest, were already at supper. They might wonder where she was but she thought it unlikely they would trouble themselves to send anyone to search for her.

She already had her hand on the latch when she heard the sound of someone walking purposefully along the passage in her direction. She stepped back just as her door was flung open to reveal Joseph Yelverton.

"You are wanted below, Mistress Wainfleet."

She did not like the way he smirked at her, but that did not stop her from accompanying him. It was only when she was descending the stairs that she realized she was still wearing her cloak. If he had not been so intent on hustling her along, she might have taken it back to her chamber and left it there.

Mouth-watering smells issued from the kitchen and the level of noise from the front of the house indicated the Otleys were in the dining parlor, but Yelverton herded Blanche in the opposite direction, past the buttery and out into the courtyard. A man she had never seen before awaited them.

"Here is Mistress Wainfleet, Constable," Yelverton said, and gave her a shove in the other man's direction.

The man was of middling height with broad shoulders and hands like hams. He caught her by the arm and spoke in a gruff voice. "You are to come with me to Waverley House."

"What? Why?" She tried to pull away but he held her with a bruising grip.

Blanche's mind raced. Waverley House was the home of Sir Eustace Lewknor, the magistrate. Why was she to be taken there? Had Sir Stephen's plan failed after all? Had the coroner ruled Edith's death a homicide?

"You will come with me now," the constable insisted when she dug in her heels. He jerked on her arm, nearly lifting her off her feet.

Yelverton had disappeared and no one else was in sight. It would do her no good to call for help. Given no other choice, Blanche accompanied the constable from the courtyard to the stable yard. His horse, a broad-backed piebald, was saddled and waiting. Without ceremony, he mounted and hauled her up in front of him.

The journey to the other side of Little Mabham was a short one, but long enough to give Blanche time to think. The sun was just setting, and it had been dawn when she discovered Edith's body. There had been time enough for a coroner's jury to be convened, but if she was the one suspected of committing the crime, why had the coroner himself not talked to her? The constable had not accused her of anything, she reminded herself. He'd just ordered her to come with him.

She breathed a little easier. Perhaps her present situation had nothing to do with Edith's death. If Sir Stephen's lie had been believed, the constable had never had cause to call in the coroner, let alone report the matter to the local justice of the peace. The alternative explanation that occurred to her was mildly annoying but much less alarming.

Joanna's husband, Arthur, had been concerned for her safety from the start. He had insisted she remain in Colchester gaol no longer than a week. Even before she was taken there as a prisoner, he'd planned out how she would be released. If he'd decided that she had been at Otley Manor long enough, it would be just like him to take steps to spirit her away. He'd doubtless persuaded the same justice of the peace who had facilitated her incarceration in Colchester Castle to reach out to Sir Eustace and ask him to remove her from Otley Manor.

Arthur's timing was inconvenient. Blanche had wanted to take Sarah away with her when she left, but perhaps Sir Eustace could suggest a way to accomplish that. With another magistrate and a respectable country squire to vouch for her, he might take her word over Sir Stephen's. She regretted that everyone in the Otley household would suffer when she told her story, but Yelverton and Mortimer deserved their fate.

By the time Waverley House came in sight, Blanche was eager to speak to the magistrate, but instead of taking her to Sir Eustace, the constable shoved her into a small, windowless room. She heard the key turn in the lock with an ominous click.

"Come back!" she called. "You cannot leave me here."

Her shouts were ignored. Beating on the door with her fists did nothing but bruise her knuckles.

At first Blanche refused to believe she had been condemned to spend the night in solitary confinement without light or food or drink. She was certain there had been a mistake and that someone would soon come and release her.

She was wrong. As the hours dragged past, she knew firsthand the terror the Trott sisters had felt during their imprisonment at Otley Manor. The conditions under which she was held were less daunting only in that her prison did not stink of vile herbal concoctions.

Chapter Thirty

Sir Eustace Lewknor, stern-faced, sat behind a sturdy oak table in his parlor and peered at Blanche through small, round spectacles. From her side, the glass magnified his eyes, making them seem to bulge. The sight might have amused her under other circumstances, but not when her hands were bound behind her. The constable who'd fetched her from Otley Manor once again held her arm in a painfully tight grip.

Although it was already mid-morning, Blanche had not been given anything to eat or drink. Hunger made it difficult for her to focus on the proceedings, but she understood that she had been charged with a crime.

One man sat on each side of the magistrate. The plainly-dressed fellow to his right was doubtless his clerk and a village man. The gentleman to his left was taller and more slender than the others, with long-fingered hands that were almost skeletal in appearance. Blanche supposed he was a second justice of the peace, but she had no clue to his identity. As she stared at him, he leaned over to speak with Sir Eustace. His words were clearly audible.

"She is younger than I expected, and more comely."

He sounded as if Blanche's appearance affronted him. She wondered if he would have been happier to pass judgment on an aged crone with wrinkled skin and a hunched back.

"Youth is no excuse for evil, Sir Thomas," Sir Eustace declared.

Blanche tried desperately to order her thoughts. "Begging your pardon, your honors," she said in a hoarse voice, "but why have I been brought here?"

The stare Sir Eustace directed at her was as malicious as any she'd ever seen. "Read the charge," he ordered his clerk.

151

There followed a recitation, part in Latin, part in French, and almost wholly incomprehensible. The one item Blanche did understand filled her first with confusion and then with an overwhelming sense of dread: "The said Blanche Wainfleet did willfully injure or kill humans or their property."

Did she stand accused of murdering Edith Trott? She swallowed convulsively, her throat dry. If it was growing more difficult to think coherently when she felt so weak and light-headed, it was even more of a challenge to manage rational speech, and if they thought her hysterical, they would pay no heed to anything she told them.

"I have harmed no humans," she said. "What property am I accused of injuring?"

Sir Thomas consulted one of the papers in front of him. "By the complaint of Lucy Dunster, you did cause a cow belonging to the said Lucy Dunster to fall sick and die, and when she accused you of striking down her chattel, you cursed her."

Lucy Dunster? The name teased at her memory but for a moment she could not call any image to mind. If she'd ever met the woman, it had been a brief encounter.

"It is clear you have mistaken me for someone else. I know no one by that name."

"I have her statement here." Sir Thomas tapped the page. "You accosted her in the meadow near Otley Manor."

Belatedly, Blanche remembered the old woman with the cow, the one whose wits had wandered. She started to say that she had a witness to that meeting who would swear nothing untoward had been said. She remembered just in time that she could not ask Father North to come forward in her defense. As a Jesuit, he would at once be arrested, and any Catholic priest caught in England faced an inevitable sentence of death.

"That is only one charge against you," Sir Thomas said. "By the complaint of Sarah Trott, Jane Kenner, and Clemence Otley, you are accused of using witchcraft to find an item that was lost."

Shock left Blanche speechless. The terrible significance of what she'd been accused of doing to Lucy Dunster and her cow was made manifest. It was not the death of the animal that condemned her. It was using a curse to cast a spell.

"I have no such powers," she said when she at last found her voice. "I did not bewitch a cow or curse its owner, nor did I use any supernatural means to find a lost ribbon. It is against the law to use magic. Everyone knows that."

"I see you are familiar with the Act Against Conjurations, Enchantments and Witchcrafts," Sir Eustace said.

"I have heard of it." Blanche's voice was steady, but inside she was quaking like a leaf in a windstorm.

"Some provisions deal with more serious crimes than killing a cow. Those found guilty of murder by witchcraft are hanged."

Blanche's heart beat fast and loud. Blood pounded in her ears, making it difficult to hear. What she could make out only increased her terror.

The magistrate waved another piece of paper at her. "Sir Stephen Otley, Joseph Yelverton, and other witnesses accuse you of willfully bewitching one Edith Trott, a maidservant in Sir Stephen's household, causing her death."

Yelverton. It must have been Joseph Yelverton who made that small noise outside Lady Otley's withdrawing room. He must have overheard what she and Sarah said to each other and decided she was a danger to everyone at Otley Manor. If only they had retreated sooner to Blanche's bedchamber.

The most likely sequence of events was as clear as crystal in her mind. To prevent her from betraying their secrets, Yelverton must have convinced Sir Stephen there was less risk in involving the coroner and the magistrate in Edith's death than in leaving Blanche free to cause trouble in the future. By accusing her before she could speak out against them, they had made anything she might say suspect. They had been desperate enough to gamble that Sir Eustace's hatred of witches ran deeper than his distrust of recusants.

Adding lesser charges to the greater one created a case against her that was even more damning. Father North had likely mentioned her encounter with Lucy Dunster. If that addlepated old woman had suffered a recent loss of livestock, it would have been a simple matter to convince her to blame Blanche for her troubles. As for the matter of the ribbon, Blanche knew already that Edith had told Yelverton how she'd found it. Edith hadn't known the true story, and she was no longer able to testify against Blanche, but that must have made it even easier for them to persuade young Jane Kenner to accuse her of being a witch. Jane had been angry when Blanche discovered that she's stolen the ribbon from Edith. She'd have been glad of a way to assure that any claim Blanche might make against her would be discounted. Lady Otley would have gone along with whatever her husband and brother decreed. And Sarah? Blanche felt that betrayal most keenly of all, but she understood it. They'd only have had to threaten the girl with another exorcism to coerce her into lying for them.

Blanche squared her shoulders, took a step closer to the magistrates' table, and assumed what she hoped was a confident facial expression. "You say I killed Edith Trott. Why would I do such a thing?"

The challenge might have been more effective had her words not come out at a higher pitch than she'd intended, but she stood her ground, boldly staring back at the justices.

Sir Eustace consulted another document. "You were heard quarreling. Then, when she fell ill, you were seen giving her an unknown powder."

"None of that is true. There was no powder."

She would put her faith in sweet reason and the fact that she was not a penniless, friendless outcast. As the wife of a prominent London merchant and the sister by marriage of an influential Essex gentleman, she was not entirely powerless. She opened her mouth to reveal her true identity and make an accusation of her own, but before she could get a word out, Sir Thomas held up a hand to silence her. He had been staring fixedly at her for some moments.

"Constable, remove the woman's coif."

He pulled Blanche's hair in the process, so that several pale stands came loose to tumble down her back and over her shoulder. Their unique silver-gilt hue immediately became apparent.

"Look at that color," Sir Thomas said. "The Devil's at work in that, I warrant."

"My hair was given to me by God," Blanche protested, "and it was not though my doing that there was a death at Otley Manor. The charges against me are all lies. I—"

"Sir Stephen Otley is an important man in Little Mabham," Sir Eustace interrupted before she could finish. "Despite his wife's weakness in matters of religion, I have no reason to disbelieve him. He and I do not see eye-to-eye on a great many matters, but we are in perfect agreement on the wickedness of witchcraft. Confess now and you may have some small hope of salvation."

It was as she had feared, as she had warned Sarah it would be. Gentlemen took one another's part, even when they had differences. Her only hope lay not in confessing, but in convincing these men that she was as well born as they were.

"I am a gentlewoman," she announced, "and as such I am as worthy of being believed as he is. I have done nothing wrong. Rather it—"

This time it was Sir Thomas who cut short her attempt to cast blame where it belonged. "Who is it that can unwitch that which another witch doth bewitch?"

Blanche gaped at him. It was a question to which there was no safe answer, but one to which she had to reply. If she did not respond with alacrity, she would be assumed to be a witch. As she fought to keep her wits about her, Sir Thomas repeated the question.

If she agreed that witches existed, it could be construed as an admission of guilt, but if she denied the effectiveness of witchcraft, she could then be accused of repudiating scriptural teaching on the matter—of heresy. Heretics were burnt at the stake, a fate even worse than hanging.

"Who is it that can unwitch that which another witch doth bewitch?" Sir Thomas asked for the third time. His face had turned the color of beetroot and his fury at being ignored was a palpable force in the chamber.

"Another witch," Blanche blurted, "or so I have been told by many a Godly vicar."

"Who are you that Edith Trott died of witchcraft?"

Another trick! This question contained the veiled accusation that she had either killed Edith by bewitching her or by failing to unwitch her.

Blanche wanted to shout at him that he was a fool to be so gullible, that witches did not exist in the great numbers he supposed, if they existed at all, but she dared not anger him further. She attempted to sound humble and to hide her anger at the unjustness of her treatment.

"I do not know, sir."

"Have you access to a garden or yard?" Sir Eustace sounded only slightly less hostile than his fellow justice of the peace.

"The *Otleys* have a yard and a garden." Blanche was painfully aware that the clerk was taking down every word she uttered.

"How many times did you lay flat or kneel in that yard?"

It took Blanche a moment to understand the reason for Sir Eustace's question. He was insinuating that she had engaged in ancient but forbidden rites associated with medicinal herbs.

"I never knelt or lay flat in the yard."

That was naught but the truth, and yet Blanche could see where such a question could succeed in tricking many a poor woman into condemning herself. Someone who made her living by offering simples to cure her neighbors' ills would have to kneel in her garden if she was to weed it and pick the herbs she sold.

"Did you ever, in the yard or in the house, kneeling, standing, or lying flat, speak these words: 'Christ, my Christ, if thou be a Saviour come down and avenge me of my enemies, or else thou shall not be a Saviour.'"

"Never."

In that moment, Blanche was glad her hands were bound behind her. That position hid their trembling. The words Sir Eustace had quoted had horrifying implications. Anyone who said such a thing was issuing a threat, promising that if Christ did not do what she wished, she would turn for help to another supernatural power—to the Devil himself.

"Do you deny that you killed a cow by witchery?" Sir Thomas looked down his long, thin nose at her, a sneer on his lips.

Blanche rallied. "Lucy Dunsters's cow may have died, but not by my hand nor through my words."

More questions followed, most of them designed to test Blanche's conformity in matters of religion. She answered those with ease, although she did once become muddled when a passage from *The Exercise of a Christian Life* sprang to mind before one from the *Book of Common Prayer*. Still, she had faithfully attended the Church of England far longer than she had pretended to be a papist. She thought she'd acquitted herself well until Sir Eustace asked his next question.

"Do you keep a cat or a dog or a toad as your familiar?"

"I do not." Her traitorous voice hitched in mid-denial.

"Did you tell Edith Trott that she would rue the day she failed to arrange your hair as you wanted it?"

"No."

"The victim's sister claims you did."

"Then she was forced to tell a lie."

Dire as Blanche knew her present situation to be, she could not find it in her heart to blame the younger woman. After what they had done to her, Sarah was right to be terrified of both Joseph Yelverton and Father Mortimer. She would say whatever they told her to say, even if it meant sacrificing Blanche to save herself.

As the two justices continued to fire questions at her, Blanche came to the stomach-churning realization that it would do her no good to hurl accusations of her own. They would believe the Otleys celebrated forbidden rites and hid priests and be more than happy to learn the location of the two hides, but they were so convinced of her guilt that they would also turn anything she said against her.

No one at Otley Manor would come forward to defend her. The entire household was already convinced that a witch had cursed Alison. Persuading them to accuse the newcomer, the stranger in their midst, of doing the same to Edith must have been simple to accomplish. Blanche would not be surprised to learn they now believed her responsible for Alison's death, as well.

"Do you claim that Edith Trott never dressed your hair?" From the way Sir Eustace bellowed the question, Blanche surmised it was not the first time he had asked it.

"Once only. I was pleased with her work." She did not think it would help her case to mention that they had both been prisoners in Colchester gaol at the time, or to admit that was the occasion on which she'd given Edith the ribbon she'd just been accused of finding by supernatural means.

Blanche responded to each succeeding question as best she could. She denied every one of the vile slanders against her, but it was obvious that her inquisitors found her answers unsatisfactory. She tensed when Sir Eustace shuffled his papers into a neat pile and then removed his spectacles to rub the bridge of his nose.

Poor man, Blanche thought. *I have given him a headache.* She was so giddy from fear and hunger that she very nearly suggested a herbal remedy for the pain. It was fortunate, perhaps, that she was no longer capable of stringing two sensible thoughts together. When her stomach growled, she was hard put not to laugh.

There was nothing amusing about the formal indictment the clerk read aloud. His words chilled Blanche's blood. By the time the magistrate stood to give his orders to the constable, a strange numbness had come over her.

"Take her to Colchester Castle," Sir Eustace commanded. "She is to stand trial for witchcraft at the next Assizes."

Instinctively, Blanche resisted when she was tugged toward the door. She knew it was useless to struggle, but she could not seem to stop herself from twisting in the constable's grip. With her hands bound behind her, she was at a great disadvantage, but she still had the use of her feet. She kicked him in the shin and opened her mouth to demand that her kinsman be sent for.

Not a single syllable made it past her lips. The constable retaliated by cuffing her. With no more effort than it would have taken to swat a fly, he sent her stumbling backward. Unable to prevent herself from falling, Blanche landed flat on her back, striking her head on the hard wooden floor with enough force to make her see stars.

Rough hands jerked her to her feet. Dazed and in pain, she was dragged outside. When she tried once again to protest, to tell them they had made a mistake, someone struck her from behind. She sank into blackness without uttering another sound.

Chapter Thirty-One

I t was a blessing, Blanche thought afterward, that she was unconscious for most of the journey from Little Mabham to Colchester. The few times she was aware of her surroundings, she'd longed for oblivion. She had been manacled and shackled against any further attempts at escape and transported in a cart, lying on bare boards without even a layer of straw for padding. With no canopy overhead, a steady, cold, drizzling rain added to her discomfort, but that was as nothing compared to the pain in her head and the dizziness. She'd alternated between bouts of nausea, uncontrollable shivering, and profuse sweating.

By the time the cart reached its destination, she was a pitiful sight. Bedraggled and wet, her unbound hair was a mass of tangles. Although she could not see them, she could feel dozens of bruises, the result of being struck and then flung from side to side over close to thirty miles of uneven road.

She had only a vague impression of the castle as the cart crossed over the bridge leading up to it, but that was more than enough to recognize her once and future prison. The keep rose ominously from the surrounding fortifications. A wall and a ditch protected it, and it had a peculiarly complex entrance way that required the cart horse to make three right-angle turns before passing under the main archway with its massive portcullis.

Once inside that barrier, they circled a good portion of the castle before stopping. Blanche was hauled out of the cart and set on unsteady legs. It was fortunate she did not have far to walk, since her lower limbs felt wobbly as a newborn colt's. She fought to keep her balance as she was taken into a ground floor room and turned over to the keeper. The door shut behind her with a final-sounding thump.

"Witch, are you?" Luke Fludd's sneer was as contemptuous as ever. "Thought you were a recusant. Ah, well, we've had witches aplenty here before you. You'll not get away with trying any of your tricks on me."

Blanche thought it wisest to say nothing. He would think her mad if she demanded that he send a message to one of her sisters. She would do better to contrive a way to bribe a guard. Once she'd managed to smuggle a message out of gaol, Arthur would mount a rescue.

Fludd came out from behind a table and walked around her in a slow circle, his eyes hot. She did not need a fortune teller's skills to realize that he was imagining her naked. An involuntary shudder wracked her body. It was not entirely due to the lack of warmth in the room.

As an accused witch, she was no longer protected by her gentle birth. The keeper could strip away her clothing if he chose, on the pretext of searching for witch's marks. He could do anything he liked with her and she would be powerless to stop him. Her stomach twisted as she imagined what she might have to endure.

"Have you money?" Fludd asked, his lips close to her ear, "or did you spend it all the last time you were here?"

She shuddered again and tried to shuffle away from him. He did not attempt to stop her, but neither did she get very far before another wave of dizziness brought her to a swaying halt.

"Well? Have you?"

Blanche swallowed hard. The money Philippa had given her was still safely hidden on her person, half in the strip of fabric tied around her waist beneath her kirtle and the rest sewn into the hem of her cloak, but she could not afford amenities if she meant to reserve enough for bribes.

"I have the wherewithal to pay for exemption from ironing." She was already bruised and sore from the shackles around her ankles and the heavy iron manacles circling her wrists. She extended her hands. "You will have to remove these if you want me to produce your fee."

Her attempt at haughtiness seemed to amuse him, but he unhooked one of the keys from his belt. With gratifying promptness, he unlocked the fetters. As she'd expected, her wrists were badly abraded despite her gloves. Her ankles, protected by her boots, had fared better. The sight of the deeply gouged leather turned her stomach. That could have been her flesh.

Bending forward, this time prepared for the wave of nausea and lightheadedness that accompanied the movement, she folded back a portion of her cloak. Removing one glove, she began to pick at the stitches in the hem with her fingernails. She glanced at her captor.

"This would be easier if I had a knife." She did not wish to reveal that she still possessed the small one she used for eating. He might take it away from her for fear she would use it as a weapon.

Fludd unsheathed an evil-looking dagger, but instead of handing it to her, he wielded it himself, cutting where she indicated. His eyes lit up when he saw the size of the coins she'd secreted in the lining of the cloak.

For a moment Blanche was afraid she had made a mistake. There was nothing she could do to prevent him if he decided to seize them all, but at least she'd still have the other half of the money Philippa had given her, the coins that rested secure in the pouch she wore around her waist.

The keeper liberated two crowns and an angel, nearly half of everything she'd revealed to him. She made no objection. Her previous experience with Luke Fludd led her to believe he would deal honestly with her ...up to a point.

"That should be enough to pay for food and drink, heat and light," she said after the coins vanished into Fludd's purse. "Especially food."

Provided with these necessities, she would regain her strength. Once she was rested and the fuzziness in her mind receded, she would find a way to send a message to her family. For the nonce, however, it was a wonder she could still stand upright. She did not think she had ever been so hungry or felt so weak.

"Come with me," Fludd ordered.

Alternately limping and staggering, Blanche was hard put to keep up with the pace he set. Her need for sleep and sustenance had grown desperate. Even the foul stuff they served in Colchester gaol would do to fill her belly and keep body and soul together.

As she'd remembered, the castle held the ice of winter in its stark stone walls. The wood in the keeper's small fireplace had been ablaze, but it had done little more than warm the person positioned directly in front of it—Fludd himself. The passage was far removed from any vestige of heat.

The sounds of helpless weeping and hacking coughs taunted her as she was led past dank, dark cells. She recalled all too well the glimpse she'd been given of the misery and despair of those confined within.

Fludd led her up a narrow flight of steps, catching her arm when she stumbled. Revolted by his touch, she pulled away and kept climbing.

The door to her cell was as heavy as all the others in the gaol and boasted a sturdy bar on the outside. Blanche entered cautiously, expecting to see other prisoners, but it seemed she was to be housed in a private cell. The tiny, stone-walled chamber had a single narrow window to let in light. That was enough to show her it was completely empty. Not only was it uninhabited, it was also unfurnished. There was no bed and no chamber pot and not so much as a stool to sit upon.

With a growing sense of panic, she turned to the keeper. "I paid for a brazier and fuel, washing water, food, drink, and candles."

Fludd laughed. "They are on their way, as are other luxuries."

Even before he finished speaking, Blanche heard the tramp of heavy feet. While the keeper's men installed the minimal necessities she'd paid for, she once again rubbed the chafed skin at her wrists, wishing she had some of the soothing salve Philippa made with marjoram, borage, and chamomile flowers.

Be thankful for what you have, she chided herself. When she was handed a cup of watery beer, she sipped gratefully. After one swallow, her throat already felt less raw. It took a concerted effort not to gulp down what remained. She knew that if she drank it too quickly, her stomach would rebel.

In her present state, even the bowl of lumpy porridge awaiting her attention looked and smelled appealing. If she'd had any saliva to spare, her mouth would be watering. She had already consumed the first spoonful by the time the keeper locked her in.

She limped to the small barred window cut into the heavy wooden door, expecting to see Fludd walking away. Instead he stood just on the other side, staring back at her. Blanche ate another spoonful of porridge, thinking of that old saying about honey being preferable to vinegar and wishing she had some honey to add to what she was eating.

"I thank you for your kindness, Master Fludd. I know full well you could have flung me into one of the common cells."

"Accused witches are kept separate from the rest of the prisoners," he informed her.

"Then I thank you for the amenities you have provided." The brazier was already giving off welcome warmth.

He smirked. "Your coins are as good as the next person's, witch, and all of them will be mine by the time you leave here."

Blanche's jaw tightened. So much for trying to be polite to the man. She read into his words the threat that when her money ran out he would take away everything he'd just supplied. He was already halfway to the turn in the passage before it occurred to her that his words might have another meaning.

"Master Fludd! Wait! Can you tell me when the next Assizes are to be held?"

"The circuit judges convene in Chelmsford on the fourth day of March." He began to whistle a merry tune as he continued on his way.

Blanche's appetite abruptly fled. She collapsed onto the narrow field bed that now took up most of the space in her cell. The fourth of March was less than a month away. That was an eternity in some respects, long enough that she would likely run out of funds, but it was also alarmingly soon. What if she could not bribe a guard to send a message to her kin? What if she could, but they did not receive it in time? Letters often went astray. She could very well be tried, convicted, and hanged before anyone with enough influence to help her had any idea that she'd been accused of witchcraft in the first place.

She might never see Kit again.

Overwhelmed, Blanche burst into tears.

Chapter Thirty-Two

When she had control of herself again, it was all Blanche could do to wrap herself in her cloak and the one thin blanket she'd been given and fall into bed. She slept deeply, or mayhap returned to unconsciousness, but she was the better for the rest when she awoke. Her head still ached, but her mind had cleared most marvelously. She ate and drank everything that was brought to her and felt her exhaustion retreat a little more with each passing hour of the new day.

In her attempts to subvert a guard, she was less successful. Two of them came close enough to her cell to talk to but both had been warned that she was a witch. The moment she opened her mouth they ordered her not to speak. One of them went so far as to make the sign against the Devil.

The second night in her prison cell passed with excruciating slowness. Everything Blanche knew about courts and the law swirled in her brain, preventing her from falling asleep. In addition to the details she'd read in pamphlets about convicted witches and other criminals, she had sometimes listened as Kit and his friends discussed trials of local interest at the quarter sessions or the twice yearly Assizes. Lawsuits were common, most of them waged over property. Cases of theft, robbery, and burglary were not unusual. Violent crimes—murder, manslaughter, and rape—cropped up less often.

If she was put on trial, she would face a jury made up of men selected from the minor gentry of Essex. A prosecutor would present to them the facts as he knew them. If Blanche understood the process aright, this prosecutor acted as a representative of Queen Elizabeth and could call witnesses to testify in court and present depositions taken from others who did not appear in person.

It seemed reasonable to Blanche that an accused person should be given a chance to prove her innocence, but that was not the way the law worked. She would not be allowed to call any witnesses. Once she was formally charged, she would be assumed to be guilty. The prosecutor would offer her little more than an opportunity to confess.

Two judges presided at the Assizes, in this case the two who rode the Home Circuit—Hertford, Essex, Surrey, Sussex, and Kent. They customarily spent only a few days in each county. Blanche remembered the time she and her sisters had witnessed the arrival of the visiting judges in Maidstone, when they'd been staying there with her mother's parents. She'd been a child of ten or so and had been much impressed by the pomp and ceremony. The judges had worn crimson robes and caps and they had passed by twice in procession, once on their way to attend church with the justices of the peace and again going from the church to the place where court convened.

No doubt most judges were honest men, but they did not spend long enough in any one place to understand local politics or local people. They relied upon the justices of the peace to apprise them of the significant details of each case. That would not work in Blanche's favor. Sir Eustace and Sir Thomas were already convinced of her guilt. They would urge the judges to sentence her to death.

She wondered, as she shifted restlessly on the narrow bed, just who Sir Thomas was. She had never heard his surname. She supposed it did not matter. What did was his passionate dislike of witchcraft. He had not been disposed to listen to common sense, not once he'd heard that Sir Stephen Otley, a gently born *man*, had denounced her.

Blanche's last thought, before she finally fell into an uneasy sleep, was that when the judges passed sentence it would be carried out without delay. She was not likely to be pardoned because she would not be given time to sue for one.

She woke in a sweat, still caught in a dream in which she was in a cart on her way to the gallows to be hanged. She had come awake just as her dream self, a noose around her neck, stepped off into nothingness.

166

Blanche got up and stirred the coals. When Sarah had been plagued by a similar nightmare, Blanche had been there to soothe her fears. She wished she had someone to do the same for her. She paced. She cried a little. She thought of Kit and of her sisters and of the many things in her life that she wished she had done differently. When she heard footsteps approaching her cell door, she was pathetically grateful for the distraction.

The guard, one of same two she'd seen the day before, brought the usual morning rations—a thick slice of rye bread, a pint of lumpy porridge, and a pint of beer. There was also a trifling portion of boiled beef that looked as tough as old shoe leather. She accepted these offerings and then spoke quickly, before he could order her to remain silent.

"I wish to purchase paper, pen, and ink."

He was a heavy-set fellow with breath like an open sewer. His speech, like his movements, was slow and ponderous, but he did not seem as wary of her as he had been. "It will cost you."

"Bring them. I will pay you well for your kindness."

Hours passed. Blanche alternated between pacing the confines of her cell and staring out her single window, even though it was noticeably colder there than near the brazier. She could not see much of the outside, only a nearby wall. The bars were set too close together to allow her to poke her head out and widen the view.

At last she heard the guard returning and ran to the door. Her heart sank when she realized he'd not brought the supplies she'd asked for.

"Where is the paper? Where is the pen and ink?"

"Master Fludd says you are not to have writing implements lest you use them to cast a spell."

Blanche stamped her foot and swore. She was tempted to mutter gibberish at the messenger who'd brought her such bad news. That would give him a scare! She thought better of the notion before she uttered a single word. It would be foolish to give the judges one more reason to believe she possessed supernatural powers.

When she was alone again, she despaired. She had been denied the means to reach out to Joanna or Philippa or anyone else who might help her. Since she had little expectation of either acquittal or pardon, her death by hanging now seemed inevitable.

Once again, tears fell. At one point she heard herself wail aloud, but this bout of self-pity was mercifully brief. If one means of escape was cut off, she would find another. She would not abandon hope.

Determined to discover a way out of captivity *before* her trial, she spent the next two days formulating and discarding one plan after another. The most elaborate scheme, and the one she liked best, involved waiting until she was taken to Chelmsford for the Assizes. Chelmsford was more than twenty miles south of Colchester and that much closer to London. Once she had eluded her captors, she would go straight to Holborn. Even though the authorities knew her name, they believed her to be an impoverished, unmarried orphan. They'd have no reason to seek out the respectable wife of prosperous merchant Christopher Wainfleet.

Blanche's optimism did not last. She was too aware of the many obstacles to her escape. She would no doubt be shackled on the journey to Chelmsford. She and the other prisoners to be delivered from gaol would be well guarded. Then, too, if she had to pay the keeper for "luxuries" until the fourth day of March, she would have very little money left with which to offer bribes.

Along with the ever-present fear of execution, the issue of money preyed on Blanche's mind. If she did succeed in getting away, she would need even more of it. In order to have the wherewithal to reach London, she would have to take care not spend all her coins beforehand.

Blanche contemplated how she might contrive to escape at an earlier date, before she was taken from Colchester Castle. There had to be a way. She had only to find it. How much would it take, she wondered, to persuade one of her gaolers to look the other way while she walked out of this cell?

"Fool," she muttered.

Even if she could pay the price, an unlocked door alone would not guarantee her freedom. She would also have to contrive to leave the castle without being caught.

It was a pity, Blanche thought, that she had nothing to barter. She had no jewelry, and since she'd been obliged to leave everything else she owned behind at Otley Manor, she was left with only the clothing she stood up in.

She looked down at herself and grimaced. She was allotted only enough washing water to cleanse her face and hands. The rest of her body was filthy and everything she wore was stained and encrusted in grime. That would present a problem if she did manage to escape. If she lacked a respectable appearance, she risked arrest for vagrancy.

It was when she considered whether or not to spend a few precious halfpennies on a comb, a clothes brush, and an additional supply of water for washing that Blanche realized she *did* have something with which to bargain. As the odious Sir Thomas had pointed out, she was comely. Although she'd never been accounted a great beauty, she was pleasing to look at and men seemed to admire the shape of her body.

Blanche invested the halfpennies. She made herself as tidy as possible under the circumstances. When her next meal was delivered, she set about charming her guard.

"I am much obliged to you, good sir." She accompanied the words with a saucy smile.

This unexpected expression of gratitude seemed to confuse him. "Eh?"

"It is kind of you to bring me food."

"Call that slop food?" He hawked and spat. "Pigs wouldn't eat it."

Blanche avoided looking at the trencher he'd handed her. She knew it would contain the same offering it always did, twice a day, every day. Meals varied only on fish days, when a half pound of cheese or one herring would be substituted for the leathery strip of meat. With an effort, she kept her smile in place.

"It will suffice to keep body and soul together, but there is something I *would* like."

The guard hesitated just outside the door. "Oh, aye?"

She nodded and continued to beam at him even after her jaw had begun to ache from the effort. "A bit of fresh air."

He snickered. "I'd think you'd have enough of that, what with the wind blowing through that window and every crack in the walls besides."

The castle *was* in a dilapidated state. The observation lifted Blanche's spirts. On the day she arrived for her first incarceration, she'd noticed gaps in the castle defenses. She'd even seen a hole in the roof of the hall. It was possible there were other weaknesses in the structure that she could exploit. It was something to ponder, after she'd succeeded in achieving her current goal.

"I was hoping for a walk on the leads," she told the guard. "Is such a thing ever permitted?"

"You want me to let you out of your cell?" He gave a snort of laughter.

"I do. Where is the harm?" She attempted to appear winsome. "I can scarce attempt an escape from that height, and I am not such a fool as to leap to my death."

The guard continued to look doubtful, as if he thought that, since she was an accused witch, she might be able to fly away. She did not think he could guess her real reason for wanting to walk on the battlements. From above, she would be able to see the layout of both castle and grounds and make a mental map of the most likely route to freedom.

"I will make it worth your while," she wheedled. "There is no need for the keeper to know about that end of things."

"Useless beggar. He only got his post because of his wife."

"Who is she when she's at home?"

"Daughter to the last keeper, that's who. Married the baker's son. He weren't even good at that." This time the glob of phlegm nearly struck the toe of Blanche's boot. She ignored it.

"Keeps an eye on him, does she?"

"Oh, aye. A close one. And I wager she's keeping an eye on you, too."

"On me?" Blanche did not like the sound of that.

"Afeared he'll help himself to one of the women prisoners, she is."

Blanche repressed a shudder, remembering how Fludd had looked her up and down. She'd felt like a slab of meat in the marketplace. That he had not acted upon his inclination had doubtless been due to his desire for domestic harmony. She prayed his wife continued to keep a *very* close watch on his activities.

The guard turned to go. Blanche called him back.

170

"You are kind to stay and talk with me." She fished a halfpenny out of the pocket into which she'd transferred a number of small coins and handed it to him. "It is lonely being locked in here by myself."

"Better than the common cell." Chortling at his own wit, he took her coin and left.

When his footsteps had faded away, Blanche sank down on her narrow, uncomfortable bed. She tried to find cause for optimism in the guard's behavior. He had shown himself to be amiable enough to engage in conversation. He had made no attempt to take liberties. Indeed, despite his rough appearance and untidy habits, he seemed to prefer to keep some distance between them.

Because he believes you are a witch!

She sighed deeply. Was it the fear of being bespelled that kept him respectful? That was a good thing, but not if that same fear prevented him from helping her to escape. He had taken her coin, but that did not mean he was open to bribery. Even if he was, even if he took her out onto the leads, that did not guarantee he would also agree to escort her out of the castle and send her on her way. He would rightly suspect that he would be blamed for her escape, and that abetting her would cost him his position and possibly his freedom. She did not think she had enough money to tempt him to take such a risk, and he had not appeared to be much taken with her charms.

A considerable time passed as her thoughts whirled around and around. The best she could hope for, she decided, was that she would be allowed out of her cell and given the opportunity to reconnoiter. It might take an act of God—an earthquake, mayhap—to provide her with the chance to escape.

Without much appetite, she reached for her food, only to discover that a rat had already been nibbling at it. She forced herself to eat what was left. If the rodents who shared her cell could choke down Colchester gaol's porridge, so could she.

She caught herself scratching her arm and forced herself to stop. Persistent itching—arms, legs, and backside—was inevitable. Rats were not the only vermin with which she shared her lodging.

It was the second guard who brought her first meal the next day. He was a bold, black-haired fellow with a look in his eyes that suggested he believed that a witch was the same as a whore. Having already observed this, Blanche did not try to engage him in conversation when he delivered her food and drink. She was relieved when he left it and retreated, locking the heavy door behind him. She was prepared to use her womanly wiles but she hoped to avoid the need to grant any favors.

She was startled when he spoke from the other side of the small barred window. She'd thought him gone.

"Ralph may settle for halfpennies, but I'd prefer a kiss for my trouble."

There was danger inherent in encouraging such talk, but when the alternative was execution, Blanche knew she must keep all her options open. That did *not* mean she had to fall into the arms of the first man to show an interest in her. She kept her back to the door.

"You have not yet gone to any trouble for me, sirrah."

To her relief, he laughed at the rebuff. "Just ask for Jack if you get lonely."

This time he did go away, leaving Blanche shaken and faintly nauseated. It did not seem likely that any of the guards had been chosen for their sense of honor or their decency. Luke Fludd might live in fear of his wife, but few of the others would pass up the offer of a fast coupling with a willing female prisoner. Most would not care if she was willing or not.

Blanche did not sleep well that night. Every creak and thump woke her, leaving her to lie in the darkness, wondering if that guard, Jack, had decided to take advantage of her helplessness. Mayhap, she thought, there were benefits to *not* washing. Surely a foul-smelling woman would cease to be desirable. Then again, perhaps not. The guards themselves stank of stale beer, onions, and sweat.

Even after she fell into a deeper sleep, there was no respite from her fears. Nightmare scenes assaulted her, and not only to do with her own likely fate. In one she saw her husband clinging to a spar, adrift at sea. She was in a rowing boat, struggling to reach him before he disappeared forever beneath the waves. With every sweep of the oars, he seemed to float farther away.

When she awoke, her face was wet with tears.

Chapter Thirty-Three

F ive long days and nights passed before Blanche at last persuaded the guard named Ralph to escort her high onto the battlements of the castle. In exchange for sixpence, she was allowed to walk up and down for an hour. She made good use of the time, memorizing the layout of the grounds and fixing possible escape routes in her mind.

On both north and east, deep ditches and earthen ramparts added to the castle's defenses. On south and west stood strong walls. She picked out two gates, but she thought there had once been another entrance to the north. She could just discern the remains of a landing place and steps. She stared long and hard at the river flowing between the castle grounds and the center of Colchester, the town which had grown up around its ancient walls. Would it be possible, she wondered, to steal a boat?

She made and discarded several schemes, each more unlikely to succeed than the last.

Two days later, during her second outing on the leads, she memorized further details of the landscape. To her north was a park, part of the castle grounds. The whole appeared to slope downward toward the riverbank. Again, she considered the idea of stealing a boat, but in case she could not find one, or if all the watercraft were closely guarded, she gave particular attention to the road. It ran from Colchester all the way to London.

Later that same day, Blanche forced herself to smile invitingly at the black-haired turnkey. He was not the most repulsive of the guards she had seen and she had found him to be refreshingly stupid. The risk of trying to entice him seemed worth taking, now that she had a definite plan.

"Do you know what would be my greatest joy?" she asked him in a sultry whisper.

He preened a bit. "I can guess."

She shook her head in a playful manner. "I warrant you cannot. I desire more than anything else to bathe."

"Immerse yourself in water?" A look of horror crossed Jack's face. "Bathing is dangerous. If you take a chill, it will carry you off."

"Then mayhap a swim?" Reaching through the barred window, she ran her fingertips over the aglets that held the front of his leather jerkin together.

"In winter? Out of doors?"

"It is passing mild for mid-February." She could tell that much even confined in her cell, and on her two excursions to the battlements, the sun had been bright enough to keep her warm.

Jack shook his head in disbelief. "You must be mad, woman, as well as evil."

"Do you truly believe I am a witch?" She contrived to sound wounded.

He pondered that, his lower lip protruding just a bit, as if that small movement could stimulate thought. "I've yet to see an accused witch do anything but die, but there are those who say a witch thrown into a pond with both hands and feet tied will float."

"If she does, she is hanged, and if she does not, she will drown. What sense does that make?"

Jack's brow wrinkled in confusion. His was not a mind adept at solving riddles.

"Never mind, Jack. I feel certain you know what I *really* mean when I speak of swimming with you. If you take me down to the riverbank, to some private spot among the trees where we may disport ourselves unseen, I will make the outing worth your while."

Jack was all but drooling at the prospect of such an assignation. Blanche waited with bated breath, afraid he would go along with only part of her suggestion. She wanted him to picture her naked and willing, but not *too* willing. If he entered her cell instead of taking her out of it, her plan to escape would be in shambles and what else she would be forced to endure

174

did not bear thinking about.

"I long to be outside the castle walls," she whispered, "just for a little while. I yearn to see the night sky once more."

"What can you see at night?"

"Why the stars and the moon."

"There's not much of one at this time of the month," he said doubtfully. "It will be passing dark."

"A pity, I agree." She spoke in what she fondly hoped was a seductive purr. "Would it not be a fine thing, Jack, to see me dance naked in the light of a full moon?"

"Aye, but then you would be seen and reported. We would never make it past the gate."

"Then this is the best time to go, and surely there is another way out. Some old, unused entrance, one through which no one will see us go out or return."

He swallowed convulsively.

"No one need ever know what we do, Jack. Not unless you tell them yourself."

Men liked to boast of their conquests, or so Blanche had always heard. Even as she ran her tongue over her lips, making yet another promise she had no intention of keeping, she wondered at her own boldness. She should be appalled, but all she felt was elation. Tempting Jack was having the effect she desired. There was a glazed look in his eyes.

"I will come for you after dark," he promised in a hoarse whisper. As he strode away, he had a new purpose in his step.

Blanche felt her knees go weak with relief. She rested her forehead against the bars. Then she prayed for the courage to carry out the rest of her plan.

Chapter Thirty-Four

The wait for Jack's return seemed endless. Blanche had no idea what time it was when she finally heard heavy footsteps approaching her door. Suddenly as nervous as a cat sighting a mastiff, she hugged her cloak more tightly around her.

The bar lifted with a thunk. A key scraped in the lock and then, with tortuous slowness, the heavy door creaked open. Her heart in her throat, Blanche stepped through it.

Their way lit by the closed lantern Jack carried, they made their way in silence down several flights of stairs and at length emerged into a courtyard. It felt much warmer there than inside her cell, which she supposed went a long way toward explaining Jack's willingness to fall in with her plans.

There had indeed been a thaw, but as her boots made squishing sounds on the soggy ground, she worried that Jack might have thought better of lying with her on the bank of the river. If he took her somewhere else, somewhere dry, her scheme would fail.

She endured a bad moment when he pulled her into the shadow of the keep to claim a kiss, but before she could succumb to panic he released her again. He had no intention of lingering over the business in a place where they could be easily caught.

She reflected, as they continued onward, that the quick brush of his lips across her own had not been as unpleasant as she had imagined. She'd had to fight an urge to wipe her mouth with the back of her gloved hand, but he'd chewed on cloves to freshen his breath, a small act of consideration that raised him in her estimation and made it slightly less likely that he would rape her.

They sidled along the wall in single file, slipping like ghosts across the open spaces. Blanche had always had excellent night vision and her extended captivity in a poorly illuminated cell made it easy for her to maneuver in the near darkness. She saw of most of the obstacles in her path before she fell over them, only stubbing her toe twice. A full moon would have made the going less hazardous, but it would also have increased the danger of being seen.

Once through the old, little-used gate—the one she had hoped Jack would know of—they followed the castle's outer wall until they came to a path that led down a gentle slope toward the river. Jack walked faster and faster, heading straight for a stand of trees that would provide sufficient cover to conceal them from anyone looking out a castle window.

The trysting place he had chosen suited Blanche most excellently. The town of Colchester was off to her right as she faced the Colne. The bridge she had marked in her memory lay in the opposite direction. Her only regret was that she could see no boats drawn up along the shore. An escape by water did not appear likely.

"If we lie on our cloaks," she whispered, "they will make a soft, dry bed."

Liking that proposal, Jack tried to kiss her again. Blanche held him at bay with a coy laugh and a hand on his chest.

"Not yet."

For such a big, rough man, he was blessedly biddable. He doffed his heavy wool cloak and spread it on the ground while Blanche pretended to remove the fur-lined garment she wore. Her sharp little eating knife was within reach, but she hoped to avoid using it. There was a better way to disable her escort.

In among the trees, with only the sliver of a moon showing overhead, Jack could not see well. He took the rustling he heard for the sound of Blanche disrobing and eagerly untied the points that held up his breeches. She waited until they were around his ankles, then rushed toward him, arms outstretched.

The force of her shove sent Jack straight into the river. He landed with a loud splash and a louder curse. By the time he surfaced, sputtering and swearing, she had already put a goodly distance between them.

Chapter Thirty-Five

B lanche took her direction from the stars. If she meant to reach London, she needed to head south and west and find the wide thoroughfare, well-traveled during daylight hours, that ran from Colchester through Chelmsford and then on to England's largest city.

What should have been a simple task took far too long. In the darkness it was easy to become disoriented but she did not dare stop moving. If she stayed in one place, she would surely be caught. Alert for any sign of danger, she kept walking, moving steadily away from both castle and town. After a bit, as much by luck as design, she stumbled onto the deserted highway she'd been seeking.

She fell twice before she had sense enough to slow her pace. The night was both her friend and her enemy. It would not serve to tumble into a ditch. If she broke an ankle or a leg, she would never make good her escape.

Blanche waited until she was a goodly distance from Colchester before she stopped to rest and catch her breath. There was stillness all around her, but it was a quiet that felt wrong somehow. After a moment, she realized that it was because she could not hear any creatures stirring. There should have been scurrying sounds as nocturnal hunters went about their business. Where were the rustling noises when one of the bigger predators brushed past shrubbery? All was silent, as if the animals were waiting, expecting—

In the distance, an owl hooted. As if that signaled safety, the night came alive again with the small, reassuring sounds of nature.

Blanche resumed her journey, chiding herself for letting her imagination run away with her. What had she thought to see? A demon, mayhap? A ghost? The creatures of the night would not harm her. They were doubtless more frightened of her than she was of them.

After a bit, she began to enjoy the solitude. Once darkness fell, most people never went farther from their hearth than a privy in the garden. Some said that diseases traveled in the night air. Others insisted that dangerous beings were abroad in the blackness, not just thieves but fairies and tommyknockers and other mystical beings with dubious intentions toward mankind. It was not until Blanche reached the outskirts of a village—she had no idea what it was called—that she saw anything more frightening than a rabbit.

There were men with torches moving toward her along the highway. She hastily left the road to conceal herself in a stand of trees. A woman alone, out in the dark, would arouse profound suspicion even if no one suspected that she was an escaped prisoner from Colchester Castle. Standing still as a statue, she watched a party of three approach her hiding place.

"Who goes there?" one of them shouted.

Startled, she nearly betrayed her presence. She plastered herself against the nearest tree trunk and held her breath, waiting in an agony of suspense for discovery. Sweat broke out on her forehead despite the chill of the February night. Were they moving toward her? She had to know. If they came too close, she would run. She eased out of concealment far enough to catch a glimpse of the man who had called out.

He was looking the other way. There was a house in the distance, barely visible in the light from that sliver of a moon. When a dog barked, the man gave a nervous laugh.

"Only Sam'l Hart's toothless old hound," he said.

The torches were rush dips, allowing Blanche to see enough of the men to judge that they were common laborers. What she could not tell was the business that had brought them out into the night. Were they on their way home after an evening in the local alehouse? Or were they up to no good, mayhap bent on stealing cattle or robbing some poor widow who lived all alone in the countryside? Either way, she did not want them to notice her.

After the men had passed out of sight, Blanche made her way through the village. The rest of the residents were all snug in their beds, as was only to be expected. For the most part, the villagers would be hard-working country folk whose day would begin just a few hours hence.

Only two houses were close to the road. Moving from shadow to shadow, Blanche took care that her boots made no sound on the uneven surface. She had become increasingly surefooted as the night wore on. With as much speed as she could safely manage, she once again left civilization behind. She breathed more easily when only an empty ribbon of highway stretched ahead of her.

Blanche had never before attempted such a long journey on foot and she had not had a single substantial meal in more than two weeks, but she was determined to reach her goal. What other choice did she have? All the same, her slow progress was discouraging. At a steady pace in daylight, she should have been able to walk the twenty miles that separated Colchester from Chelmsford between sunrise and sunset. It was impossible to proceed at anything approaching that speed at night, even though she put forth her best effort, and she was resolved to travel as far as she could before dawn.

By the time the sun poked its head above the horizon, Blanche had just passed through a good-sized town. She was no longer alone on the highway. A wagon rolled past her, the sort with sides that folded down to display goods for sale. Peddlers owned such vehicles, keeping them packed and ready to travel to the next fair or market. That thought brought Father North to mind and she wondered how he was faring in his disguise.

Moments later, a farm cart rumbled by. The husbandman's wife peered down at her, her expression disapproving and suspicious. Blanche understood her reaction. Even in the daylight, a woman alone was regarded with disfavor. A woman wearing a fine garment like Blanche's hooded, fur-lined, well-made cloak and walking rather than riding or being carried in a litter, provoked comment.

To be remembered was dangerous. Even if no one realized she was an escaped prisoner, careless tittle-tattle to the wrong person might result in an accusation of theft. The last thing she needed was to be detained by some local constable who thought she had stolen the clothes on her back.

As soon as the cart was a safe distance ahead of her, Blanche removed her cloak and folded it as small as it would go. The rest of what she wore had been Alison's. Her sister had not needed adornment for her beauty to shine through. She had preferred country living to city and the practical to the gaudy in her manner of dress. Her clothes were of good quality but had been made with cloth dyed in plain, sad colors.

Blanche's greatest difficulty came from her distinctive pale blond hair. The hood of her cloak had hidden her lack of any other head covering. Her jaunty little hat had been left behind at Otley Manor and she had lost her coif at Waverley House. To go bareheaded was to invite unwanted attention, even if her hair color had been the most ordinary of browns. Only young maidens left their tresses unbound.

Blanche kept walking, tucking the bundle she'd made of her cloak under one arm. With her free hand she reached through the placket in her skirt to find the suspended pocket hidden beneath and pull out her comb. She spent the next few minutes restoring what order she could to her long, thick locks before stopping by the roadside to twist it into a braid and tuck most of it inside her collar.

She thought about rubbing dirt into the hair still showing to disguise its lack of color, but all that was available to her was mud and slush. She abandoned that idea and continued on her way.

The morning was crisp and not much warmer than the night had been, but between the exercise and the bright sunshine, Blanche did not feel unduly chilled without an outer garment. She drew in deep breaths of the fresh crisp air, hoping it would revive her, but nothing could completely dispel her growing weariness. Her pace slowed. Her feet ached and her limbs were sore. She was in desperate need of rest.

You are free, she reminded herself. *You are on your way to safety. You must keep moving forward.*

And she must think of a credible reason for being on the road alone. Sooner or later someone was bound to challenge her. Her bundled-up cloak would never be mistaken for goods she was taking to sell at Chelmsford market.

Were the authorities searching for her? By now, her escape from

Colchester Castle had surely been discovered. She doubted Jack had reported it. He'd have looked like a fool if he had, and would have found himself in trouble besides. Doubtless he'd let Ralph be the one to discover that her cell was empty.

Would they bother to hunt for her? Perhaps, if they truly believed she was a witch, they would decide she had used a magic spell to disappear, thereby making pursuit futile.

She wished she could count on that misconception, but she dared not.

The good news was that only a few people at Colchester Castle knew what she looked like—the keeper and her guards. That was to her advantage. There was no likeness of her and her description—of medium build and slightly above average height—would fit half the women in the kingdom. If only her hair was not so distinctive, she would feel confident that no one would recognize her.

As Blanche soldiered on toward Chelmsford, she considered how she might disguise herself further. A kerchief or a coif, even a hair net, would help. So would traveling with a group, but that would mean taking another sort of risk. Could she trust strangers not to give her away? She thought not.

No more than a mile later, at the point where a narrow track joined the highway, she encountered another solitary woman. This one entered the main road riding one horse and leading another. The second animal was piled high with bundles.

"Good morrow to you," Blanche said in a friendly fashion. Just walking beside the other woman made her less conspicuous.

Bright blue eyes stared down at her along a long, thin nose. Blanche could not begin to guess the woman's age. Her face was tanned and weathered, as if she regularly exposed herself to the elements. Her gaze settled on Blanche's carefully-folded cloak.

"Good quality, that."

"You are well-dressed yourself."

Although the woman's outer garment was plain black wool, the kirtle beneath was made of fine camlet and the bodice and sleeves, visible when

183

the woman shifted in her saddle, were embroidered with colorful silk thread.

Of a sudden, Blanche had a queasy feeling in her belly. Had she made a mistake? She'd taken the woman for a farmer's wife on her way to market with produce, but this was the wrong season to sell crops. Even baskets of eggs were unlikely at this time of year. Most of the bundles on the pack horse appeared to be soft. Whatever this woman was selling, it was not food.

They continued on toward Chelmsford for another quarter mile, silently assessing one another. The woman spoke first.

"Running away, are you?"

Blanche took her time answering. She had heard no undertone of condemnation in the question. Mayhap the woman thought Blanche was a daughter escaping from a violent father or a servant fleeing a lecherous master. Or did she imagine Blanche to be a faithless wife with a lover waiting for her in another town? It scarce mattered what she believed, so long as sympathy inclined her to help.

"Yes," Blanche said. "I am."

"Have you broken your fast?"

Blanche shook her head, suddenly ravenous. She had not eaten enough to keep a dog alive since well before she'd been carted off to gaol. It was no wonder she had so much difficulty putting one foot in front of the other.

With a grunt, the woman reached into one of the leather bags attached to her saddle and produced bread, cheese, and a small crock of barley water. All the while Blanche ate, still walking beside the horse, the woman watched her. Blanche expected a barrage of questions the moment she finished her meal. Her companion asked only one.

"Have you ready money?"

Of a sudden Blanche wished she had not been so quick to accept the food. She slanted a suspicious glance in the other woman's direction, wondering if she was about to demand payment for the meal.

"A few pennies." Blanche had more than that in coins of various denominations, but she felt justified in telling the lie. The woman's intent might be to cozen her out of all she possessed.

"Pay me a groat and I will let you lead my packhorse. If you keep your head down, it will appear that you are my servant."

"A groat! I could bespeak a room in an inn for an entire night, supper included, for such a sum."

The token protest seemed in order, lest she seem wealthier than she was. The groat was an old-fashioned coin compared to sixpence and shilling coins. Her father had told her once that under old King Henry it had been valued at fourpence, but these days it was worth only half that amount.

Blanche's objection made the other woman chuckle. "And what sort of room would you be getting for a tuppence? You'd do better to take my offer. A woman traveling alone attracts attention."

"I am aware of that," Blanche muttered.

She had by now been walking for many hours, not daring to stop for more than a few minutes at a time to rest her aching feet and legs. She regarded the pack horse with a deep sense of longing. "For a groat, I should be allowed to ride."

That earned her a sharp look. "Atop my bundles?"

"Why not?"

"That poor beast is already overburdened. Do you know nothing about horses?"

Stung, Blanche did not reply. In truth she knew a good deal about them and was an avid rider. She lacked experience only with pack animals. She had never stopped to think that there might be a limit to what they could carry.

They walked a little farther in silence.

"They call me Long Nell that do talk of me," the other woman said. "I ride a regular circuit on horseback, transporting my goods on this pack animal and setting up a standing on market day in each of the bigger towns. I sell at the fairs as well as in markets. You will have to walk, but I will trade a less conspicuous cloak for the one that you carry and even add something to cover your hair into the bargain."

"How is it that you have an extra cloak, and head coverings too?"

Long Nell chuckled. "That is what I deal in—clothing bought from those who have fallen on hard times and must sell it to put food on their tables. I am a blessing to them, and to you."

Blanche made one last half-hearted suggestion. "You might walk some part of the distance while I ride your horse."

"She that owns the horse rides. And to tell you true, it is difficult for me to walk far since I have much pain in my knees."

With a sigh, Blanche surrendered to the inevitable. "Let me see the cloak."

"Let me see your groat."

Since, for the nonce, the road was empty of other traffic, they stopped long enough to make the exchange. When Blanche had relinquished two pennies and her cloak and donned the clothing Nell offered, she took up the pack horse's reins.

Side by side, they trudged on toward Chelmsford.

Chapter Thirty-Six

"Have you tried a poultice of rue and borage mixed with honey for your knee?" Blanche asked after a time. She remembered that her mother had been wont to use that remedy when Father's game leg bothered him.

"I have, but it did me little good."

"There is another cure I have heard of," Blanche said. "It is an ointment made of butter, rue, frankincense, and threepenny worth of Blessed Water—*Aqua Benedicta Rulandi*. You must buy it from an apothecary."

"Expensive, then?"

"Yes. And it must be applied three times a day for a summer month to be effective."

There followed a spirited discussion of recipes. Blanche racked her brain to come up with more. Every young gentlewoman was supposed to know something about the common cures with which to treat the members of her future household. Although many of her mother's lectures had gone in one ear and out the other, a few of her lessons had stuck in Blanche's mind.

Mother had taught all four of her daughters simple remedies. Philippa, who had a keen interest in such things, was still a great one for sharing any new discovery she made. Although Blanche had lacked both skill in the stillroom and interest in the subject, she *had* absorbed random bits of the information thrust upon her, and she was possessed of a most excellent memory.

"A distillation of primroses does much to ease the pain of gout," she said, quoting her sister.

Long Nell responded with a cure for hiccoughs.

They spent the next half hour in pleasant debate over whether or not mummy was a useful ingredient in medicines. Long Nell was convinced that a man's flesh, dried, cut up small, and put into a glass vessel with spirits of wine, was a proven preventive against the plague. Blanche did not agree.

Their speculations came to an abrupt halt when they heard the sound of rapidly approaching horses' hooves. Blanche ducked her head, grateful for Nell's cloak and its concealing hood. The garment was the dull gray known as rat's color. Its generous head covering shielded her features and completely covered her hair.

Even with eyes downcast, Blanche could see enough to count four horses. The nags slowed to match the plodding pace of Nell's animals and a familiar male voice addressed the peddler.

"We are looking for a white-haired woman wearing a fur-lined cloak," he said. "Have you seen her?"

Blanche's breath backed up in her throat. She did not need to see the man's face to recognize Jack, the black-haired gaoler from Colchester Castle. The man she had tricked. The man who now had a very personal reason for wanting to hunt her down and return her to her cell. If he captured her, she would not fare well at his hands.

"Nary a sign of such a one," Nell said in a cheerful voice. "What has she done?"

"She's a witch," Jack said bluntly. "She killed a woman with her evil spells and then she chanted in her cell and worked magic to escape from Colchester Castle."

Long Nell made appropriately horrified sounds.

No one questioned the mute servant holding the pack horse's reins. That was just as well. Blanche doubted she'd be able to force a single word past the constriction in her throat.

When Jack asked Nell how long she had been on this road and whence she had come, the roaring in Blanche's ears grew louder, drowning out their words. She had to cling to the packhorse to keep herself upright. It was all she could do not to press her forehead into the bristly warmth of its mane in the futile hope that if she could not see the riders, they would fail to notice her.

After what seemed like hours, the men rode on.

"God be with you in your search," Long Nell called after them.

Slowly, Blanche lifted her head and watched the riders until naught but a cloud of dust remained to mark their passage. Only then, her heart filled with dread and her chest tight, did she look up to meet Nell's speculative gaze.

"It was not a cruel husband or a lecherous master you ran from."

"No."

Nell's brow furrowed. "A pity I have no rue."

"Rue?" It was an herb with many properties and uses but Blanche could not begin to fathom what Nell had in mind.

"They say rue can give you second sight. Carry a bunch of it, mixed with broom, maiden hair, agrimony, and ground ivy, and you can see into a person's heart and know if she is a witch."

Blanche sighed. "I wish it could be that simple."

"Did you use witchcraft to kill someone?"

"Indeed I did not, but neither did I hesitate to take advantage an opportunity to escape when one arose."

"Stand up straight then, lass, and stop trying to make less of your courage. I warrant you created that opportunity."

Nell's bracing tone was exactly what Blanche needed to hear. She met the other woman's eyes without flinching. "And if I did?"

"Then you did well. Colchester gaol is a terrible place." That said, Nell used her heels to urge her horse into motion.

Blanche tugged on the pack animal's reins and followed her. After the first a few steps, her legs ceased to wobble.

"You might have turned me over to them."

"I might have," Nell agreed, "but to what purpose?"

"To rid the world of a wicked witch?"

Nell snorted, a sound that much resembled one made by her horse. "Do you know the name Elizabeth Lowys?

Blanche shook her head. "Another notorious witch, I presume."

"She was tried and hanged for bespelling several people in Great Waltham. What a great lot of nonsense that was! My mother knew her well. She was an unpleasant woman, but not evil. Because her neighbors disliked her, they spread rumors. The chief witness against her was a twelve-year old child who'd been told frightening stories by those who interrogated him. He was terrified that the Devil would come and get him if he did not do as he was told and what he was told to do was accuse Goody Lowys."

Nell's face flushed as she urged her mount to increase its speed. She had known the woman herself, Blanche thought, and perhaps even liked her.

Now that she had been reminded of the case, she recalled seeing a woodcut in a published account of Elizabeth Lowys's trial. It showed a woman hunched over with age, walking with the aid of a staff, and wearing a strange-looking hat. What she remembered of the text, to the contrary, had clearly indicated that Goody Lowys was a woman still young enough to bear children. She had postponed her execution for a year by pleading her belly.

That Blanche and Nell were not alone on the highway made it unwise for them to speak further of witchcraft, even in whispers. Dangerous talk alone had sent more than one careless speaker to gaol. Blanche kept a sharp eye on their fellow travelers, wary of anyone who looked too long at her. Some walked. Others rode on horseback or in carts. At one point, a long, four-wheeled goods wagon passed by and shortly thereafter they were overtaken by a closed litter with outriders. Doubtless some gentlewoman was making a long journey.

Although Blanche saw no indication that anyone else was hunting for an escaped witch, she was not easy in her mind. What if Jack and his fellow gaolers turned back? What if, belatedly, he became suspicious of a nondescript woman in an all-concealing, rat's-color cloak?

"Where will you go when we reach Chelmsford?" Nell asked after another lengthy silence.

"To London."

"A wise choice. My travels take me in that direction only as far as

190

Chelmsford. It is a pity you cannot remain with me while I conduct my business there, but the people I deal with know I work alone. Afterward, I am bound for Great Waltham, far and away from your destination."

"I will miss your company."

"You will miss my protection. How will you disguise yourself after we part?"

"I have no idea," Blanche admitted.

After a time, the spires and rooftops of Chelmsford appeared in the distance. By then, exhausted by the long hours of walking, it was all Blanche could do to keep moving forward. Like one who had been asleep, she started at Nell's exclamation.

"There's your answer!" She pointed out a woman plodding along the road ahead.

Blanche stared at the solitary figure, noting the way she kept glancing over her shoulder and stayed close to the side of the highway. At the first hint of trouble, she appeared likely to dash into the underbrush and hide. Blanche's sympathy for her was immediate, but she was too tired to follow Nell's reasoning.

"Answer?" she repeated.

"To a prayer. You dare not call attention to yourself in Chelmsford lest those men searching for you hear of it, and since you and I must part company before we enter the town, you need a new identity. What better way to establish one than for you to be accompanied by a servant?"

"A maidservant of my own." At last Blanche caught Nell's drift. "I could say I am ...a merchant's wife ...on the way to meet my husband in London." There was nothing like the truth for ease of remembering.

"In that guise you can bespeak a room for the night at an inn," Nell said.

Blanche's incipient smile vanished. "This ploy will never work. I have no baggage with me. That alone will give the lie to my claim. And these clothes are not the garments worn by a person with funds."

"A wise woman does not display her wealth when she travels, and no woman wears her best on a long journey when it is apt to be soiled. As for your boxes and trunk, simply tell the innkeeper they have been sent on ahead. You there!" Nell addressed the woman keeping to the side of the road. "A word with you."

There was something about Long Nell's forceful nature that compelled others to listen. Although the plodder's manner put Blanche in mind of a dog that had been whipped, she approached when commanded to do so. She appeared to be of middle years. Her long, thin face looked careworn and her muddy brown eyes were dull but wary.

"My companion has need of someone to pretend to be her maidservant," Long Nell said. "Are you interested in the post?"

"I have been in service." The woman spoke so softly that Blanche had to strain to catch her words.

"What is your name?" Nell asked.

There was a telling hesitation before the woman answered. "I am called Mary."

Blanche felt certain this was a lie, but she had no intention of challenging it. The odds were excellent that the woman was a servant who had unduly departed her employment, as Sarah Trott had attempted to. They would both be safer if they traveled together.

It did not take much effort for Blanche and Mary to come to an agreement. When they reached a narrow track leading away from the main road, Nell led them down it. As soon as they were out of sight of the highway, she brought her horses to a halt and dismounted. She stood eye-to-eye with Blanche and studied her face with disconcerting intensity before she spoke again.

"You need rest, my girl, or you will be good for naught. Take yourself and your new servant to the Three Tuns of the far side of Chelmsford. It is small but much frequented by carters. If you tell the landlord I sent you, he will do well by you. How much money have you?"

"Enough for a room and to pay a carter to take me to London." Even after the peddler's many kindnesses, Blanche did not feel comfortable revealing that she still had coins tucked into the cloth tied around her waist. Those once sewn into the hem of her cloak had dwindled to a pitiful few, but should be sufficient to satisfy the innkeeper.

Nell grinned. "And if I double that, I warrant I'll have the true reckoning. You had the right of it earlier. You must have better clothing if you want this ruse to succeed." She stopped Blanche's protests with an impatient gesture. "Do not argue. It will cost you nothing. That cloak you were wearing when we met has already assured me of my profit."

She produced garments of richer fabrics than those Blanche wore and another cloak that was nearly as fine as the one Blanche had given her but far less conspicuous. Unlined, it was dyed the shade of brownish-green called pease-porridge tawny. Best of all, she supplied a headdress that would completely cover Blanche's hair. It was made in a style long out of fashion, but a frugal country woman would not be averse to wearing such a thing.

"You should also have a small chest to hold your possessions," Nell said. "It will look better when you arrive at the inn. No one will know that it is all but empty." She found one in the collection of goods carried by the pack horse and transferred the contents to the spaces left by the garments she'd taken out.

Blanche was moved nearly to tears by the other woman's generosity, and grateful, too, that Nell had chosen such a secluded spot to stop in. She made haste to change her clothing, but when she caught the older woman staring at the cloth belt revealed when she traded one kirtle for another, she could not help but have misgivings. She very nearly turned and fled into the surrounding trees.

As if Nell had read her mind, she gave a bark of laughter. Turning her back, she produced another modest repast and indicated that both Blanche and Mary should sit on a nearby stone wall to partake of it.

Sharing the meal eased Blanche's concerns. Breaking bread with someone was a good way to take her measure. When they had eaten, Nell used the stone wall to help her mount and signaled for Mary to take the pack horse's reins.

"Come along, my girl," she called to Blanche, "unless you are such a fool that you still think you have aught to fear from me."

193

Chapter Thirty-Seven

Evening found Blanche and Mary safely ensconced in a chamber at the Three Tuns. They had both slept for a time after arriving, after which Blanche persuaded her new companion to risk being seen long enough to go below and give orders for their supper to be brought up.

"This is the plan," Blanche said as they waited for the meal to be delivered. "I will pay the servant who brings us our food to act as a go-between. He will make arrangements for us to travel to London on the morrow with one of the carters supping in the common room below. If Nell was right, there should be several to choose from, each transporting goods from the country to the city."

Blanche's scheme received its first setback when it was the innkeeper's daughter who brought their supper. A saucy brown-haired lass of no more than fifteen, she listened to Blanche's proposition and agreed to help, but not for the farthing Blanche had intended to spend.

"It will cost you a penny."

"That is four times as much!"

"Deal with them yourself then."

It took an effort, but Blanche held on to her temper. "Ha' penny now and another when you have secured passage for myself and my servant."

As soon as the girl left, Blanche and Mary tucked into an excellent meat pie. Blanche's diet in gaol made her especially appreciative of well-prepared food. The wine was an excellent vintage and had not been watered. She had eaten every crumb and downed every drop by the time the innkeeper's daughter returned.

"You're to have two seats atop furniture, boxes, packs, and bundles piled into a two-wheeled cart. It will cost you four shillings and sixpence."

Blanche sent the girl a skeptical look. "That seems a high price for a perch so precarious."

"You will not find one cheaper. In truth, it is a bargain, since you will travel as cargo. Most carters charge three shillings a hundredweight to transport goods and I warrant you two together weigh more than that. Besides, I have saved you an additional shilling. That's what carters usually charge for loading the cart. You look spry enough to climb aboard on your own."

"Have we no other choices?"

"There is an empty farm cart set to travel south at first light, but it was last used to haul night soil."

Accepting her fate, Blanche paid the girl the rest of what she owed her.

"And so to bed," she said when she and Mary were alone again. "A good night's sleep is a necessity given the long day we have ahead of us."

A short time later, Blanche lay on the soft featherbed between clean sheets and covered with warm blankets. There was a goodly fire burning in the hearth and her belly was full. She longed for a bath, but in all other ways she was content. Her one and sixpence had been well spent.

She soon drifted into sweet dreams. She was at home and so was Kit, returned from a successful voyage. They were in each other's arms, anticipating other pleasures, when Blanche was jerked from sleep by the sound of shouts and alarums in the courtyard beneath the chamber window.

Stumbling from the bed, still half asleep, she looked down upon her worst nightmare. The men from Colchester Castle stood just below, locked in a loud dispute with the innkeeper. To ease a throat gone suddenly dry, Blanche swallowed hard.

"It is necessary that we search every room," Jack argued. "This woman cannot be allowed to escape."

"There is no lone woman here!" the innkeeper insisted. "This is a respectable inn."

Mary appeared at Blanche's side, clutching her arm when she caught sight of the men and horses milling about and heard the shouting. "Are they here for me?"

"No," Blanche whispered. "Be silent."

"She is not just any woman," Jack said. "She is a witch and a murderess! She bears the mark of the Devil in the unnatural paleness of her hair."

For a moment Blanche feared Mary's squeak of alarm would give away their presence, but the men in the stable yard were too intent upon their quarrel to hear such a small sound. Blanche risked a glance at her companion. Mary could still betray her. The other woman had released her grip on Blanche's arm and moved a little apart from her. She had seen the color of Blanche's hair. Simple as she was, she knew Blanche was the one these men were seeking, but she also had enough sense to realize that if she called out to them she would also put her own safety at risk.

Slowly, the frantic pounding of Blanche's heart subsided into a dull, steady thump. She looked away from Mary and back at the men still quarreling beneath the window.

"You will drive away my custom with this foolishness!" the innkeeper argued. "Never mind that you waste your own time. I tell you that I would never allow a woman traveling alone to bespeak a room. I know what *that* sort of female is up to!"

Silently, Blanche blessed Nell for her foresight. A respectable-looking merchant's wife traveling with her maid was above suspicion. Still, she dared not risk Jack getting a glimpse of her. If he insisted upon seeing and speaking to every guest, she was doomed. She was wracking her brain for ways to hide herself during a search of the premises when the innkeeper tried a new tactic.

"I warrant you could do with a bit of food and drink." He flung one brawny arm around the black-haired gaoler's shoulders. "You'll have been searching all the day long. Come into the common room, where we won't disturb my patrons, and I'll give you descriptions of all who lodge here this night. No need to roust them out of their beds, eh?"

The other men from Colchester, weary from their long day on the road, prevailed upon Jack to agree. Blanche breathed a sigh of relief when they all disappeared into the inn together. Neither the innkeeper nor his daughter had seen the color of her hair. Thanks to Nell, it had been completely covered that old-fashioned headdress. Her host knew her only as a friend of his old acquaintance, the peddler in used clothing. He could tell the searchers nothing that would harm her.

She turned to find Mary staring at her with wide, frightened eyes.

"Should we go back to bed, mistress," she whispered, "or must we dress and flee into the night?"

"To run away will only attract unwanted attention," Blanche said. "We stay."

Her words reassured the other woman, but to Blanche The Three Tuns no longer felt like a safe haven. The innkeeper believed he spoke the truth, but she could only pray he would prevail, convincing Jack's men not to search the inn themselves. She did not breathe easily until, a long time later, she heard them return to the courtyard, mount their horses, and ride away.

Chapter Thirty-Eight

T he last rays of sunlight struck the spires of more than a hundred churches as England's greatest city came into view. Off to Blanche's left rose the imposing bulk of the Tower of London, dominating the landscape. She sat up straighter, the discomforts of the journey momentarily forgotten.

The feeling of euphoria did not last. Her neck had a painful crick in it from repeatedly looking over her shoulder for any sign of pursuit. She was not safe yet. Not entirely.

The carter, a taciturn sort, had said little throughout a day that had begun before dawn. Mary, too, had been largely silent, although Blanche had caught her stealing more than one wary glance at her temporary mistress. The other woman remained a potential source of danger. Blanche could only hope that she was too afraid of calling attention to herself to denounce Blanche as an escaped prisoner and accused witch.

At the Crowne without Aldgate, a large and well-known inn, the carter announced that he would go no farther that day. Blanche reckoned he'd brought them just far enough. The Crowne was situated outside the ancient Roman wall but within the city limits. They had left Essex. It was possible but unlikely that Jack would pursue her beyond the boundaries of the county.

Blanche felt a great longing for her own house in Holborn, but if she were to continue on it would perforce be on foot. Exhaustion already clawed at her, draining her of strength and befuddling her mind. She was in no fit state to bargain for the use of a horse or hire a litter to carry her home and it would be unwise in any case to leave such a clear trail.

Be sensible, she told herself. *Leave the remainder of the journey until morning.* She needed to be well rested and have all her wits about her when she told her story to the people she hoped would help her to bring charges against Joseph Yelverton and Father Mortimer. And if she was to rescue Sarah Trott from Otley Manor, she would have to watch what she said. A careless word could condemn that poor young woman as well.

Head high, shoulders squared, Blanche entered the Crowne and bespoke a chamber for herself and her maid. "And I shall require extra water for washing," she informed the innkeeper, a sturdily built woman with face like a horse.

"I've twenty chambers above the ground floor, fifteen of them heated," the innkeeper boasted, leading the way inside.

Blanche willingly paid for the best accommodations in the house.

The Crown was larger than most inns. Three ranges rose three stories high overlooking a courtyard. The interior was sweet smelling. The floors had been freshly strewn with straw mixed with rosemary clippings. Blanche's chamber was generously proportioned. The walls were covered with linenfold paneling and the floor with tiles. A huge bed with ceiler, tester, and side-curtains of green say held pride of place and, as promised, a fire in the hearth already gave off welcome warmth.

Their hostess left them with the promise of supper within the hour. Blanche sank down onto the softness of the cushions on the window seat, limp with relief and gratitude. Tonight there would be no riders in the courtyard. Tomorrow she would be home.

Mary remained standing, shuffling her feet and looking ill at ease. She refused to meet Blanche's eyes. It did not take much imagination to guess what worried her.

"Well, Mary," Blanche said in a bracing voice, "here we are in London. On the morrow we will go our separate ways. Is there someone in the city who will take you in? Kinfolk? A friend? A lover?"

Mary shook her head. Her plain face revealed no emotion but her eyes were sad.

Blanche spoke more gently, sincere in her regret. "I cannot keep you with me, even if you truly wished to stay, but if I can help in any other way, I will. Do you want to return to the place of your birth?" That was what Sarah had intended when she ran away.

A single tear escaped and ran down one pale cheek. "I cannot go back to my village. That is the first place my master will look for me."

Her answer confirmed that she was a runaway servant, subject to arrest, just as Blanche had suspected. "Did he mistreat you?"

Mary refused to answer and Blanche did not have the heart to press her.

"Do you mean to seek new employment in London?"

"I am a hard worker, mistress. I will never give cause for complaint. But I do not know where to go to find a new master."

"In London men and women offer their services for hire by going to Paul's Walk. That is the middle aisle of the cathedral. If you wear a blue ribbon and hold a broom, those looking for a housemaid will consider hiring you."

Mary looked uncertain.

"Have you the wherewithal to buy a broom and a blue ribbon?" Blanche asked.

Mary shook her head.

Blanche sighed. "I owe you a debt. Your presence kept me safe last night." She gestured toward the box Nell had given her. "You may have that and the few items that contains. There is a comb and a spare shift. If you sell them, you will have money enough to buy the broom and the ribbon and have a little to spare. In return, I would have you forget my name. Forget my appearance. Forget that you ever met me."

"Oh, yes, mistress. Gladly." Mary's entire face lit up.

Blanche returned the smile with a slightly sour one of her own. She wished Mary well, and would add a few coins to the contents of the box before they parted, but she sincerely hoped their paths never crossed again.

Chapter Thirty-Nine

I t took Blanche more than three hours to walk across London. The streets were crowded, as they were every day. It took constant vigilance to dodge riders, who tended to think they owned the road, not to mention avoiding the steaming piles of dung their horses left behind. With every passing month more coaches seemed to appear in the city. In the narrower lanes, pedestrians had to press themselves against the sides of buildings or shelter in doorways to keep from losing their toes.

While eluding these dangers, Blanche continued to keep an eye out for others. She was not worried about pickpockets. Her few remaining coins were safely hidden beneath her clothing. It was pursuit she feared. Her heart nearly stopped when she caught a glimpse of a man with jet-black hair. For a moment she was certain it was Jack, still hunting for her. Then he turned, and she saw that he was older and had a distinctive hooked nose. Furthermore, he showed not the slightest interest in her.

The way out of London proper into the suburb of Faringdon Ward Without required Blanche to pass beneath the gatehouse at Newgate. The fortification guarded one entrance to the city, but it was also a notorious prison. The condemned on their way from there to Tyburn to be hanged were taken through Holborn dressed in shrouds and with the ropes already around their necks. Blanche could not see such processions from her house, but she had often heard them.

She wanted to run through that gateway. Instead she forced herself to walk at a sedate, unhurried pace. When she looked up at the barred windows, her heart went out to those imprisoned there, helpless and without hope of freedom. At her first opportunity, she resolved to donate money for food and blankets for the prisoners. It was the least she could do.

The tightness in her chest began to ease a little once she'd passed the Saracen's Head and turned her steps toward home. She crossed the stone bridge over the Fleet and began to climb Holborn Hill. It ascended sharply from that point, leading up to the parish church of St. Andrew. Next came Hatton House and the extensive gardens at Ely Place, famous for its roses and its strawberries, and a few minutes later she was descending to Holborn Bar, the limit of the city's jurisdiction.

Once she made her way through Middle Row, a series of buildings that partially obstructed the street, the landscape began to change. She was very nearly in open country by the time she passed the road that led north to Gray's Inn, where lawyers were trained and where she planned to seek legal advice on the morrow. She spared a glance for the Earl of Southampton's palatial home to the south, but her focus was elsewhere. She had nearly reached Wainfleet House.

The property was small and plain compared to Southampton's mansion or Hatton House, where the Lord Chancellor lived, but it had once belonged to a member of the minor nobility and Kit's wealth had allowed them to refurbish it and add many amenities. Blanche entered through a passage beneath the street range, surprised to find both the outer and inner gates standing open, as if visitors were expected.

When no one emerged from the porter's lodge to challenge her, she grew alarmed. Dreading what she might find when she emerged into the courtyard, she broke into a run, only to stop short at the unexpected sight that met her eyes.

Two men, one of them the missing porter, stood beside a horse that had been saddled and equipped as if for a long journey. The second man was Blanche's husband, Christopher Wainfleet.

Kit turned and froze, staring at her as if he'd seen a ghost. The next instant he was racing toward her. Blanche flung herself in his direction and they met in an embrace that left them both breathless.

"I am so glad you are home," Blanche whispered when she was able to speak again.

She lifted a hand to his face. It wasn't enough to have his arms wrapped around her or to still feel the tingling sensation his kisses left on her lips. She needed this added touch to reaffirm that he was real.

"I have been here for two days," Kit said, "frantic with worry. None of the servants knew where you were and I found letters waiting for you from two of your sisters, each demanding that you write to them the moment you returned."

Two of your sisters.

Kit's words reminded her that he did not know Alison was dead, Blanche's happiness dimmed and she stepped away from her husband.

"I will tell you everything," she promised, "but first let us go inside and sit down. I have been walking for a very long time."

Matching her slow pace, he looked her up and down, frowning as he took in the physical changes spending time in prison had wrought. A mirror at the Crown without Aldgate had shown her that she'd lost weight. Her skin had an unhealthy pallor. As a merchant, Kit would also notice the inferior quality of her clothing.

He made no comment, only calling for servants to bring food and drink to their bedchamber. Once there, he helped her to change into her own clothing, a kindness that gave him the excuse to examine every inch of her. She sensed he needed to make certain she was unhurt.

Kit's care and concern soothed Blanche, and inclined her to do something other than talk, but when she wound her arms around his neck and lifted her face to be kissed, he did no more than brush his lips against hers. Resting his hands on her shoulders, gentle but firm, he waited for her to meet his eyes.

"You must keep your promise of an explanation first, I think. How is it that you arrived home on foot and without an escort and wearing clothes I have never seen before?"

Loath to speak of serious matters, although she knew she soon must, she fell back on banter. "I do not suppose you would believe I've been with a lover?"

"Because I abandoned you to go to sea?" He shook his head. "I think it most unlikely."

She pretended to pout. Leaving his side, she collected the tray a maid had brought and carried it to the bed, settling herself upon it tailor-fashion and reaching for a wedge of cheese. "You might at least do me the courtesy of appearing to be jealous."

He joined her, tearing off pieces from a loaf of freshly baked bread and offering them to her. "Most husbands would also be angry. They'd lock you in your chamber, mayhap even beat you at the merest suspicion that you'd played them false. You said you would tell me everything, my love. I am holding you to your word."

She nibbled the bread and sipped a little of the wine Kit poured into her goblet, savoring the flavor. Even such simple food and drink tasted wonderful after what she'd been forced to eat in gaol.

"I wish I could pretend none of it had ever happened," she confided.

"Is it so bad as all that?"

"I fear it is."

He shifted his position until he could slide one arm around her. "Tell me."

"You were already at sea when Alison left Philippa's home in Kent," she began.

The telling took the best part of the next two hours. Kit did not interrupt her, and Blanche left out nothing of importance. His hand rested on her arm throughout the narration, but the fingers that began by idly stroking her wrist went rigid as she told her tale, at times curling into a fist. Still, as much as he might disapprove of the decisions she'd made and abhor what had happened to her as a result, he was her love, her second self, and most of all, her partner. He understood her well enough to know that she could have acted in no other way than she had.

"I am sorry to hear of Alison's death," he said when she at last fell silent. "The four of you have always been close."

It was beyond comforting to rest her head against his shoulder, even when he was vibrating with anger on her behalf.

"You have the right of it, my love," he continued. "Those who performed such devilish rites and then sought to sacrifice you to save themselves must pay for what they've done. That they caused the deaths of your sister and the maid may be impossible to prove, although their guilt is plain enough to me, but the other crimes they have committed will assure that they are condemned to death."

By the time he stopped speaking, his voice was tight with suppressed rage. Blanche found her husband's vehemence was both reassuring and frightening. She lifted her head so that she could look straight into his eyes.

"I will not cry over Yelverton or Mortimer, but I do not want the entire household to suffer."

"Not even Sir Stephen? He is the one who convinced the magistrate you are a witch. As for Lady Otley, she does not deserve your sympathy. She did nothing to stop your arrest, nor did she act to save her servants from being tormented by the priest. If you had not contrived to escape from gaol, taking a risk that makes me shudder just to think of it, you might be facing execution yourself."

"You would have found me before the Assizes. You were going to ride into Kent to question my sister, were you not? She'd have told you I was at Otley Manor and you'd have looked for me there. If no one in that house would tell you where I was, you'd have spoken to Sir Eustace next and he, I am certain, would have directed you to Colchester Castle."

"All that would have taken time." Kit gripped her hand with crushing force. She read the anguish in his face even as she heard it in his voice. "Mayhap too much time. And if I had been longer at sea—"

She touched a finger to his lips. "But you were not, and I did escape, and with your help I will have justice for Alison and Edith."

"If only I had come home sooner. I should have been here to—"

"Prevent me from spying on recusant women in gaol?"

"To *help* you, as I will help you now. First thing in the morning, we will go to someone with the authority to act and tell him everything that transpired at Otley Manor."

"I need to return there, Kit."

"For Sarah Trott?"

She nodded.

"Are you certain she was coerced into giving false testimony? Hers was one of the accusations that led to your arrest."

"She was forced into making a false claim. Only think how terrified she must have been. To witness an exorcism is horrifying enough. I can only imagine how being subjected to one must have affected poor Sarah. If they threatened to put her through that torment again, or worse, it is no wonder she agreed to say whatever they wanted."

"I do not think it would be wise for you to go back there."

"I must. Throughout the journey from Chelmsford to London, when I was not worrying about being caught and taken back to Colchester Castle in chains, my thoughts most often centered on Sarah's plight. I made a promise to her. I am determined to do my best to keep it."

"Next you will be wanting to rescue all the Otley servants."

"Would that I could, especially the stable boy, Rafe." Were there others, she wondered, who had been coerced into converting? At least those who were true believers knew the risks they were taking to continue to practice their faith in secret.

"I can see I will not be able to talk you out of attempting to save Sarah," Kit said after a moment, "but I do have a condition. Before you set foot in Essex again, let alone revisit Otley Manor, we must try to clear you of the charges against you. As it stands now, you are an escaped prisoner, and when you fail to appear at the Assizes, you will be declared an outlaw."

"All the more reason, then, to report what I know." She glanced at the sky beyond the window. It was already growing dark. "Who should I talk to, Kit? Who can best resolve these matters?" She gave a small, self-deprecating laugh. "Who is most likely to believe my story?"

He considered for a moment, and then a smile overspread his face. "We will go to Hatton House and you will tell your tale to our good neighbor, Sir Christopher."

"Will he agree to see me, even if he is at home and not at court?" Blanche asked. "He is a very important man." Not only was Sir Christopher Hatton England's Lord Chancellor, he was also one of Queen Elizabeth's favorites.

"He may not grant you an audience," Kit admitted. At her instant frown, his smile broadened into a grin. "That is why *we* will go to see him together. Indeed, until this matter is settled, my dear wife, I do not intend to let you out of my sight."

Chapter Forty

I t was a wretched day, so cold that a steady rain turned to icy pellets by the time it reached the surface of the highway. Heads bent, huddled in their cloaks, Blanche and Kit made no attempt at conversation during the walk from Wainfleet House to the elaborate gates that marked the entrance to Ely Place. Sir Christopher had built his grand new house on but a portion of the land that had once belonged to the Bishop of Ely.

A servant answered the door to the Lord Chancellor's house and appeared to recognize Kit. He let them inside without hesitation. As Kit shook icy water off his cloak, he sent his wife a reassuring smile. She was too nervous to smile back, and feared she looked like a drowned rat, but they'd have been just as wet if they'd ridden here, and then their horses would have been drenched as well.

The first setback came when the servant informed them at Sir Christopher was not at home.

"And Master Flower?" Kit asked. "Is he on the premises?"

The servant escorted them to a small, cheerless antechamber to wait while he inquired.

"We do not need to talk to the great man himself," Kit said in answer to her questioning look. "We need only capture the ear of someone who can set the wheels of justice in motion. It is a pity Sir Christopher did not keep Samuel Coxe on as his secretary after he became Lord Chancellor. I knew Coxe well when he held the post of packer in the port of London." Kit's mouth curved into a wry smile. "Then again, he might not have had enough clout to help us. He was suspended from those duties at one point, accused of taking bribes. The truth of the matter was that he had quarreled with another of Sir Christopher's dependents, Francis Flower, and Flower was in a position to do him harm."

"The same Flower you just asked after? What makes you think he will be inclined to do us any favors?"

"He is known to have an extreme dislike of all recusants."

"And you are acquainted with him?"

"He knows who I am. We have spoken once or twice when we happened to patronize the same alehouse."

Blanche supposed it was not so odd that two men with so little in common should know each other. Alehouses and taverns were a prime source of information for merchants and statesmen alike and Holborn Street, as a main road leading into London, had its fair share of both.

She experienced equal parts of delight and trepidation when they were led through rooms floored with Purbeck marble and hung with exquisite tapestries to reach a smaller chamber where a man sat alone at an enormous desk piled high with papers and books. He looked up, dark eyes watchful, when Blanche and Kit were presented to him.

"Wainfleet." The man greeted Kit but looked straight through Blanche.

"Flower. I will not take much of your time, but my wife has told me a story that I believe Sir Christopher will wish to hear."

Narrowing, the eyes shifted to Blanche, seeming to take her measure in a glance and dismiss her as unimportant. In spite of the warmth of the room, she shivered. She could not attribute the reaction solely to her sodden clothing.

Could they really trust this man? What if he did not believe her? Worse, what if he believed only part of what she said and insisted that she be sent back to Colchester Castle to await trial for witchcraft?

"What is it you would have him know?" Flower asked.

Since the Lord Chancellor's man clearly expected Kit to speak for her, Blanche kept silent and let her husband tell the tale. He began with her decision to look into her sister's death.

Flower listened, his expression growing ever more grave, but Blanche did not deceive herself into thinking it was because he appreciated her initiative or because he cared about the death of an unimportant gentlewoman. She could not even tell if he believed what he was hearing. Knuckles drumming on a stack of papers signaled his impatience and made her wonder if he would let her husband finish. It was not a story that could be told quickly, no matter that Kit had promised not to take up much of Flower's time.

As he repeated what Blanche had told him, he left out her desire to rescue Sarah Trott. She supposed that was only to be expected. She had left out a few details when she'd told her story to him. One of those details would most assuredly have interested Francis Flower—the location of the hides at Otley Manor—but she did not think it wise to interrupt.

Kit ended his narrative by outlining the false charges leveled against Blanche. He made it clear that his wife was innocent of any wrongdoing.

"Save for attending Mass during the time she was pretending to be a Catholic convert," Flower observed.

"Wholly justifiable in this instance," Kit insisted.

Flower folded his hands into a pyramid atop the desk and stared over them at his visitor. "You say they harbored at least two Jesuit priests at Otley Manor?"

Blanche was unable to remain silent any longer. "*And* murdered two innocent young women."

"Treason is a more serious crime than murder," Flower said without looking at her, "and a greater threat to England."

Anticipating his wife's reaction, Kit caught her hand and squeezed it in warning. When she took a step toward the man on the other side of the desk, he slid an arm around her waist to prevent her from reaching him. Blanche bit back a tart comment and checked her forward motion. Flower's disapproving expression suggested that he was not the sort of man who would ever take well to being told what he should do by a woman. As much as it pained her, she held her tongue.

"Master Flower," Kit said, "I have every confidence in your ability to deal appropriately with these traitors, but the matter of the charges lodged against my wife also gives me great cause for concern."

"So long as she does not return to Essex, she is in no danger of arrest."

Something in the way he said them made his words sound like a threat, one Blanche interpreted as "stay out of the way of those sent to deal with the Otleys or *she* will be found and prosecuted."

Kit kept his voice smooth and reasonable, but the arm that encircled Blanche was rigid. "That might prove …inconvenient. As I have mentioned, one of my wife's remaining sisters lives in that county. They have just lost a much loved younger sibling. Would you deny them the comfort of time spent together?"

"Let the sister come to London."

Blanche told herself to be glad he showed no interest in interrogating her. And the bitter truth was that, for all her efforts, she had no proof her sister had been murdered. Even the cause of Edith Trott's death could not be established with any certainty. Her only hope of obtaining justice for those two young women rested with the laws that made traitors of Catholic priests and all the secret Catholics who sheltered them.

"There must be something you can do to rid my wife of these charges." Frustration and fear leaked into Kit's voice. "Without intervention, she will be declared an outlaw if she does not appear at the next Assizes."

Flower looked as unconcerned as ever about her fate, but he was willing to throw them a bone. "I will recommend to Sir Christopher that he support your petition to the queen for a pardon …after the priests are taken into custody and everything Sir Stephen Otley owns has been seized by the Crown."

Flower's sardonic smile made it evident that he was well aware of how far short this fell of what they'd hoped for. He was still smiling when he dismissed them with an arrogant wave of one hand.

They had no choice but to go.

"We are most grateful for your assistance," Kit said through gritted teeth.

Blanche had to fight an urge to tell this self-important underling what she thought of him, but when she glanced back over her shoulder, it was to see him reach for a sheet of paper and begin scribbling furiously. She took heart from that. If he was making a record of everything Kit had told him and if he was as active against recusants as Kit believed, he would keep his promise to raid Otley Manor and take Father Mortimer and Joseph Yelverton into custody.

The rain had stopped, allowing them to converse as they made their way home.

"How quickly do you think he will act?" Blanche asked.

"He will have to consult with Sir Christopher, and with Sir Eustace Lewknor, since Otley Manor is in his jurisdiction." Kit shrugged. "It is likely to be a week or more before they can stage another raid."

"Then we still have time."

He sent her a long-suffering look, although she felt certain he knew what was in her mind, he asked anyway. "Time to do what?"

"Time to rescue Sarah Trott and return her to her parents."

Chapter Forty-One

B y the time Blanche and Kit had walked the remaining distance to Wainfleet House, the sun had come out, but despite the improvement in the weather, Blanche was cold and wet. She thought it a fine idea when Kit suggested that they return to their bed to warm themselves, but she could not resist teasing him.

"It is the middle of the day. What will the servants think?"

"They should be accustomed to our ways by now. Besides, it is no sin for a man to make love to his wife."

"On the contrary, it is very nearly a Commandment."

They were halfway across the courtyard, lost in each other's eyes, when someone called Blanche's name. Her *given* name. She could count on the fingers of one hand the number of people who would address her in public as Blanche rather than as Mistress Wainfleet.

All of them were related to her.

She turned to discover her sister Joanna clattering across the cobblestones. The sound came from the wooden pattens strapped to her shoes to keep them out of the mud and slush. With a cry of pleasure, she gathered Blanche into a violet-scented embrace.

"Thank the good Lord you are safe! We have been so frightened for you."

Over Joanna's shoulder, Blanche stared with mixed feelings at the rest of the newly arrived party. She'd have welcomed a few more hours alone with Kit, but her heart felt lighter at the sight of Philippa and Joanna's husband, Arthur. The love and concern on their faces was as comforting as the feel of Joanna's arm around her waist.

"I did not mean to worry you," she apologized. "I wanted to send word to you, but I was not able to."

"But where have you been?" Joanna stepped back, the better to scold her. "When Arthur and I went to Otley Manor, you had already left, and no one would so much as acknowledge that you had ever been there."

Blanche felt a prickle of concern. "You ...you asked for me? By name?" The vague plan she'd had in mind for Sarah's rescue would fail if her sister and brother-in-law had revealed too much.

Joanna shook her head. "We pretended to be lost and in need of directions, but since we arrived just at the dinner hour, we were perforce invited in. It was a simple matter for me to chatter about the difficulty of staffing my household and Lady Otley was only too happy to share her woes. It seems that she has been unable to find either a companion or a tiring maid to suit her." Joanna's lips twisted into the semblance of a smile. Her tone was dry when she added, "I feared, from what you told Philippa about Alison's death, that they had done away with you, too."

Blanche saw nothing to smile about. "Someone did kill Lady Otley's tiring maid. Her name was Edith."

Philippa, overhearing, made a tut-tutting sound and in a quiet voice suggested they retire to more private surroundings. There were an extraordinary number of Wainfleet servants lingering in the courtyard, all of them with their ears stretched.

"You are looking rather damp, Blanche," Philippa added, this time in carrying tones, "as are we. Let us go in and find a fire and send for cups of mulled wine." Without further ado, she steered her sisters toward the door.

Blanche's response was softly spoken. "I owe my safe return to the coins you left with me."

Kit and Arthur followed, talking quietly to each other. All three of them, Blanche thought, Philippa, Joanna, and herself, had been fortunate beyond words in their choice of mates. Even Philippa, who had lost her husband to a hunting accident, had enjoyed a decade of marital bliss. She only wished Alison had been as blessed. Their youngest sister had turned down more than one otherwise suitable admirer because she did not feel the same deep emotional attachment that her sisters shared with their husbands. She had wanted that for herself. It had been her tragedy that she'd believed she had found it with Joseph Yelverton.

Blanche ordered refreshments to be brought to the chamber above the hall, her favorite in the house. It boasted a bay window that projected out and caught the best of the day's sunlight. Philippa and Joanna promptly ensconced themselves on the cushioned window seat. Blanche chose to stand closer to the hearth, where a goodly fire gave off welcome warmth.

Her two older sisters might have been twins, she thought. Joanna was five years younger than Philippa but they shared the same light brown hair and pale skin. Only Blanche had been gifted with near-white hair. Alison's locks had been spun gold.

There had been other sisters once, and brothers, too. Their mother had given birth to thirteen children in all, but only the four girls had lived to adulthood. Philippa had five children of her own and Joanna four. Now that Kit was home again, Blanche hoped she'd soon be able to provide her husband with an heir.

A wistful smile on her face, she let herself dream of the future until the servants had brought food and drink and taken themselves off again. Then she drew one of the newfangled, lightweight wicker chairs across the glazed floor tiles to a position near her sisters. The fire had warmed the room to a comfortable level, aided by the thick tapestries that adorned its walls. One, made in London, displayed red roses on a blue ground. Another, imported from Arras, was a forest scene.

Kit stood with one shoulder propped against the linenfold paneling to the side of the hearth, giving every appearance of being at ease until one looked into his eyes. "I believe it will be helpful to garner suggestions from everyone present," he said, addressing his wife, "but first you must tell your tale again."

Blanche obliged. This time she mentioned the hides but did not go into detail about where they were or how to open them. What she did her best to recall was everything Father Mortimer had said about the herbs he used in the exorcism. She stopped at that point in the story, well before the part where she had been accused of witchcraft, to address her oldest sister.

"Does my memory serve me well, Philippa?" she asked. "You are the one with most experience in the stillroom. Could Alison and Edith have been poisoned with white bryony?"

"It is impossible to say for certain since I was not there to examine their bodies. Although the herb is poisonous, it also has medicinal uses. Mixed with nightshade, it relieves pain. The juice diluted in water is helpful in treating chilblains. With a tincture of wine, it can alleviate coughing." She lowered her voice. "The berries, distilled, can also be used to cause a miscarriage."

"What of the blisters? And the convulsions?"

Philippa's lips pursed as she considered. "Those could be signs of ingesting white bryony, but other poisons can cause similar symptoms. There are also a good many diseases that produce nausea, vomiting, diarrhea, even convulsions, and you did say Alison was ill before she was accused of being possessed."

There was still some question in Blanche's mind about that, but she did not allow herself to be distracted. "Edith was not sick, nor was there anything wrong with her lips the last time I saw her alive. I think it likely the blisters signify poisoning by white bryony."

"What a terrible way to die." Joanna's voice was filled with sympathy.

"You may well be correct in your conclusion," Philippa conceded, "but if you are, then you are fortunate you did not meet the same fate yourself. We should never have devised such a foolish plan. It could have cost you your life."

"We all agreed there was something strange about Alison's sudden death. How could we not try to uncover the truth?"

"But why was the maid killed?" Arthur asked. "If it had been the younger girl, that Sarah, I could understand their need to silence her. Like Alison, like you, she might have betrayed the family and the priest alike. But from what you've said, the older sister was sincere in her beliefs. She was no threat to them."

"I have no answer to give you," Blanche said, "nor do I know why I was not killed outright. I can only suppose they feared that another death in the household would be difficult to explain."

"If that is the case, then Sarah will not be harmed." Philippa sounded confident in her opinion.

Blanche shook her head. "They may not kill her, but she is still at risk. I saw their faces—Mortimer and Yelverton—when they were tormenting those two young women. Both of them derived a sick pleasure from inflicting pain and degradation. It had naught to do with religious fervor. They no more thought they were doing God's work than I believe I can fly. Sooner or later, they will want to resume their wicked games and Sarah will once again be chosen as their victim. I must find a way to get her out of that house."

"Otley Manor will be raided," Kit said. "That will put an end to these foul practices." He gave the others a brief account of their visit to Hatton House. Without explaining why, he ended it by telling them that Blanche had been forbidden to return to Essex.

"But a raid will send Sarah back to prison," Joanna objected. "Blanche has the right of it. That girl has suffered enough." She turned to her husband. "Can Ned Peyton help?"

Arthur looked doubtful.

"Blanche told me how your friend cooperated in sending her to Colchester gaol," Kit cut in, "and that he was making arrangements to bring her out again when the inmates were pardoned, but the situation has changed since then. Another Essex justice of the peace has become involved." He pinned Blanche with a look. "You had best tell them the rest of the story."

When, amid gasps and expressions of sympathy for her ordeal, she had recounted how she had been arrested, arraigned, and sent back to Colchester gaol, and had briefly summarized how she had contrived to escape and return to London, Blanche was forced to agree with Kit. "Even with the best of intentions, Master Peyton cannot assist me without appealing to Sir Eustace Lewknor, and if Sir Eustace learns of your connection to me and discovers where I am, he could send men to take me into custody."

Joanna worried her lower lip. "I fear you have the right of it, and in this matter, I am not certain we can trust Ned Peyton." Arthur opened his mouth to object, but his wife talked right over him. "Peyton had his own reasons for assisting us. He was honest enough about that. He hoped Blanche would discover how priests are being smuggled into Essex. In all other ways he is a most pleasant fellow and a good neighbor, but he is rabid in his hatred of Jesuits. He'd help Sir Eustace and Master Flower raid Otley Manor and he'd keep Sarah Trott out of their clutches, but only so that he could keep her close and persuade her to give him further information about other priests. She'd be as much a prisoner as if she'd been sent back to gaol."

Blanche refused to admit defeat. "There has to be some way to rescue Sarah."

"You will think of something." Philippa was nothing if not loyal. "You lived at Otley Manor, Blanche. Did you learn nothing during your time there that could be of use?"

Blanche stared at her sister. There *was* something, but not from her days as Lady Otley's companion. She had still been in Colchester gaol when that gentlewoman told her about the ways Catholic prisoners contrived to communicate with one another.

She sipped at the wine Kit had poured for her and pondered the possibilities. Could it be that the answer was right here in London?

"I must go out again." She rose abruptly from her chair, filled with new energy and determination. "There is a question I need to ask one of our neighbors."

Chapter Forty-Two

After changing into her finest garments, complete with farthingale and ruff, Blanche ordered up the litter she rarely used and instructed the bearers to carry her the short distance to Southampton House. Although it was the London residence of the earls of Southampton, it was the dowager countess who held a life interest in the property and made her home there.

Lady Southampton was not yet forty, but she led a restricted existence. Suspected of clinging to the Old Religion, she was not welcome at the royal court. Her seventeen year old son, who had inherited the title at the tender age of eight, did not live with her. He was being raised in the faith of the Church of England by a guardian.

Too nervous to appreciate the splendor of her surroundings, Blanche assumed an arrogance she was far from feeling and swanned into the house as if she owned it. She had the advantage of having lived in Holborn for several years, long enough to have heard rumors about the countess's household.

"Take me to Master Harrington," she told the servant who admitted her. If she could win over Lady Southampton's chief gentleman in waiting, an audience with the countess would be sure to follow.

Harrington turned from a window in surprise when she was shown into the anteroom where he awaited his mistress's pleasure. As soon as her name was announced, she saw recognition dawn in his eyes. He gestured for her to make herself comfortable on one of the settles that furnished the chamber.

"I have heard of you, Mistress Wainfleet," he said after the servant had left.

"I have no doubt you know of my husband," she replied.

He shook his head. "Your fame exceeds that of Master Wainfleet. You are the one they call the Finder."

Taken aback, Blanche was at first uncertain how to respond. That she had an ability to find things that were lost had been used against her in the Otley household. The expression on Harrington's moon-shaped face appeared benign, but she did not want to do or say anything to make him distrust her.

"You assisted Lady Digby when she misplaced a rope of pearls," Harrington continued. "Locating that necklace was a clever piece of deduction, Mistress Wainfleet."

"I used no more than old-fashioned common sense." Blanche affected as much modesty as she could muster.

Lady Digby, who lived hard by Wainfleet House, was nearly ninety, careless with her possessions, and apt to blame her servants when anything went missing. After Blanche's success in locating the pearls, she'd taken to sending for her neighbor rather than the constable when such situations arose, especially since having one of her retainers arrested satisfied no one. In almost every instance, Blanche had been able to trace the lost object by asking a few pointed questions about its last known whereabouts. Carelessness, not dishonesty, explained most of the disappearances.

"Have you come here in search of something?" Harrington asked.

Blanche felt a smile overspread her features. Her plan might just work, after all. "In truth, I have," she said. "There is a most delicate matter in which I hope the countess can help me. I am seeking the location of a man named Adam North, recently come to London from Essex. It is possible that Mistress Cecily Hopton knows how to find him. Her name, I think, is known to… some in this household."

She did not wish to come right out and say that she knew Lady Southampton was a secret Catholic, despite the fact that the countess, her late husband, and the man her daughter had married were all members of known papist families. If the rumors were true, Lady Southampton had a priest living permanently in her household, although of course he went about in the guise of a clerk or secretary. Or of a gentleman in waiting? Harrington's expression gave nothing away.

If Lady Otley had been telling her the truth, devout Catholics had the means to communicate among themselves. Blanche's hope was that the countess could tell her how to find the notorious Cecily Hopton, the woman who had brought aid and comfort to prisoners in the Tower of London during her father's tenure there. If anyone would know how to locate Father North, the real object of Blanche's search, it would be Cecily.

Harrison considered her request for what seemed an inordinate amount of time before coming to a decision. "There is no need to trouble Lady Southampton," he said. "Her clerk, Master Butler, is in communication with Mistress Hopton."

Was Butler the household priest? Blanche admired Harrison's circumspection, but regretted that she could not simply ask that question.

He led her through the domestic offices to a small, out-of-the way chamber where a somberly dressed gentleman appeared to be working on the countess's accounts. The wary look on his face when he beheld Blanche in all her finery prompted her to bend a knee and slowly, deliberately, cross herself. At once she felt like a hypocrite, but there was too much at stake for her to tell them the whole truth.

"I have urgent news to convey to Adam North," she said. "I was of late in Essex, at Otley Manor, and learned of something that concerns him."

"I do not know anyone named North."

"He is newly come to London."

"I cannot help you."

"But you can," Blanche insisted. "Only tell me how to find Mistress Cecily Hopton, for I feel certain she will know his whereabouts."

That she knew Mistress Hopton's name gave Master Butler pause. He glanced at Harrington. They exchanged a long, silent communication. Then the priest told Blanche what she wanted to know.

Chapter Forty-Three

When she returned home, Blanche was smiling. Looking anxious, Kit waited for her in the stable yard. His expression did not alter when she abandoned her litter only to call for a horse to be saddled.

"Two," he amended before the groom could scurry away to carry out her orders.

He followed her up to their bedchamber, where she at once began to change into clothing more suitable for riding. The farthingale would have to go in any case. Even sitting sideways on the horse, as a gentlewoman must, the bulky undergarment was a nuisance. She exchanged her fine garments for a plain kirtle with an overskirt to protect it from the dust and selected a matching bodice that had mannish buttons like a doublet. A felt hat, also masculine in design, completed the ensemble. She'd still have to wear her cloak, as the day grew colder with each passing hour, but so long as she did not have to raise the hood, she would have a clear view of her surroundings.

"Where are we going?" Kit asked as he helped her tie the laces that held bodice and kirtle together.

"To Wentworth House in the city."

She glanced out the window at the sky. Despite all that had happened so far that day, the afternoon was not yet far advanced. On horseback they could make good time and would be home again before darkness fell.

"*Lord* Wentworth's house? Why?"

"Because the baron's wife is there, together with her unmarried sister. They await the birth of the next Wentworth child. Help me with these aglets and I will explain everything on our way there."

Once they were mounted, she related the story Lady Otley had told her when they'd been prisoners together in Colchester gaol—how Cecily Hopton, daughter of the Lord Lieutenant of the Tower of London, had given aid and comfort to Catholic prisoners.

"Sir Owen retired to his country estate last year," she said when she'd recounted the rest of the tale, "but Cecily is still in London."

"Cecily is Lady Wentworth's unmarried sister?"

"She is, and although there is no question about the Wentworths' religious beliefs, Cecily is known in Catholic circles to continue her practice of relaying messages to prisoners in the Marshalsea. If she cannot help me find Father North, then no one can."

"The priest you told me of? The first one you met at Otley Manor?"

"The same. He is a good man, Kit, for all that he is a Jesuit."

"That may be, but even assuming you can convince Mistress Hopton to pass along your request, what do you imagine he can do to rescue Sarah Trott?"

"The request will be that he meet with me. If I can talk to him in person, I am certain I can enlist his aid."

When Kit continued to look skeptical, she told him in more detail about her encounters with the priest. He remained dubious. As she had, he'd been indoctrinated in the belief that all Jesuits were conspiring against the Crown.

"Trusting one of them is not only foolish, it is dangerous."

"There are good and bad men in every religion," Blanche argued. "Have you forgotten that it is a gentleman of the puritan persuasion who wants to see me hang for a witch?"

Prevented from answering by their arrival at Wentworth House, Kit just shook his head. Once Blanche had extracted a small parcel from her saddlebag, they turned their horses over to a groom.

"I have come to deliver this to Mistress Cecily Hopton on behalf of a mutual friend," Blanche told the servant who opened the door. She held up the paper-wrapped package. "I have instructions to give it only into Mistress

THE FINDER OF LOST THINGS

Hopton's hands."

That she was well-spoken and wore rich apparel and that her escort was respectable-looking convinced the fellow to admit them. He left Kit waiting below and showed Blanche into an upper chamber where Cecily and her sister's gentlewomen kept Lady Wentworth company.

"Mistress Wainfleet," the servant announced, "come to speak with Mistress Hopton."

"Well, come closer," Lady Wentworth called in a peevish voice. She was great with child and plainly uncomfortable. "Let us have a look at you." She peered at Blanche in the manner of those who are short sighted before turning to the younger woman seated next to her. "Do you know this woman, sister?"

Did the suspicion in her attitude come from a knowledge of Cecily's past exploits, Blanche wondered, or from some other cause? She wanted Cecily to believe she was a fellow Catholic, but if Lady Wentworth were to think that, she would never permit them to speak in private.

"We have a mutual friend," Blanche said quickly. "She asked me to bring this to you."

Holding up the little box like a talisman, she tried desperately to think of a name for this imaginary friend. None came to mind that would not make one woman or the other leap to a disastrous conclusion.

"I have been expecting this," Cecily announced. "Will you excuse us, sister? I have something for Mistress Wainfleet to take back with her in return."

Without waiting for permission, she hustled Blanche out of the room and into a nearby gallery. Instead of strolling up and down while they talked, admiring the view of London on one side and the portraits of assorted Wentworths on the other, Cecily turned on her.

"Who are you and what do you want with me?"

"I need your help."

Cecily eyed the parcel. "Is that a bribe?"

"Only if it pleases you." She handed it over.

Undoing the string and the wrappings, Cecily opened the box and peeked inside. "Ginger candy?"

224

"If you dislike it, I will take it away with me. It was but an excuse to be let into Wentworth House. Please. I have heard wonderful tales of your cleverness and your devotion to your faith. If they are true, you are the one person in London who can help me right a terrible wrong."

"I have no idea what you mean."

"And I cannot fault your caution, especially living in this household."

Cecily appeared to be about Blanche's age. Shorter and stocky, she had reddish-brown hair, a high forehead, a long nose, and a small mouth. At the moment her lips were pursed and her eyes narrowed.

"We have much in common," Blanche said. "We are both gently born and both accustomed to going our own way." She leaned closer, speaking rapidly. "It is urgent that I speak with a man named Adam North. Three weeks ago, he left Otley Manor in Essex to travel to London in the guise of a peddler. If you have the means to send a message to him, I beg you to ask him to come in all haste to Wainfleet House in Holborn."

As she said the words, Blanche was astonished to realize that it had been only three weeks since she'd last seen Father North.

Cecily shook her head. "I cannot help you."

Blanche persisted. "The life of an innocent may be at stake. I cannot tell you more, but I will ...confess to him."

Were there code words secret Catholics used to identify themselves to one another? If there were, she did not know them. Belatedly, it occurred to Blanche that Cecily might have regretted her conversion to Catholicism and returned to the faith in which she'd been raised. That might explain why she had not been imprisoned for her past actions. Cecily had not plotted the death of the queen or the overthrow of the state, but that she had smuggled at least one priest into the Tower of London and delivered messages to accused traitors were also treasonous acts.

Nothing in Cecily's manner or facial expression betrayed her thoughts, but after a moment she bestirred herself to walk halfway along the length of the gallery. She came to a halt in front of a portrait of a woman dressed in the fashion popular at the beginning of Queen Elizabeth's reign.

"This is a likeness of one of the daughters of the first Baron Wentworth."

"She is holding a book in one hand," Blanche observed. "Do you think it is a Bible?"

"More likely the *Book of Common Prayer*."

That Cecily's voice had a slight edge gave Blanche hope. "If I were to have my portrait painted, I would be depicted holding a copy of *The Exercise of a Christian Life*."

She scarcely dared breathe as she waited for Cecily's response. It was slow in coming. They continued on to the end of the gallery and circled back again before the other woman said a single word.

"How do you know Father North?"

"I was imprisoned with Lady Otley and her friends in Colchester gaol. We were released by the queen's general pardon of recusant women. Father North was one of the priests who came to Otley Manor while I was living there."

This answer seemed to satisfy the other woman. "I do not know where he is at present, but I can send word to someone who may be able to find him. Whether he will meet with you or not must be his decision."

"God bless you, Mistress Hopton."

"Do not make me regret trusting you, Mistress Wainfleet."Still carrying the box of ginger candy, Cecily left Blanche to find her own way back to the antechamber where Kit was waiting for her.

She had succeeded in implementing the first part of her plan, but the victory felt oddly flat. To achieve her own ends, she had been obliged to deceive a woman she admired. She had, in truth, become a most excellent liar.

Chapter Forty-Four

Three days later, two days after Blanche's sisters departed for their respective homes, a peddler arrived at Wainfleet House. He no longer had a cart, only a pack bulging with caps, gloves, trinkets, and bits of ribbon and lace. The porter was about to turn him away when Blanche saw what was happening from an upper window and rushed outside.

"I am in need of amusement," she announced. "Let him come in and show me his wares."

Father North looked older and more worn than he had just a few short weeks earlier, and at least some of the concern in his eyes was for her. Even so, he betrayed none of the fear a sensible man should have shown at discovering the "impoverished orphan" he had met at Otley Manor was instead the mistress of a fine house in Holborn. When Kit barged into her solar before she could begin to explain herself, clearly intending to remain, the Jesuit threw himself into the role of itinerant seller of smallwares, hauling out a sampling of hair laces, long laces with which to close a kirtle or tighten a corset, and men's points with metal aiglets.

"I have these in leather, cloth, or braid," went his peddler's patter, "but long-lasting silk is by far the best material."

Blanche fought an urge to laugh. "Be at ease, Father North. This man is my husband and he already knows who you are."

This seemed to shock the priest, but he was quick to recover and accept Blanche's offer of a seat in one of the room's two turned chairs. They sat facing each other while Kit remained standing near the door. He might have appeared to be acting as a guard, protection against unwanted intrusions,

227

but it was no coincidence that he was also positioned to prevent any attempt Father North might make to escape.

After a considering glance at the other man, North bestowed a gentle smile on Blanche. "You asked to speak with me, my child. What is it that troubles you?"

"I could lie to you," Blanche said, "perhaps convince you of my continuing desire to convert to Catholicism, even though you can plainly see that I am not at all what you thought I was."

"That would be a mistake."

"Because you would see though it?"

He shook his head. "Because it would burden you with yet another sin on your conscience."

In spite of the seriousness of the situation, that made her laugh. "Bad enough I am a heretic, eh?"

His faint, answering smile gave her hope that she had chosen the right tactic.

"It is worse than you think, Father. I was pretending to be newly converted to your faith in order to spy on those at Otley Manor."

When North's eyes hardened. Blanche put one hand on his arm.

"Hear me out before you consign me to Hell. I had a good reason. I needed to discover how a young woman named Alison Palmer came to die. She was my sister."

In as concise a manner as possible, she related the facts: Alison's decision to go to Otley Manor, her illness, exorcism, and death, and the similar fate of Edith Trott.

"Father Mortimer performed these exorcisms?" The appalled expression on Father North's face told Blanche all she needed to know. This was not common practice.

To make certain of his support, she described the ritual in detail and finished her story with an account of her own ordeal. "I was accused of witchcraft because Joseph Yelverton overheard me making plans to take Sarah away with me. The fear that we would make accusations against him and Father Mortimer once we were safely gone, and mayhap reveal the location of the hides at Otley Manor, drove the Otleys to consign me to a hangman's noose."

She did not tell the Jesuit about her visit to Hatton House, or of Master Flower's promise to secure support for a pardon from the Lord Chancellor. She had not been pardoned yet. Until she was, she risked arrest the moment she set foot in Essex.

Father North appeared to be in a state of shock. "It is not part of our mission to take innocent lives."

"I am glad to hear it."

"If you are telling me the truth, your sister was in need of medical care and prayers, not exorcism, and in the case of the Trott sisters, the goal appears to have been the forced conversion of young Sarah rather than the banishment of any demon."

"And the chance to fondle female flesh." Kit's disgust was palpable.

North flushed but nodded in agreement. "This practice must not be allowed to continue."

"I fear for Sarah's safety," Blanche said. "Aside from the horror of the experience, the smoke these young women were forced to inhale contained a poison, almost certainly the same poison that was used to kill Alison and Edith."

North shifted in his chair, frowning as he considered her words. "I can believe one of my fellow priests was misguided in the matter of the exorcisms, but why would Father Mortimer, or anyone else in that household, commit the sin of murder? Priests are charged with saving souls."

"There is a great deal that does not make sense about those two deaths," Blanche admitted. "That is another reason why I must return to Otley Manor." She heard Kit's sharply indrawn breath but did not look his way. "I can do so safely if you escort me. As long as you are present, no one in that household will dare harm me, let alone report my presence to the magistrate."

"I have responsibilities here in London."

"More important that preventing the abuse of an innocent young woman? Do you really believe Sarah will be spared further indignities?"

He bowed his head and closed his eyes. Was he praying? Or merely mulling over all she had told him? Blanche folded her hands in her lap and waited. Kit shifted his weight from one foot to the other but he, too, remained silent. Neither of them mentioned the coming raid on Otley Manor. If her plan succeeded, she would be safely away again, along with both Sarah and Father North, before it took place.

After a considerable time, Father North spoke. "You have persuaded me, Mistress Wainfleet, that I must return to Otley Manor to convince Father Mortimer of the error of his ways. I give you my word that I will escort Sarah Trott back to her family in Stisted. There is no need for you to risk your freedom by accompanying me into Essex."

"On that, at least, we can agree."

Blanche ignored Kit's muttered comment. "I must go with you, Father. I have yet to discover with certainty what person fed poison to my sister. With your help, that matter, too, can be resolved. The murderer is far more likely to confess to you than to me."

"That may be true, but you know I cannot break the seal of the confessional."

"There will be no need to if I am present to overhear the admission of guilt."

Blanche held her breath, waiting for the priest's decision. For all she knew, it was also forbidden to knowingly allow a lay person to eavesdrop.

After another eternity, Father North reluctantly agreed to take Blanche with him, although he did not make any specific promises about what he would allow once they reached Otley Manor.

"Be prepared to travel light," he instructed her. "We will leave for Essex at dawn."

Chapter Forty-Five

K it watched with an unrelenting scowl as Blanche packed clothing and a few other necessities into a capcase. Arms folded across his chest, he had a formidable appearance, but she knew full well he would never use his greater strength against her, not even to protect her from her own folly.

"I'll not change my mind," she said without looking up from her task.

"I am aware of that."

"And you cannot go with me. While I am at Otley Manor, I must maintain the fiction that I am an unmarried woman of limited means."

"I am astonished that the good father is willing to go along with such a deception."

"It is a matter of expediency. He can more easily deal with Father Mortimer if I do not confuse the issue by telling anyone else the whole truth."

"North does not know the whole truth himself."

She turned, hands on hips, to glare at him. "Do you think I like lying to him? It is necessary, and my plan is a good one." Or at least it was the best she could cobble together in time to rescue Sarah before the raid.

Blanche's annoyance faded when she caught a glimpse of Kit's face. He was afraid for her, afraid of losing her. Abandoning her packing, she ran to her husband, sliding her arms around his waist and resting her head against his chest. After a moment's hesitation, he embraced her in return.

"I can never adequately convey to you the horror of witnessing that exorcism, and it was so much worse for Sarah. Worse still when she woke the next morning to find her sister dead beside her. Can you imagine it, Kit?

231

Can you?"

She felt as much as heard his deep sigh.

"She will not trust Father North, but I am sure she will come away with us if I am there, and because *he* is there, the Otleys will allow it."

"Have you thought, my love, that having failed to get rid of you one way, those at Otley Manor may resort to more direct means? One of that lot is a murderer. Your return is certain to be perceived as a threat."

As it should be, Blanche thought. Aloud she spoke in soothing tones. "Father North's presence will protect me."

"Are you certain you can trust him? He is a Jesuit. They are trained to deceive, the better to foment rebellion among English Catholics."

"I saw no sign of duplicity in him at Otley Manor, nor did I hear him speak any seditious words. I know there are some Catholics who would like to overthrow Queen Elizabeth, but most of those I've met seem only to want to be left alone so they can worship in peace."

Kit wasn't listening. "North has no *reason* to protect you. What are you to him but a heretic and a traitor to God?"

Blanche slid her hands back to the middle of his chest and pushed herself a little away from him. "I do not *entirely* trust him, but it is to his advantage to convince the others to let Sarah leave. Once he has done me that favor, I will be in his debt, and my best means to repay him will be with my silence."

"I have my doubts about how gullible that priest is."

"Then consider this. He knows, as the Otleys did not, that I have you to avenge me if I come to any harm."

"It is not only those at Otley Manor who concern me. We have no idea when the raid will take place. If you are still there, Sir Eustace will show you no mercy."

"That is why I must not delay. If we leave at first light, I will reach Otley Manor and be well away again before Master Flower and Sir Eustace have time to take action."

"Is there nothing I can say to persuade you to change your mind?"

There was. He could offer her an ultimatum, pitting the future of their marriage against her determination to carry out her quest for justice. That he did not force her to make that choice made her love him all the more.

"Have faith in me, Kit. I will go back to Otley Manor. I will make one last attempt to learn who killed Alison, and then, whether I have my answer or not, I will take Sarah to Stisted and return to Wainfleet House in all haste."

"I do not doubt you can accomplish all you set out to do, but you cannot expect me to wait patiently in London while you place yourself in danger."

"You cannot come with me to Otley Manor. What possible reason could Father North give for your presence? You can scarce pretend to be a priest. You would not even make a convincing papist."

"But I can go with you as far as Little Mabham and find lodging there. That will place me near at hand in case of trouble, and I will be in a position to hear of it if a raid is imminent."

Blanche did not argue. It was a most excellent compromise.

Chapter Forty-Six

After two days of traveling, stopping for the night at the Three Tuns in Chelmsford, where Blanche gave the innkeeper a package to pass along to Long Nell with her gratitude, she once again entered the Otleys' modest brick and timber house. As they had agreed, she kept silent and let the priest explain her presence. He did so with simple eloquence. God had aided her escape from gaol because she was innocent and had led her to him to right the wrong that had been done to her.

"Now see here, Father," Sir Stephen blustered. "There were witnesses to her wickedness."

"False witnesses." Father North looked directly at Joseph Yelverton.

They were gathered in Lady Otley's withdrawing room, just the family, Blanche, and the two priests. Father Mortimer, prune-faced, glowered at his younger colleague. Father North presented a picture of calm reason, his manner grave, while rage turned the other man's countenance an unflattering, blotchy red. North had an aura of righteousness about him, enhanced by the way the sun coming in through the windows turned his pale hair into a halo. He stood tall and slender and straight, diminishing the other man simply by his proximity. Mortimer's balding pate, bulging eyes, and obvious paunch had never been more apparent. All the blustering in the world could not obscure Father North's soft-spoken words of condemnation.

"The first witness was Goody Dunster. Her claims were false. I witnessed her meeting with Mistress Wainfleet myself. I know what happened and what did not. The second witness was a child, easily swayed. I took her confession when I stopped at her parents' home on my way to London and

234

know why she wished to do Mistress Wainfleet harm."

"My maidservant—"

Father North cut short whatever excuse Lady Otley might have been about to make. "Sarah Trott was too terrified to do or say anything but what she was told. An accusation of witchcraft should not be made lightly, and exorcism is not a ritual to be undertaken without a great deal of forethought and the approval of those more knowledgeable than any simple man of the cloth."

He did not say who had to approve, but Blanche assumed there was a hierarchy within the church that decided such matters. How inconvenient for Father Mortimer!

Sir Stephen, Joseph Yelverton, and Father Mortimer seethed under Father North's condemnation. Only Lady Otley showed true contrition. She asked if Father North would hear her confession.

"No!" Father Mortimer advanced upon Father North, angrily gesticulating. "You have no authority to disparage what I have done here. I am the one who returned to Otley Manor to minister to this flock. I return time and again at great risk to myself while you, after but two visits, were content to go haring off to London."

Even the Otleys seemed to realize what a weak argument that one was.

"Have you been here and gone again since Mistress Wainfleet's arrest?" Father North asked in a mild voice.

"What has that—?"

"Did you, mayhap, visit your poison upon another household?"

The question surprised Blanche and left the others bereft of speech. She felt certain Father North had known nothing of Father Mortimer's proclivities before she told him about the exorcism, but he had returned to his lodgings in London the night before their departure for Otley Manor. Had he had time enough to discover more about the other priest's past?

Whether he had some specific incident in mind, or this was a stab in the dark, his accusation hit its mark. Father Mortimer's face went from blotchy red all the way to purple. He sputtered in indignation but no coherent words came out of his mouth.

Lady Otley fell to her knees in front of the younger priest. Her face was deathly pale, her eyes wide and tormented. "How can we redeem ourselves, Father?"

Before Father North could answer, Lady Otley's brother seized her by the shoulders and yanked her to her feet. "Don't be a fool, Clemence." He sneered at Father North. "This so-called priest has been compromised. He has brought a witch among us. Is that not proof enough that he lies?"

"The so-called witch can speak for herself," Blanche interrupted. "You made accusations against me only to protect yourself. You overheard me talking to Sarah. You knew we planned to leave and took steps to prevent that from happening. You were afraid we would testify against you, just as you feared Alison would."

"Alison?" Yelverton was taken aback by the mention of her name.

"She was going to return to her sister's house. You stopped her with your absurd contention that she had been bewitched. The exorcism was not intended to free her of a demon but to cause her death."

Everyone save Father North stared at Blanche as if she had run mad. After one quick glance at their faces, she kept her gaze on Yelverton. Although she searched most assiduously for some sign of guilt, all she could find was astonishment.

"Who *are* you?" he demanded. "What do you know of Alison Palmer?"

"She was my sister."

A gasp from Lady Otley drew Blanche's attention. The gentlewoman's eyes narrowed, examining Blanche's face in minute detail. "Alison had three sisters," she said. "Oh, what I fool I was to believe you."

Sir Stephen sent his wife a sharp look. "What are you talking about, Clemence?"

"Mistress Wainfleet spun a fine tale back in Colchester Castle, all about a cousin whose husband threw her out into the cold for owning a forbidden text. She even told me his name—Arthur Chapell."

Comprehension dawned on Lady Otley's husband and brother at the same time.

"The lost travelers," Yelverton said. "The people who came here after

CHAPTER FORTY-SIX

Mistress Wainfleet's arrest—they were looking for her?"

"Oh, yes, and very cleverly, too. Mistress Chapell and I had a most delightful discussion about the difficulties of finding reliable servants."

"And that other party?" Yelverton asked, addressing Blanche directly. "The woman from Kent with the suspiciously lame horse? Was that another sister?"

Blanche drew herself up straighter and looked him square in the eye. "Yes, it was. Alison wrote to her shortly before she died. Somehow you discovered she'd sent that letter and feared what she would reveal to the authorities. That is why you killed her."

"I did not kill Alison Palmer. I was …fond of her."

"So fond of her that you subjected her to torture?"

"She was possessed by a demon. We tried to save her."

"Enough!" Father North's command silenced them both. "I will hear confessions now, and while I do, Mistress Wainfleet will assure herself that Sarah Trott is unharmed and help her pack her belongings."

Father Mortimer continued to grumble about upstart young priests, but the others agreed, almost eagerly, to everything Father North proposed. He had that effect on people. He made them believe that all they had to do was follow his lead and all would be well.

Lady Otley summoned Sarah.

Blanche was shocked by the girl's appearance. In the short time Blanche had been gone, Sarah had shrunk to a shadow of her former self. She reacted with alarm rather than elation when Father North told her that Blanche had come back to escort her to Stisted.

As they trudged up the stairs to the garret, Sarah was visibly trembling. There was deep suspicion in her eyes when she looked at Blanche, suspicion that bordered on fear.

"I am not angry with you, Sarah," Blanche said. "I know you were coerced into claiming that I bewitched Edith to death."

"I was not coerced." She thrust out a defiant chin but her voice shook. "They showed me plain what you had done."

Shocked, Blanche did not at once have the words to respond. Sarah truly believed she was a witch? How could that be?

"What did I do?" she asked when she'd managed to gather wit enough to voice the question.

"It all began when you came here."

"What did?"

"Illness, exorcism, and death."

"What happened to Alison Palmer had naught to do with me. That began well before we met in Colchester gaol."

Sarah frowned. "A witch does not have to be present to cast a spell."

Blanche prayed for patience. "And why should I wish harm to anyone in the household, least of all Alison?" She took a step closer and waited until Sarah met her eyes. "She was my sister."

"Then why did you kill her?"

Blanche held onto her temper with an effort. The girl had been lied to so often that it was not surprising she was confused. She wondered if there was anything she could say that would convince Sarah that she had, for the most part, told her the truth.

"I am the last person in the world who would wish to harm Alison, and I did not kill Edith, either."

At least she had Sarah's full attention. Although the younger woman kept as much distance between them as possible and looked as if she was prepared to take flight at a moment's notice, she was listening.

Blanche perched atop the wardrobe chest, trying to look harmless. "When my other sisters and I learned of Alison's sudden death, we already knew how unhappy she was here. We found it hard to believe that she could have been carried off so quickly by any natural means and resolved to discover what had led to her death. With the help of friends, it was arranged that I might share your imprisonment in Colchester gaol. I meant to deceive Lady Otley and win her trust. I thought it possible that someone murdered Alison. I still believe that was the case."

"You admit you lied to us? To me?"

"Not about wanting to help you, Sarah, and my name really is Blanche Wainfleet, but I have a husband and a house just outside of London, and as you already know, I never truly wished to convert to Catholicism."

Sarah no longer looked as wary, but neither did she seem anxious to trust anything Blanche told her. "If you did not bewitch Mistress Palmer, who did?"

"No one. Think back on what you yourself observed. Alison was ill, not possessed. Father Mortimer and Joseph Yelverton used her symptoms as an excuse to perform an exorcism, just as they used your attempt to escape and Edith's defense of you to excuse another."

A shudder wracked Sarah's too-thin frame. She squeezed her eyes tightly shut, as if to shut out the memories of that terrible experience. They popped open again almost at once. She stared, unseeing, at some distant point.

Blanche kept her voice gentle. "Alison was poisoned, Sarah. So was Edith."

"No!" Sarah's lower lip trembled until she pressed the back of her hand to her mouth. Her brow furrowed as she tried to gather her thoughts. "Why should I believe you?"

"Because I promised to take you home to your parents and I have returned to keep my word, even though I have placed myself in great danger by doing so."

"Who killed my sister?"

"I believe it was Joseph Yelverton." She'd thought him guilty of Alison's murder, too, but although she had not believed everything he'd said during the confrontation just past, his denial of guilt in Alison's death had rung true. She was still puzzled by that development.

Sarah seemed to shrink further into herself at the mere mention of Yelverton's name.

Blanche reached out to her. "You need to come away with me now, Sarah. We do not have much time."

Sarah shook her head with such vigor that her kerchief came loose.

"After all you have endured, I would not trust anyone either, but it is important that we leave Otley Manor as soon as possible." She hesitated, then chose honesty over further deception. "There is going to be another raid. If we remain here much longer, we both risk being sent back to Colchester gaol."

Chapter Forty-Seven

Blanche and Sarah returned to the withdrawing room to discover that Father North intended to stay the night and celebrate Mass the next morning.

"I had hoped you would leave with us," Blanche said when she managed to take him aside for a private word. She had also hoped to eavesdrop on the confessions he heard, but that now seemed unlikely.

There had already been stirrings in Little Mabham when they'd passed through on their way to Otley Manor. Kit was not the first stranger who had sought lodging there that day. After he bespoke a room in a ramshackle inn on the outskirts of the village, he passed on the news that Sir Eustace was entertaining important guests from London. Father North did not understand the significance of that information, but to Blanche it meant only one thing—the raid on Otley Manor would occur very soon, mayhap as early as tomorrow.

"My duty is here," Father North said. "These people have sinned and need my guidance. Word has already been sent to the Farleighs and I am about to leave with Master Yelverton to fetch Mistress Kenner and her daughter."

Torn, Blanche came close to warning him that another raid was imminent. She did not want him to be caught in Francis Flower's net, and the thought of sending old Mistress Farleigh and young Jane Kenner back to gaol made her stomach clench. Her distress was such that it took her a moment to realize how odd it was that Father North and Joseph Yelverton should be dispatched on an errand that would ordinarily be performed by a servant. Had the priest learned something from Yelverton that he hoped to pursue in the course of a ride to a neighboring estate?

"I expect you will be gone before I return," Father North said. "Your husband will see you safely to Stisted and then home to London. I wish you well, Mistress Wainfleet. You have a good heart …for a heretic."

Again, Blanche hesitated. She wished she could warn him, but she could not think of a way to do so without also allowing Father Mortimer and Joseph Yelverton to escape the justice they so richly deserved. Moreover, she and Sarah needed to depart before Sir Stephen changed his mind about following Father North's advice.

"Where is Father Mortimer?" she asked. In North's absence he might well try to regain his earlier influence over the household.

"He is in his chamber, contemplating his sins. He has confessed and been forgiven. He will be a better man and a better priest from this day forward."

Blanche took this assessment with a grain of salt. She thought it more likely that Mortimer was sulking, stung by the sharp rebuke he had suffered at his colleague's hands. As for forgiveness, she had none in her heart for either him or Yelverton.

A short time later she stood in the stable yard watching the two men ride away. Instead of continuing in his disguise as a peddler, the priest had made the journey from London as Kit's servant, but he'd brought along his pack. He had it with him now. The vessels, vestments, and portable altar went with him everywhere he traveled.

Her own horse waited, saddled and ready for the short trip to the inn on the outskirts of Little Mabham. She even had a mount for Sarah. They'd used the extra animal to carry their baggage on the outward journey. They could be well on their way to Stisted by nightfall, but only if they left at once.

Instead, Blanche delayed her departure to return to the house and seek out Lady Otley. She found the gentlewoman in her withdrawing room.

"I am not sorry to have put an end to the exorcisms," Blanche told her, "but I bear you no ill will. You have been nothing but kind to me." That was a slight exaggeration, but she meant what she said.

Lady Otley's features had a ravaged look. "I did not believe them at first—my brother and Father Mortimer—when they said your sister was possessed. I saw no signs of aught but an ague. But when your priest tells you something is true, how can you not accept that he is right and you are in error?"

It was indeed a quandary, and today Lady Otley had been forced to make another difficult choice in deciding which of two priests she should believe. The outcome would have been far different if she and Sir Stephen had sided with Father Mortimer.

While Sarah watched anxiously from the doorway, the small bundle holding all her belongings clutched to her chest, Blanche racked her brain for a way to persuade Lady Otley to temporarily leave her home and keep the other women away until after the raid. The truth would not do. If she warned Lady Otley that a raid was imminent, Father Mortimer would escape as well. Worse, if she admitted to alerting the authorities, everyone at Otley Manor would turn on her. She had no wish to sign her own death warrant.

Father North had been gone for no more than a quarter of an hour when Blanche realized there was nothing she could say or do without jeopardizing her own safety and that of the girl she'd come to rescue. She bade Lady Otley farewell and had just turned toward the door when there was a great to-do in the courtyard. Horses' hooves clattered on the cobblestones and men shouted.

The east-facing windows of Lady Otley's withdrawing room offered a clear view of the courtyard and the stable yard beyond. The late-day sun cast them in shadow, but there was more than enough light to confirm Blanche's worst fear. Sir Eustace and Master Flower had arrived at the head of a large party of armed men.

Lady Otley came up beside her. As soon as she recognized the magistrate, she let out a shriek and collapsed onto the window seat, burying her face in her hands. Despite all the fine plans she and Sir Stephen had made for dealing with another raid, now that it had come upon her, she seemed incapable of taking action.

Confronted with the very fate Blanche had warned her about, Sarah abruptly came to life. She seized Blanche's arm to pull her away from the window. "You must not be found here. If Sir Eustace recognizes you, he will hang you on the spot."

"It is too late to escape."

The men below had already begun to spread out. Some guarded exits while others swarmed into the house. Blanche tried to tell herself that Master Flower would intervene to protect her, but she was far from certain he'd bother to exert any effort on her behalf.

Her best hope was Kit. When he'd seen what was going on, he'd have followed the raiding party to Otley Manor…unless something had happened to prevent him. Fear for her husband's safety momentarily rendered her incapable of rational thought.

Her mind in turmoil, Blanche allowed Sarah to guide her steps, unaware at first of the girl's intentions. It was not until they mounted the stairwell that hid the hide that she understood what her companion meant to do.

Grim-faced but determined, Sarah worked the nail that opened the trap door, hauled it up, and shoved Blanche so hard that she had to step down onto the first rung of the ladder to keep from falling. Her voluminous skirts covered the opening from side to side, preventing her from descending any farther. Sarah pushed at the heavy material, forcing it through the hole.

Blanche descended along with it. "There is room for both of us. Come in after me."

Sarah bent down so that they were eye-to-eye. "I have not been outlawed, and if we are both inside, who will let us out? It is your turn to trust me, Mistress Wainfleet. When I will show Sir Eustace the location of the hide in the garret, it will prove I am loyal to the Crown. He will take everyone else away and leave me behind to release you."

She pushed on Blanche's shoulders with unexpected strength. Blanche resisted, nearly losing her balance again before she gave in to Sarah's urging.

There was a flaw in the girl's plan. Blanche tried to warn her, but the younger woman was already closing the trap door above her head. It came down so fast that Blanche had to duck to avoid being struck. The heavy wooden panel fell into place with a solid thump, leaving her in darkness.

She rapped on the underside of the panel. "Sarah, wait."

The Otleys concealed their holy relic in the smaller hide, along with their portable altar, several forbidden books, and the consecrated vessels. Once the magistrate had found those, he would indeed arrest everyone in the house, but he would take Sarah away, too. Even if he believed her claim to have converted only under duress, he would not set her free. He would do what Joanna had warned them Master Peyton would do and keep her close, mayhap for months, hoping she could give him information about other recusant activities in this part of Essex.

Blanche drew breath to shout, to make Sarah aware of her danger. Before she could utter a sound, she heard someone approach the top of the stairwell and start down.

"Open the hide," Father Mortimer ordered.

"So you can escape the punishment you so richly deserve?" Sarah shot back. "Never."

"Out of my way, girl."

Blanche had no difficulty interpreting the series of bumps and thuds or the cry of rage that followed. Sarah had pushed the priest, propelling him past the entrance to the hide, and then given him another shove for good measure, one that sent him tumbling down the stairs. He had failed to take into account the strength of long-pent up emotions ...or the power of arms made muscular by hours of scrubbing floors, washing sheets, and lifting everything from buckets of water to pails of slops.

Father Mortimer survived the fall. Blanche heard his muffled curses. Then came the shouts of Sir Eustace's men when they discovered a priest trying to scramble to his feet and run away.

Accepting that she would gain no advantage from making her presence known to the raiders, Blanche made her cautious way down the few remaining rungs of the ladder. She was annoyed but not surprised to realize that she was shaking uncontrollably. She'd just had a narrow escape but she was far from safe.

Still clinging to the ladder, she attempted to discern something of her surroundings. The walls felt as if they were closing in on her, even though she knew she had plenty of room to move about. Father North had told her that the hide was nine feet deep and six feet square. It was even warm, since it nestled up against the house's main chimney stack.

If only the whole were not surrounded by solid stone.

A wave of panic swept over her. This might be a hide, but it was also a trap. If everyone in the house was taken away to gaol, she could die in here of thirst and starvation. Even if Kit came looking for her and was able to get into the house, he might not be able to rescue her. She'd never told him where the hides were or how to get into them.

Her heart raced faster as fear threatened to swamp her senses. There was no way to escape on her own. The mechanism that held the trap door shut was a spring bolt of the same sort as the one on the smaller hide in the garret. It required someone on the outside to open it, and that person had to know which nail controlled the lock and move it sideways to draw back both the cord and the bolt.

She willed herself to be calm. Sarah had been right about one thing. It would not have gone well for her if Sir Eustace had found her at Otley Manor. To avoid discovery by the magistrate, she would have to stay silent as a little mouse until such time as someone who did *not* want to imprison and execute her, preferably her husband, came within earshot.

At first there was a great deal of noise. Heavy footfalls sounded directly over her head as Sir Eustace's men climbed to the upper floors. Sarah must already have told them about the small hide in the garret. There were sounds from other parts of the house as well—shouts, screams, and curses.

She took comfort in her certainty that the searchers would not capture Father North. She was grateful for that small favor, although it galled her to realize that Joseph Yelverton, having gone with the priest to the Kenners, would likewise escape arrest.

Slowly, Blanche became aware that the interior of the hide was not as dark as she'd first thought. Moving with great care, she shuffled toward the single source of light, a small circular opening cut into one wall. When she pressed one eye to this spy hole, she was rewarded with a bird's eye view of a small portion of the hall below. It appeared that the entire household had been herded together there to await their fate. Several rough-looking men in leather jerkins, variously armed with halberds and cudgels, held their weapons at the ready to discourage any attempt at escape.

For an interminable length of time, nothing happened. Then Sir Eustace and Master Flower appeared, and with them Sir Eustace's clerk carrying the contents of the garret hide. Lady Otley's gasp was clearly audible. Sir Stephen looked as if he was on the verge of apoplexy. Neither seemed to notice when Sarah was brought into the room, or that one of Sir Eustace's men kept a tight grip on her arm.

Although distance and the thickness of the hide's walls muffled their voices and made their words indistinct, Blanche understood enough of what was being said to realize that everyone was to be taken to Waverley House for a hearing, after which they would be transported in chains to Colchester Castle. They would not have to wait long for trial. The Chelmsford Assizes were less than a week away.

Powerless to do anything but watch, she kept her eye glued to the peephole until all the prisoners had been led away. She waited until she could no longer hear any sound but the beating of her own heart before she felt for the ladder. In this place, even the keen night vision she had been blessed with was inadequate to show her what was at the top.

In the darkness, she used her fingers to trace the cord that connected nail and bolt, thinking that there had to be a way to work the mechanism from the inside, but nothing she tried produced any positive results. When she pulled hard on the cord, she felt it give in a way that alarmed her. She remembered her first thought upon seeing the mechanism—that the cord might easily fray and break—and a little sob escaped her.

Slowly, spirits drooping, she descended once more to the bottom of the hide, accepting the hard truth that she would never be able to escape from this place on her own.

Kit would come, she told herself. When he entered the house, he'd hear her calls for help and break through the trap door to rescue her.

Unless he was already in gaol himself.

If he had attempted to delay the raiding party, Sir Eustace would have dealt harshly with him. She had no confidence that Francis Flower would have come to his defense.

As silent tears streamed down her cheeks, Blanche she sank to the floor of the hide. Her back braced against the wall, hugging her knees, she gave in to despair.

Chapter Forty-Eight

A long time later, at the sound of voices above her head, Blanche stirred. Despite the closeness of the air, the sensation of walls pressing in on her, and her overriding fear that she would never see the outside of that hole again, she had somehow managed to fall asleep. Slowly, disconcerted by the total darkness—not even a glimmer of light filtered in through the spy hole—she uncurled her stiff limbs and sat up.

Someone was on the stairs. Someone who knew the location of the trap door. She stood, extended one hand until it touched a rung of the ladder, and craned her neck.

Silently, its hinges well oiled, the trap door opened. An impossibly bright light shone down on her, forcing her to fling her free arm across her eyes to protect them.

"That is not Father Mortimer." Joseph Yelverton sounded much-aggrieved by the discovery.

Shrinking back, Blanche felt her heart sink to her toes. Would Yelverton rescue her or kill her? The question did not hang in the balance long.

"Mistress Wainfleet," said Father North, taking Yelverton's place at the opening into the hide. "I am glad to find you safe. Do you need a hand to climb out of there?"

"Leave her where she is!" Yelverton's voice rose to a shout. "Let her rot! She is the cause of all this trouble."

Blanche hastily scrambled up the ladder and emerged from the priest hole. She glared at her accuser. "I am not the one who brought false charges against an innocent woman."

"You were born sinful, as all women are."

"Joseph! Cease this bickering."

At the priest's command, Yelverton's mouth snapped shut. Blanche likewise said no more, although further accusations hovered on the tip of her tongue. If Father North's mild rebuke could silence Lady Otley's brother, then during their ride to the Kenner house he must have found a way to make Yelverton fear for his immortal soul. She glanced around her but saw no sign of Mistress Kenner or her daughter.

Father North answered her unasked question. "Word of the raid reached us when we were only a few miles away from Otley Manor, but we did not think it wise to return here until it was full dark. You were well-advised to conceal yourself. Had Sir Eustace caught sight of you, matters might have gone harder on everyone."

"They could scarce be worse than they are," Yelverton muttered. "From the steward to the boy who turns the spit, the entire household has been imprisoned."

"Along with Father Mortimer," said Father North. "Despite his flaws, he does not deserve the fate that now awaits him."

Blanche kept her thoughts on that subject to herself. By the light of the lanterns the two men had brought with them, illumination far less glaring now that her eyes had adjusted, she studied their faces. Yelverton was angry, and most of that anger was directed at her. Father North's expression was one of deep sadness and genuine concern, reinforcing her opinion that he was a good man, no matter what his religious or political beliefs.

"We cannot stay here," the priest said. "They may come back. In truth, I am surprised they did not set a guard."

"To watch over an empty house?" Yelverton's scorn at the idea was such that, for a moment, he forgot he was speaking to a man of God.

Father North let the comment pass without rebuke, but Yelverton's words made Blanche uneasily aware that someone else should have been watching the house. Indeed, someone else should have entered it by now.

Where was Kit? *Had* he been taken into custody? Or had he entered the house while she slept, found no trace of her, and gone away again?

"We have time enough to decide what to do with this spy in our midst," Yelverton continued. "She must have been the one who informed on us to Sir Eustace."

"When you did such an excellent job of convincing him I am a witch? He has long known that there were recusants here. Sir Stephen has been paying his wife's fines for years. It must have galled Sir Eustace to catch only women during his earlier raid. No doubt he has been planning another ever since, in the hope of arresting a priest this time around."

Yelverton came at her, arms outstretched as if to seize her by the throat and throttle her.

Father North stepped between them. "Control yourself, Joseph. If she'd had any suspicion that Sir Eustace would attack us here today, she would have been long gone before the raid. That she was forced to take refuge in the hide proves her innocence."

"It is a trick," Yelverton insisted. "We dare not let her live."

The toothsome gentleman who had briefly won Alison's heart had entirely vanished, replaced by a sniveling coward with no honor in him. Blanche had no qualms about letting the priest protect her. Yelverton would kill her if he could. She had no doubt of it.

"Your words trouble me, Joseph," Father North said. "That you are so eager to do away with Mistress Wainfleet makes me question all that you said to me earlier and wonder if you were, in truth, responsible for the deaths of Mistress Palmer and the maidservant."

Peering out from behind Father North, Blanche saw Yelverton's mouth open in a most unappealing fashion as he gaped at the priest. It was a moment before he found his voice. "I never harmed so much as a hair on either of their heads!"

"How can you say so?" Blanche demanded. "Even if you did not commit murder, you did much harm to those young women, and to Sarah, too, when you subjected them to false exorcisms."

"That is different." His gaze darted to the priest and away. "I have acknowledged my error in trusting Father Mortimer."

"You and Father Mortimer are cut from the same cloth." Blanche had seen the sick pleasure both of them had taken in tormenting those poor girls. "Both Alison and Edith showed signs of having been poisoned with white bryony, one of the ingredients Father Mortimer used in that foul mixture he forced them to inhale."

"I know nothing about herbs," Yelverton protested. "Do I look like a cunning woman?"

"You look like a liar," Blanche said.

Once again, Father North intervened, holding up a hand to silence them both. "Come with me, Joseph. I will hear your confession. Your full confession this time. Mistress Wainfleet will wait here while you and I retire to the chapel."

The priest picked up his pack and one of the lanterns and gestured for Yelverton to precede him. He took Blanche's cooperation for granted.

She waited until the two men reached the next landing. Leaving the second lantern behind, she crept after them into the nursery. When Father North closed the door of the chapel behind them, Blanche pressed an ear to the wood and listened for all she was worth.

Chapter Forty-Nine

Their voices were too low for Blanche to overhear more than murmurs, but she knew the first part of what they said would be only the ritual words of the confessional. It was after Yelverton asked for forgiveness that he would clarify just what he had done to need it.

Taking care to make no sound, she opened the door and slipped into the dimly lit chapel. The two men sat at opposite ends of the long bench, heads bent as if in prayer. Since the door was behind them, neither noticed her entrance. She moved swiftly and silently to hide herself behind the nearest tapestry, the one that depicted a scene from the Old Testament story of Judith beheading Holofernes.

Yelverton had already begun to enumerate his sins. Blanche took no satisfaction from hearing him admit them, and her indignation grew as he described how his passions had been inflamed by viewing female flesh and watching Father Mortimer touch Edith's privy parts.

When he stopped speaking, Blanche expected Father North to assign a penance. Instead, the priest remained silent, as if waiting for Yelverton to acknowledge still more transgressions. After a bit, the penitent coughed, cleared his throat, and yielded to lifelong habit, secure in his certainty that a priest would never reveal anything he heard during confession.

"I had naught to do with Alison's murder, if it was murder," Yelverton said. "I admit I instigated and encouraged her exorcism, after she denied me her body and began to speak of leaving Otley Manor, and that I had some foreknowledge of what would be done to her during the ritual, but I would never have countenanced her death."

"And yet she died."

"In prison. I was not there, and no one acted on my behalf."

Another long silence followed this denial. Blanche scarcely dared breathe. Yelverton had to be lying. Would Father North press him to admit it?

"She was going to leave," Yelverton blurted. "Return to her sister's house in Kent. She had already written to her. If she had not had the misfortune to fall ill, she would have gone and taken our secrets with her."

"How can you be so certain she would have betrayed you? Did she hate you so much that she could countenance your arrest, even your death?"

Yelverton sounded sulky. "Women are weak. She could have been persuaded to give evidence against us. When I told her of Alison's intention to leave us, Clemence feared the same outcome."

For a moment, Blanche stopped breathing. Clemence Otley? Could she have been so wrong about that gentlewoman? Lady Otley *was* Yelverton's sister, and she *had* been in prison with Alison. The possibility that she had acted to protect herself and her husband and her brother grew stronger as Yelverton babbled on, lodging further complaints against Alison, the woman he'd once claimed to love.

Blanche had thought of Lady Otley as kind, albeit gruff and set in her ways, but the more she considered it, the more likely it seemed to her that Sir Stephen's wife could have murdered Alison. Faith and family meant everything to her. Despite what her brother believed about the weakness of women, Lady Otley would not have hesitated to strike out against someone she perceived as a threat.

Remembering Lady Otley as she'd last seen her, quailing at the sight of Sir Eustace entering the courtyard, Blanche frowned. She'd been bold enough in prison, a leader among the women held there, and again when she was back home, making plans in advance to thwart another raid. But when it came to the point…

Lost in her own confused thoughts, Blanche missed a little of what Yelverton said. It was a new quality in his voice that drew her attention back to him. Was that regret she was hearing?

"Edith came to me that night," he said. "She told me she was with child.

Her death was an accident, Father. I swear it. The distillation of bryony berries I gave her was supposed to cause her to miscarry. I never meant for her to die."

Blanche bit back a gasp. Yelverton had just confessed to causing the death of an unborn child, a damning sin in and of itself.

"Go on." Father North's voice had gone cold.

"When she began to convulse, I did not know what to do. And then she stopped breathing."

"You did not seek help? Did not wake Father Mortimer to give her last rites?"

"I ...I could not think what to do. In the end, I carried her to the garret and laid her on the bed beside her sister. Sarah was deeply asleep. She never stirred."

"You crept away and told no one." The condemnation in the priest's voice was impossible to miss.

"It took me hours afterward to clean up the mess in my chamber," Yelverton complained.

Blanche's hands itched to slap him, to scratch his face, to claw his eyes out. To call him a pig would be to do pigs a disservice.

After a long pause, Father North asked, "Was the child yours?"

"So she said. She doubtless lied, hoping I'd marry her. Now that I consider the matter, I am no longer so certain that she was *not* possessed. After I lost Alison's favor, Edith exerted a most unnatural influence over me. That is when I fell under her spell, Father. She came to my bed and worked her wiles on me."

A likely story! Blanche was almost as appalled by this claim as she had been by his callous treatment of Edith's body. That Father North failed to rebuke him had her hackles rising. Even a good man, it seemed, was willing to believe in the inherent wickedness of women.

To Blanche, it was abundantly clear that Yelverton had been the seducer. He was the brother of the mistress of the house, Edith but a lowly maidservant. What choice did someone in her position have if a gentleman chose to pursue her? A complaint to Lady Otley would have earned her a

254

beating, and if she had fallen pregnant, no one would have thought it cruel of the Otleys to toss her out to fend for herself, even though it was the middle of winter.

"Despite your denials, you did take a life," Father North said. "That of the child. For penance, you must write down an account of all you have just told me."

"What will you do with it?" Yelverton's voice was unsteady.

"For the nonce, nothing, but if it becomes necessary, the document will be used to free the person who now stands accused of Edith's death."

"That heretic!"

"Mistress Wainfleet, yes. Do you deny that you coerced Edith's sister and others into accusing her of witchcraft?"

After a few indignant sputters, Yelverton admitted to that sin as well, and when Father North ordered him to go to the well-supplied desk that was the only other piece of furniture in the chamber and write out his confession, he obeyed.

Blanche watched from her hiding place as Yelverton sharpened a quill with his pen knife and dipped it in ink. By the light of the lantern, he began to write. It took him some time to finish, but when he had sanded and blotted the whole and thrust it toward the priest, Blanche felt a small thrill of triumph.

At just that moment Yelverton's head shot up. He turned her way, likely alerted by some small, inadvertent sound she had made. Pen knife in hand, raised like a weapon, he rushed toward the tapestry that concealed her.

Once again, it was Father North's swift action that prevented him from reaching her. He swung his peddler's pack with enough force to knock Yelverton senseless. Shaking his head, his expression one of deep regret, he stared down at the motionless body before bending over to collect both the knife and the confession Yelverton had recorded. He handed the closely-written pages to Blanche.

"I am indebted to you," she said when she'd deciphered enough of the crabbed handwriting to be sure Yelverton had followed the priest's instructions to the letter. She tucked the papers into the pocket hidden in her skirt.

While she was reading, Father North retrieved several sturdy lengths of braided silk from his pack and used them to bind the unconscious man's hands and feet.

"You have acted in accordance with your conscience," he said, "and so have I. Now we must both be gone from here in all haste. It might be best if you find your husband and return at once to London."

He did not need to say that Sir Eustace might choose to disregard Yelverton's written confession if Blanche herself tried to present it to him. Given the magistrate's hatred of witchcraft, there was a distinct possibility that he would decide she'd used a spell to coerce it.

"There is still Sarah to consider."

"I doubt Sir Eustace can be persuaded to release her."

That was not an outcome Blanche was willing to accept, nor was she inclined to leave Yelverton here, where he might free himself and escape. For all that she admired Father North and was grateful for his help, she was not convinced that he desired to see Joseph Yelverton arrested. For all she knew, he intended to untie the villain as soon as she was safely on her way to Little Mabham.

"You must leave at once, Father. I can see the sense in that. But I mean to wait here for Kit. Even now he will be on his way. When he arrives, he and I will decide what is best to do with our prisoner and his confession." In the back of her mind was the vague notion that she could somehow use them to barter with Sir Eustace for Sarah's release.

Father North did not argue with her. "May the good Lord bless and keep you, my child," he said, and with those parting words, he left her alone in the chapel with Joseph Yelverton.

Chapter Fifty

Yelverton was still unconscious, or pretending to be, after Blanche heard Father North ride away. She prodded the miscreant with her foot, then tugged at the bonds that held him to make certain they were securely tied. The steady rise and fall of his chest assured her that he still lived. That pleased her. He might not have killed Alison himself, but he'd been responsible all the same. She felt certain, despite his denials, that he knew who had administered the fatal dose of white bryony. It saddened her to think it had might have been Lady Otley. She wanted confirmation of her suspicion before she accused that gentlewoman of murder.

Leaving her prisoner in the chapel, she made her way to the wing that housed the pantry, buttery, and kitchen. The latter was as dark and cold as every other room in the manor house but she soon located kindling and a tinder box and started a fire. She found another lantern and a supply of candles, both wax and tallow. Even more welcome, considering the empty hole in her belly, she discovered a supply of food and drink. She helped herself to slices of cold ham and chicken and sawed off generous portions of bread and cheese to go with them. Instead of barley water, she chose a Tuscan wine from the reserves Sir Stephen kept for his personal use.

She had just tucked into this modest repast when she heard a thump from the direction of the kitchen yard. She froze with her cup halfway to her mouth. Seizing the largest of the cook's knives, she stood facing the door, ready to defend herself.

The blade fell to the floor with a clatter as soon as the door opened. She recognized Kit even before he shoved back the hood of his cloak to reveal his

257

well-loved features. She had hoped he would come, prayed that he would, but she had been most terribly afraid that he had been prevented.

When he opened his arms, Blanche gave a glad cry and threw herself into them. Despite his cold lips and clothing so wet that it rapidly dampened her own, she clung to him until he took her by the shoulders and set her away

"Enough!" He was laughing. "As much as I enjoy holding you, my love, just at this moment I need the heat of that fire more."

It was only then that she noticed the layer of white crusting his cloak. The day had been no more than overcast when the searchers came. Now, through the still open door, she saw that heavy wet snow coated the ground deep enough to make walking difficult. It appeared as if the storm was nearly over, but it must have been fierce while it lasted.

Cautiously, another cloaked and hooded figure poked its head around the doorframe. Sarah Trott's frightened eyes were huge in her pale face and she looked half frozen.

"Come in before you turn into an icicle!" Blanche pulled the younger woman into the kitchen and slammed the door shut to keep out the elements.

When all three of them stood in front of the fire, Kit spoke. "Sarah told me she'd locked you in the hide to keep you safe. I was afraid we would find you still imprisoned there."

"Father North released me. He and Joseph Yelverton returned to Otley Manor after everyone else had gone."

Sarah started and gave a cry of alarm at the mention of that name.

"He cannot hurt you. Not anymore."

"How—?"

"I will tell you everything," she promised, interrupting Kit's question, "but first I must know how you managed to persuade Sir Eustace to release Sarah into your custody."

"I lied to him, of course." Kit grinned unrepentantly at her. "But let me begin at the beginning. I was watching the road from Little Mabham to Otley Manor when I saw a large number of men ride past. I joined them, thinking to spirit you away in the confusion of the raid, but I never managed to enter the house. When the prisoners were brought out and you were not among them, I feared you were dead."

"Oh, Kit!"

"Thanks to your descriptions, I recognized stout, solid Lady Otley and her heavy-set husband with his little tuft of a beard, and the balding priest, Mortimer. Sarah was by far the youngest female and the most obviously frightened, cringing every time one of Sir Eustace's men tried to hurry her along, but when she heard Master Flower address me as Master Wainfleet, fortunately not within earshot of Sir Eustace, she sent me such a look of desperate hope that I knew you must have told her about me."

"Flower recognized you?"

"He did, but it was not to his advantage to call attention to my presence. He believed me when I told him I had come, at your request, to bear witness to the capture of the priest."

Blanche turned toward Sarah, finding the younger woman much restored by the warmth of the fire. There was a little color in her cheeks and she was no longer shivering. "Did you show Sir Eustace the location of the garret hide?"

"For all the good it did! He did not believe me when I said I was not a papist like the rest. He put me in the same cell with them when they knew I had betrayed them."

No wonder she had been afraid.

"It is as well that you were not kept in a separate place." Kit left the fireside to contemplate the food Blanche had left out on the table. "The plan I devised to set you free would not have worked if you'd been deemed a valuable witness against the others. As it was, my presence raised no alarms. At my first opportunity, I had another word with Master Flower in private."

He helped himself to some of the bread and a wedge of cheese.

"You were fortunate he did not clap you in irons and send you to Colchester gaol with the rest," Blanche said. "He must have been suspicious of your sudden appearance on the scene."

"Mayhap he was, but it was information you provided that was responsible for the success of the raid. He had made us certain promises if Father Mortimer was captured."

"He was to facilitate my pardon, but we never spoke to him of Sarah." She gestured for the younger woman to partake of the food and wine and retrieved her own goblet.

"Well there, I fear," said Kit, "is where I was forced to deceive the Lord Chancellor's man. I told him that Sarah was *your* maidservant and that she accompanied you to Otley Manor when you set out to discover the truth about your sister's death."

"And he accepted that? When he knew Sarah and Edith were sisters?"

"We never mentioned their relationship when we went to Hatton House to tell him your tale. He believed me when I assured him that Sarah was loyal to both church and state and that she'd remained at Otley Manor only because she had no way to leave after you were taken away."

"And that was all it took to secure her release?"

The sparkle in Kit's eyes put Blanche in mind of the look on a small boy's face when he'd succeeded in outwitting his tutors.

"I may have suggested that he tell Sir Eustace a slightly different tale, one designed to bolster Flower's importance. The magistrate is now convinced that Flower sent Sarah to Otley Manor as a spy, and that he's sent her back to London in the company of his manservant—that would be me—to protect her from retaliation by the others."

"I am surprised Sir Eustace was gullible enough to believe that."

"I do not see why you should be. He was credulous enough to think that you were a witch."

"And you're certain he does not know I am here?"

"Flower never mentioned your name. Why would he when he wanted all the credit for himself?"

Kit paused to take a long swallow of wine. His hand was not entirely steady, telling Blanche that, despite his protests, he still had concerns for her safely.

"Once Sarah and I were away from Waverly House, she told me where you were and assured me that you had not been harmed. We rode here as quickly as we could to release you from the hide, but the weather made the journey from Little Mabham a slow one."

"The storm seems to be easing."

He nodded in agreement. "Dawn is not far off. As soon as it is light, we will leave for Stisted. But first, it is your turn. What transpired here after Sarah left?"

"Father North convinced Yelverton to tell the truth and to write down his confession."

She produced it, giving it to Kit to read while she summarized the details. When she came to his claim that Edith was carrying his child, she sent Sarah a hard look.

"Did you know?"

Sarah shook her head, but she considered the matter with a thoughtful look on her pale face. "It may have been true. It makes sense of other things."

"What things?"

Kit interrupted before Sarah could answer. "This paper clears you of the charges of witchcraft. There is no longer any need for you to fear Sir Eustace."

"I think I would just as soon avoid that gentleman. With the Lord Chancellor's support, it should be a simple enough matter to secure a royal pardon. But I still do not know how Alison died. Not for certain. Yelverton claimed both he and his sister knew that Alison had written to Philippa, and that they were both convinced she would betray their secrets. Do you think it is possible that Lady Otley poisoned Alison?"

Kit considered the idea and shook his head. "It seems unlikely she'd have brought white bryony with her into captivity."

Blanche saw his point. It was doubtful any of the women taken in that first raid had been given much time to collect their belongings. Surely they'd have chosen clothing and coins to bribe the gaoler over poisonous herbs.

A small sound drew Blanche's attention to Sarah. The girl gripped her wine cup tightly between her hands. Staring down at it, avoiding their eyes, she began to speak in a low voice.

"Edith was secretive even with me, but we shared a bed. That is how I know that on some nights she slept elsewhere. And I know, too, how angry she was when Master Yelverton brought Mistress Palmer into the household." She glanced at Blanche but looked quickly away. "Edith was the first to suggest that your sister was possessed by a demon. She helped them during the exorcism by collecting the herbs Father Mortimer asked for."

"Did she see my sister as her rival for Joseph Yelverton's affections?"

At Sarah's nod, Blanche's conclusions rearranged themselves in her mind. Yelverton hadn't wanted Alison dead. He'd wanted to punish her for recognizing his true nature and rejecting him. Lady Otley hadn't poisoned Alison to stop her from betraying her and her fellow recusants. That gentlewoman's only sin had been in failing to protect her companion from her brother. Alison's true enemy, all along, had been Edith Trott.

"Your sister killed mine," she whispered.

Sarah's face twisted and tears rolled down her cheeks. Her words came out between sobs. "I do not know that for certain, but Edith was the one charged with caring for Mistress Palmer when we were taken to Colchester gaol. It was her task to give her food and drink and something to quell her coughing."

Philippa had said that the juice of white bryony was sometimes used as an ingredient in a cure for catarrh. Could medicine brought with them from Otley Manor have been too strong? No, Blanche decided. Not even the kindest mistress would have thought to pack herbal remedies in the midst of a raid. There was only one reason for Edith to have had possession of a lethal dose of white bryony when she entered Colchester Castle. She had already had it on her person. She had planned all along to kill Alison. If there had been no raid, Blanche's sister would still be dead.

"Dry your tears," she told Sarah. "Nothing Edith did reflects on you and she has already paid for her crime."

"Yelverton killed her and her child." Kit had placed the confession on the table when he'd finished reading it. Now he picked it up, folded it, and tucked it inside his doublet. "What kind of man is Father North to have taken a murderer away with him?"

Blanche sent him a startled look before she realized that she had left something out of her narrative. "Father North left some time ago, but Yelverton is still here. He is trussed up like a Christmas goose and lying on the floor of the chapel."

A look of alarm on his face, Kit sprang to his feet. "Show me."

Sensing his urgency, Blanche took up the lantern and led him through the house and up the stairs. Sarah did not follow them. Blanche could not blame her for being reluctant to go anywhere near the man who had abused her and her sister.

In the nursery, Blanche stopped short, seizing Kit's arm with her free hand to hold him back. "I closed the door to the chapel behind me when I left."

It stood open, a gaping hole into greater darkness.

"Are you certain?"

"I remember thinking what a pity it was that the door had no key. I'd have liked to lock him in."

How long had it taken Yelverton to free himself? Was he still in the house or had he crept out while they were all in the kitchen?

"He'll have gone straight to the stables for his horse," Kit said.

"Not if he thinks I left with Father North and he is alone in the house. He will have gone to his chamber first to gather his possessions."

"Stay close to me," Kit ordered, and turned back the way they'd come.

They had already passed the little room Yelverton and Father Mortimer had used for their exorcisms when Blanche hesitated and looked that way. Something was different. She stopped and stared at the closed door and then it came to her—the key that should have been in the lock was missing.

"He's in there," Blanche whispered when Kit turned to see why she was no longer right behind him. "I am certain of it."

Without hesitation, he threw the full weight of his body against the door, leading with his shoulder ...and bounced back with equal force. Rubbing his arm, he glared at the solid wooden panel. "Wait here."

He went into the chapel and returned with the long bench. It was heavy enough to use as a battering ram. It took Kit three tries, with assistance from his wife, but in the end, the door shuddered and crashed open.

Yelverton was waiting for them. Eyes wild, he charged, running full tilt into Kit and knocking him aside with such force that Blanche's husband fell heavily to the floor. Yelverton shoved Blanche out of his way and seized the lantern she'd set aside while they were breaking into the room.

Kit was still struggling to get to his feet when Blanche hiked up her skirts and raced after Yelverton. She had no idea how to stop him, but she was determined to prevent his escape.

At the same instant he reached the head of the stairwell, Sarah dashed up the steps. For a moment they teetered on the landing in a hideous parody of an embrace. Then Yelverton thrust her away from him. She caught her balance, turned, and kicked him hard, striking him on the back with her booted foot just as he began his descent.

The lantern flew from his hand and landed on the top step, mercifully without breaking open or starting a fire. Arms flailing, he desperately sought purchase but found nothing to grab onto. With startling abruptness, he dropped out of sight. A series of thumps marked his descent. After the last echo died away, absolute silence fell.

Kit went down first to examine the crumpled form at the foot of the stairs. He looked up at Blanche and Sarah and shook his head.

It was too easy a death, Blanche thought, but at least Joseph Yelverton would never again abuse a young woman. She descended the stairs and stopped beside the body.

Sarah followed. She stared down at Yelverton's dead face, illuminated by the lantern Kit had rescued. Then she took aim and spat.

Blanche was tempted to do the same. Instead she turned to her husband. "Give me Yelverton's confession."

When he'd handed it over, she placed it in the dead man's hand.

"As soon as we are well away from here, we will send an anonymous message to Sir Eustace, telling him there is more for him to find at Otley Manor."

"Is there more *you* need to find?" Kit asked.

"I have the answers I sought, and rough justice has been served up to those responsible for the deaths of Alison and Edith."

The first rays of the sun lit their way as they rode away from Otley Manor.

A new day, Blanche thought. *A new beginning.*

She was content.

A Note from the Author

The subplot involving the exorcism of maidservants in a Catholic household in Elizabethan England is loosely based on what happened to the Williams sisters in the 1580s. In sixteenth-century Essex, accusations of witchcraft were even more common than those of possession. Most English people at that time, no matter what their faith or level of education, believed that both witches and demons were real.

Although I consulted many sources, including my own *Everyday Life in Renaissance England* and my online *A Who's Who of Tudor Women*, details for this part of the story are drawn primarily from Jessie Childs' *God's Traitors: Terror and Faith in Elizabethan England*, Katherine Sands' *Demon Possession in Elizabethan England*, and Keith Thomas' *Religion and the Decline of Magic*. Recusants (those who refused to attend required services of the Church of England) were persecuted with fines, imprisonment, and even death. Jesuit priests were hunted and executed for spreading their "false" religion. Priest holes (called "hides") existed in many Catholic homes.

With the exception of several people Blanche applies to for aid in London, all the characters in this novel are fictional. Colchester Castle is real and was used as a prison in the 1590s, despite being in poor repair.

About the Author

The Finder of Lost Things is Agatha Award winning author Kathy Lynn Emerson's sixty-third traditionally published book. She has written nonfiction, children's books for ages 8-12, contemporary and historical romance novels, and contemporary and historical mysteries. The latter include the Face Down Mystery Series featuring Elizabethan gentlewoman and herbalist, Susanna, Lady Appleton, and its spinoff, the Mistress Jaffrey Mysteries, as well as the Diana Spaulding 1888 Quartet. Two collections of her short stories have been published. Her nonfiction includes *The Writer's Guide to Everyday Life in Renaissance England* and *How to Write Killer Historical Mysteries*. She also writes under the pseudonyms Kate Emerson and Kaitlyn Dunnett. She lives in rural Maine. Readers can learn more about Kathy and her books at www.KathyLynnEmerson.com.

Also by Kathy Lynn Emerson

Historical Mystery Series:
The Face Down Mysteries
The Mistress Jaffrey Mysteries
The Diana Spaulding 1888 Quartet

Nonfiction:
The Writer's Guide to Everyday Life in Renaissance England
How to Write Killer Historical Mysteries

Collections of Short Stories:
Murders and Other Confusions
Different Times, Different Crimes

CPSIA information can be obtained
at www.ICGtesting.com
Printed in the USA
BVHW070832081020
590503BV00015B/36

9 781947 915824